For my Dad, who ͻ
and for Debbi
her

CHAPTER ONE

You know that inevitable scene in disaster movies where the plucky hero is trying to outrun an approaching catastrophe? You can see it in their rear-view mirror, coming up fast, and you're willing them to speed up. Then, right at the very last moment, by the skin of their teeth, they somehow escape?

Well, thinks Melanie Louise McCarthy, this moment is nothing like that. This moment feels more like a 200-foot tsunami suddenly appearing over the horizon, her clapped-out car stalling, and the earth splitting open to reveal a torrent of hot lava into which said car falls backwards.

Mel takes a very, *very* deep breath before asking Aaron (father of her son, Connor) to repeat the earth-shattering, out of the blue announcement that he just made,

"Connor has asked me to talk to you about dropping out of university and coming to live with Maya and me in Ibiza, and errr, well, Maya is pregnant, we just found out. So you know, with starting a family, we really do need to sell the house. I mean, it was always the agreement when Connor was older, anyway. I'm sorry to rush you, Mel, but the flat is too small for Connor and the baby."

Knowing how huge this news is for her, he gives her his most reassuring smile; however, Mel is unable to speak. Her mind has gone into shock and is running, in high definition, back through the 20-odd years since she first met him DJing in a bar in Ibiza, as if somehow this is the actual end of her life.

Which, she acknowledges, it is, as she knows it.

She sees their whirlwind romance, the unplanned teen pregnancy, the naive dream that it wouldn't change their lives, all the years of wondering where Aaron was every weekend, him moving out, then moving on, the relentless single parenting, getting Connor through school, college, and proudly watching him off to University. She never saw a version of events in which Connor would change his mind and leave home to live with his Dad, his gorgeous Spanish wife, and their (bound to be beautiful) baby in Ibiza.

As for the 'Starting a family' comment, what were we? His practice lap?

"Connor knew it would upset you, Mel, which is why he asked me to talk to you about it. He feels like going to university is more your dream than what he wants to do. He'd like to come and work at the studio, try making a life out here, he wants to be around when his baby brother or sister is born."

The best she can do is sputter a congratulations before the tsunami washes her away.

When they came home from Ibiza, they were obviously in a *situation.* Aaron's parents had helped them out by putting a deposit down on a rundown terrace in what was then a pretty undesirable bit of the city. They were dubious, due to the amount of work it needed and the lack of skills Aaron and Mel possessed, but Mel insisted they would transform it over time, which she had. She'd loved the old Formica kitchen and the turquoise bathroom with the pop art tiles and regretted having them ripped out. Coloured bathrooms are all the rage now, she thinks discontentedly, emptying the contents of her bathroom cupboard into a cardboard box.

It had been a few weeks since Aaron dropped his bombshell, but Mel is still reeling from Connor's decision. Her instinct is to clutch him tight and say over my dead body. To tell Aaron to go back to Ibiza, 'Start his family' and leave this one the hell alone. But Connor is not a sweet-faced toddler who sleeps in her bed every night or the little boy who cried for weeks when he started school because he wanted to stay home and watch Fireman Sam. Connor is 18 years old, taller than her by a head and turning into his father so much it's unnerving. Legally, she can't stop him, and in the most ironic twist of fate, at 18, she also got a summer job in Ibiza, left home and never went back.

Is her behaviour finally catching up with her? She can't help but wonder.

Mel is well aware that she's been using Connor for years as a convenient way to keep her past at bay. However, ignoring her life before he was born has always left her feeling like she's a jigsaw with half the pieces missing. She wonders how obvious that will be once he's gone.

Her friends, trying to be positive in the face of Mel's morose mood, tell her repeatedly that this is a new start for her, a chance to make up for all those years she missed while she dealt with Aaron's addictions and raising Connor pretty much by herself. They all insist that, at 37, Mel is still plenty young enough to have a whole new life, meet someone else, get married and "Start a family" (Aaron's comment, the subject of much derision). Currently Mel feels incapable of pursuing any of those things. Maybe it's a touch dramatic, but she feels nothing but grief for her son, her home and the place she held in the world for the last 18 years.

A commotion from downstairs means Connor's back, having

been out with Aaron, who's here dealing with the impending house sale. He comes loping up the stairs, and Mel reminds herself to be happy for him; she would never voice it, but his decision does feel like a betrayal. More uncomfortable is how much it makes her think of her own Dad.

Does karma play the long game?

"Hey! How was lunch? How's your Dad and Maya?" She plastered on a bright smile. They had invited her along, but she claimed to be too busy with packing, when all she'd done was perch on the toilet and worry about what she was going to do with her life.

Connor is not insensitive enough to tell his Mum that they spent lunch looking online at houses with pools, murmurs a fine and asks if she needs him to do anything before he goes out to watch the football, "No, you go, I'm almost finished in here anyway and I need to think about what's going into storage and what's coming to Janet's with me."

"It is weird, seeing it half empty." Connor looks around, his eyes alighting on the doorframe on the landing that Mel has used to measure Connor's height over the years. The pencil scribbles faded and smudged at the bottom, and the last mark at the top, a dizzying distance from those early years. "I guess someone will just paint over it," he lines up against it, "Have I grown any more?"

Mel chokes back a betraying tear at the thought of all their history being painted over in a few swift strokes, busying herself so he doesn't notice, "Probably Connor, I swear some days you grow inches overnight." He goes off searching for a snack to fill those hollow legs, leaving her to collapse on the edge of the bath to pull herself together. She knows this move will be hard; they've been living here all of Connor's life, and when she thinks of herself 18 years ago, they both grew up here. There are so many memories, he carousel of emotions is exhausting. Yesterday, she sent Connor to empty the loft. Fairly convinced she'd given away all his childhood things years ago, she can't believe the amount of stuff he throws down. She marks the baubles for storage, clueless about where she'll spend next Christmas.

Deep breaths, Mel, she thinks.

One of the last things he passed down was a bag of baby things. Mel had clutched the musty bundle of babygro's, weeping into them for those long-gone baby days. With everything going on, she can't even begin to dissect how she feels that Connor will have a sibling that isn't hers or that Aaron will be making a different go of parenthood this time around. All these thoughts swirl around in her stomach. She puts the baby things in the wash to donate to charity, pretty sure Maya would have zero interest in them. It will be all Swedish neutrals and organic cotton for that baby, she sighs, pouring herself a large glass of wine.

Unfortunately, the student suburb they moved into nearly 20 years ago is now less takeaways and cab offices, more artisan delis and eclectic gift shops. Meaning that their three-bedroomed terrace with its long skinny garden is now desirable. It gets snapped up within weeks of being on the market. The proceeds are being split between her, Aaron, and his parents (who have decided to go on a world cruise). Mel doesn't see much of Joanne and Martin these days, but they were so helpful to her when Connor was little and Aaron was AWOL; it was good to give something back finally. As for Mel's share, after paying off the credit cards that often kept them fed and dressed over the years, and deducting fees, she has just about enough to use as a small deposit on even a smaller property.

That same gentrification, however, has now priced her out of this area of the city, so there are a lot of choices to make, which, frankly, on top of everything else, feels overwhelming. She toys with vague ideas of going to college and pursuing something different. Her head teacher suggests a teaching apprenticeship, and another friend says she should teach abroad. Until she can decide, she will be moving in with her friend and colleague, Janet, and her husband, Steve. Janet is the teacher Mel works with at Holy Trinity Primary School. They've been an unlikely tag team for six years now. Janet is nearer retirement age, but the two have struck up a solid friendship. Anyone from the outside looking in might say that Janet is a mother figure, Mel having lost her mum when she was sixteen. Janet does feel a bit like Mel is her adopted daughter, which is why she insists Mel come and stay with them, knowing how hard this is for her, and giving her the chance to decide on her next step at leisure. Janet lives in an immaculate house in the leafy suburbs where she claims they rattle around. She insists that Mel is doing them a favour. It'll stop them from facing the idea of downsizing, stay as long as you like, she insists.

That Janet tries to mother her is another issue that Mel chooses to ignore, well-versed in burying her head in the sand. She will do anything, including barely going home in twenty years, to avoid thinking about her mother. If ever she needs someone to fill those empty shoes, though, that time is now. She keeps her worries to herself, though, having grown accustomed to shouldering life on her own and hiding her feelings from Connor. She feels like a train wreck; she hasn't slept properly for weeks and seems to cry over something everyday. Looking at her tired, red-eyed reflection in the mirror," It looks like you've been in one too," she mutters to herself.

The move, in theory, is still about a month away, provided

nothing unexpected turns up in the final bits of paperwork. However, since that conversation with Aaron, Mel has been getting on with the preparations. Being methodical is her way of navigating inner turmoil that prevents a decent night's sleep. This house has so much history; her 3 a.m. thoughts often rehash all the drama with Aaron, as he battled with his numerous vices. Things calmed down between them after she made him move out, and eventually, he turned his life around, but while he was still causing chaos, she had met Ben. She sighed, turning over in bed. Ben, another ghost on her pillow. He left, ironically, because he felt haunted by Aaron. By the time it fizzled out between them, Aaron was with Maya, whom he met while DJing in a club in Ibiza.

How history just loves repeating itself.

Staring at the familiar ceiling above her like it's a projector; she sees all the nights she spent soothing Connor back to sleep when Aaron came home wasted, watches herself think up something new with pasta because it was all they could afford to eat, all the phases that Connor went through, the school photos from round faced preschooler to a grumpy looking Year 6. Her thoughts drift back to Aaron and the complexity of their relationship, recalling all the fights and the subsequent apologetic reparations. The push and pull of wanting to give Connor a proper family, and her frustration with Aaron's behaviour. That easy-going smile that would disarm her in seconds, sometimes still even now, she acknowledges with a sigh.

But they were never a good match for each other, although she kept trying for Connor's sake, long after it was clear that Aaron was the only one who could help Aaron. When they first met, she was still hurting from losing her Mum and the fallout from two serious relationship breakups; she wasn't in any kind of place to meet someone and settle down. She always knew they would never've lasted the long haul if they hadn't had Connor. After they moved back to Manchester, Aaron pushed every unresolved button in Mel; his erratic behaviour mirrored her own after her Mum died, leading to volatile arguments.

A guilty memory floods in; Connor is standing at the top of the stairs, crying, as she throws Aaron's belongings out the front door again. She has pried him about his early memories of Aaron, but thankfully, all he seems to remember are the good times. That charm that kept her in Aaron's thrall also works on children; in fact, everyone loves Aaron. That's what got him into so much trouble, but also got him out of it. The only one who never liked him was her dad, and no doubt Aaron would have won him over in the end, especially now he's sober, drives a flashy car and sports a very expensive haircut.

She often thinks back to the day that they arrived back at his parents' house in Manchester, unannounced, at the end of the Ibiza season, Mel sporting a noticeable baby bump over her tiny denim shorts (mortifying, retrospectively). Honestly, thinking about Connor doing the same thing makes her feel uneasy. To their credit, Aaron's parents were relatively calm, as she remembers. Now, as a parent, she wonders about the conversations they must have had when they were alone. She and Aaron were naive enough to think that love would keep them afloat, so his parents did their best to help them. Mel didn't even tell her own Dad for months.

Honestly, she couldn't say she would be so gracious if Connor were in the same boat. The Connor/Ibiza turn of events is surreal because it's like her own experience. Mel was all set for university until she skipped College to hang out with her new boyfriend and failed her A Levels. When that relationship came to a very sticky end, she went to Ibiza instead of retaking her exams, as her Dad had wanted her to do. She was so proud of Connor for achieving academically where she had failed, and now he isn't going to university either. She hopes that Ibiza is just a phase and he'll return and get his degree.

Before having Connor she never gave a second thought to how working mums manage, presuming that she'd have a career after Connor grew up a bit, but it turns out there aren't too many jobs that allowed her to get him to school at 8.45 and leave in time to pick him up at half past three. Then there were the school holidays, thirteen weeks a year when most jobs give you three. What should you do with your child for the extra 10 weeks? Pop them in the filing cabinet while you carry on? The most logical solution was to get a job in a school, so she worked as a lunch supervisor for a while. Before long, the head teacher, spotting her easy rapport with the kids, suggested she look into training as a teaching assistant. Teaching had never been on her career radar, not that she had much of one as she blew through her A levels in a fog of grief, boys and alcohol. As a kid, all she wanted to do was work with animals. Growing up in a farming community, she rode horses and was the kind of kid who took in all the mauled mice and battered birds the cat brought home, trying to coax them back to life. Kath, her dad's partner, always found a lamb for her to bottle feed, but somehow that dream got lost as her mum became sick.

As she got older, she imagined going to university to study something cool like Media Studies and moving far away from the little Yorkshire village she grew up in, to live in a minimalist loft where she'd drink lots of pink cocktails. It was highly possible that she'd watched too many American TV series.

Teaching fit in, the kids liked her, probably she thought, because she was still a kid herself. She completed her qualifications through the school, and when Connor became more self-sufficient, she found a full-time position at Holy Trinity Primary. She was placed in Janet's classroom to assist, and was still there seven years later. Janet is always on at her to do her teaching qualification, saying she'd fly through the training and earn a decent wage. Mel enjoys her job, but she isn't sure she wants to dedicate her life to it. Now her primary job isn't being a mum; she doesn't know what she's going to do. For the first time, she has options, and it's terrifying and liberating all at the same time.

CHAPTER TWO

Connor is trying hard to keep his elation to a minimum at home, but with his mates and his dad, he's buzzing with excitement about his new life. He was all set to go to Newcastle to study economics, but just like his Dad, his heart has always been in music, even though he never had the guts to go ahead and study it. Wary of him following in Aaron's footsteps, Mel had tried to steer him towards something more tangible. Going to university was more about pleasing his mum and doing what his friends were doing than something he cared about.

Ibiza floats his boat with its clubs, sunshine, and a job at his dad's recording studio. He wouldn't say it to his mum, but if things work out in Ibiza, he thinks returning to Manchester and attending university will be permanently deferred. Maya is cool, and his dad is like a hundred times more laid back than Mum. He'll miss her, maybe, but at 18, what thought does any kid give to how their parents feel? It's a gaping flaw in life's plan that you only realise when you have your own children, that your parents were also actual people. He's glad she's moving in with Janet; he'd worry about her if she were living alone, but Janet is nice, like a mother to his mum, so she'll look after her.

As a kid, he always thought his mum and dad would get back together. He was always around the house, even when Aaron didn't live with them. Mum wouldn't let Connor stay overnight in the flat that Aaron shared with his DJ mates (before he got what they all refer to as 'clean'), so his dad would come hang out with him at his mum's. Sometimes he'd wake up to hear the front door go in the middle of the night, and he knew it was his dad sneaking in or out, long after Mum insisted they would never be a couple again.

Until marrying Maya, he still thought there was a slim chance they'd give it another go. He sees how Mum's face changes when she sees him, and Dad always asks him if she's seeing anybody. Maya is nothing like his mum; she's Spanish and years younger than Mum, probably, he doesn't really know. She's a yoga teacher and owns a studio on the island. She converted dad to yoga, and to be fair, he does look fitter than ever.

She's threatened Connor that he must start doing it with them in Ibiza. Connor is more of a gym man, but if that's the price to pay to live there, he figures he can try it; he's not wearing leggings, though. Connor still can't quite believe that instead of running for the bus to college in the gloomy Manchester drizzle, he'll be driving around the island in the open-top jeep they use. His friends are excited, especially now that his dad works with some famous musicians. Not one to show off, he sometimes can't resist a little name drop to impress the girls. Connor's mates are all hinting at coming to stay already. He knows there is no way Maya will want a houseful of his mates once the baby arrives, so he tells them he'll find an apartment to rent nearby once he gets settled. Maybe Dad wouldn't mind them hanging out by the pool, *the Pool*, he laughs to himself.

Laters Manchester.

Janet pours Mel a cup of tea, gesturing to her to go and sit in the sun in the conservatory. Mel sinks into one of the moon-shaped bamboo chairs, staring out over Janet's well-kept garden, still not quite to grips with the fact she will be living here in a matter of weeks. It's just temporary, she tells herself, trying to quell the rising panic. She isn't technically a homeless person, but then, in the next breath, she thinks she is precisely that - of no fixed address, without a home, her chest tightens. If she weren't sitting down, she'd go at her knees. Janet comes through with a plate of freshly baked muffins, and the comforting vanilla smell perks her back up. As Mel reaches for one, she calculates how many dress sizes she'll go up if she stays here too long. Janet's baking is legendary in the staff room,

"Steve has just about emptied all the crap out of your room and he's going to put a new shower in your ensuite,"

"Jan, you don't need to do that, I'll be fine with whatever's there, I don't want to be any bother."

"When his mother stays, she never stops complaining about it, she says standing under a dripping tap would be more enjoyable, so it needs doing.Besides, it gives Steve something to do."

She signals the strangle sign as Steve wafts behind them, having smelled the muffins. She offers him the plate, then sends him off to the tip. Steve's just taken early retirement and is already driving Janet mad, drifting about the house,'Like a sad ghost,' she described him at the last staff meeting. Now he is pushing her to retire. Janet says she will be prolonging work for as long as possible, getting through the six weeks' school holidays with him around 24-7 seems like enough of a challenge.

"So how's it all going? Have you got a definite date from the estate agents? Most importantly, did you sign up for Tinder again like you promised?"

"No and NO!!"

"Mel, I don't mean to be harsh, but we all think it's time you got back out there. This is the start of the rest of your life! It's exciting!! C'mon, log in, I'm in the mood for a good swipe session!"

"Errr, I don't think so Jan, last time you'd drunk so much Prosecco you forgot which way to swipe and ended up matching me with every Tom, Dick and Harry,"

"You did get a lot of Dick, pics as a consequence,"

"My eyes are still recovering, I told you, never again…"

"You're such a spoilsport, c'mon let's just have a little look. I haven't touched alcohol today, yet." She consults her watch, "Though we could forget the coffee and have a gin, it is nearly the cocktail hour?" Mel realises she will also be doubling her alcohol units once she moves in here. Janet's measures are generous and then some.

"I was just broadening your horizons. I always said you are far too fussy,"

"I'm not fussy! I just have *standards*, I've deleted my profile, Jan, there were so many *inappropriate* matches."

She shudders thinking about it,

"The problem is your baseline is too high, you won't find many Aarons on Tinder," says Janet with a sigh. She is a staunch member of the Aaron Fan club nowadays, despite disliking the sound of him when she first heard Mel's stories. By then, however, Aaron had cleaned himself up, and Janet was willing to give anyone a second chance. She only needed to meet him once to be on Team Aaron for life; that easy charm also extends to winning over tough inner city teachers. Now they regularly share memes and moans about their beloved Manchester United. She'll still listen to Mel's grumbles about him, but is always fair in her commentary. Mental note, thinks Mel, never to introduce Aaron to any new friends,

"I didn't always go for golden boys," Mel is on the defensive, trying to shoot down the suggestion that she still holds any kind of torch for Aaron. "My first love was not like that at all. He lived on a farm. We went out for a while before... I met someone else. I suppose you would've probably called him a bit of a golden boy..." Mel trails off; she doesn't allow herself many memories of back then.

"I didn't know there was anyone before Aaron?" Janet tries to form the question casually. Mel is notoriously private about her life growing up in Yorkshire, "Is that when you lived with your Dad?"

Mel pauses, a bit lost in the past that she keeps buried deep, murmuring a yes, not having allowed herself to think about either of them for a long time. Her memories are so painfully tied up with her mum dying that she keeps them locked away. She remembers that she broke hearts and had hers badly broken, long before she went to Ibiza. Janet is curious about Mel's past. Besides knowing that she grew up in a small town in Yorkshire called Greenleigh and that both her parents are now gone, Mel never offers any other details.

"Have you told Kath, is it? About the move? " She fishes, Kath is Mel's dad's wife, aka the woman he left her mum for. Needless to say, they are not close. Kath still lives in Greenleigh, in the tumbledown farmhouse Mel moved into after her mum died. Mel sends Christmas cards and makes the occasional phone call, but to be honest, in all the chaos, Mel has forgotten about telling her.

"Kath? I guess I'll ring her once I've moved out..." She shrugs, changing the subject.

With some polite trepidation, Connor shows her the pictures

of the farmhouse Aaron is buying. With its sparkling blue swimming pool on a secluded hill with stunning views of the distant sea, it's the holiday home of dreams. Aaron insists she must come and stay once they've settled in. Mel can only imagine how weird that would be, giving him a noncommittal reply.

Connor talks her into having a leaving party, and not to seem as miserable as she feels, she agrees. She even makes an effort. Well, when Janet arrives, she insists that Mel go back upstairs and put on a dress. Mel, being more of a jeans and t-shirt type, spends the whole night folding her arms, but she does pile her hair up and even puts in some dangly earrings that she fiddles with all evening.

Connor has invited most of the guests, setting up the BBQ and chairs at the far end of the garden so his friends can steer clear of any adults. Janet and Steve come along with some of the other staff from the school. She invites all the neighbours out of courtesy, but these days it's all couples with young kids she barely knows. Connor insists that she ask some of the parents of his old school friends, with whom she has lost touch over the years. Mel isn't sure if anyone will turn up; she's always been a bit of a lone wolf, due to being an only child. Feeling a bit tipsy after a glass of the cocktail concoction Connor made with the odds and ends from the cupboards, she goes inside to find some juice to dilute it. Mindful that with teenagers around, it could get messy later. She doesn't want to spend the night holding back the hair of vomiting kids.

The house is pretty bare now. Most of the non-essential furniture has gone to a spooky storage facility that she hopes she never needs to visit alone at night. Connor's flight is booked for a few days after he gets his A Level results, which seem a bit null and void now that he isn't going off to university. He tells her that he will do his degree someday, but Mel suspects he's only saying it to make her feel better.

As she swirls a carton of cranberry into the punch, she tries not to let her worries spoil the evening. Sitting down on the bench, she looks down the garden, seeing the ghost of the old swing set Martin bought for Connor one birthday. He'd hurt himself jumping off it from a height more times than she could count. After several dashes to A&E for minor cuts and bruises, she dismantled it before he broke something. She remembers the paddling pools that would sag limply after a few uses, the sand pits cats used as litter trays, if you forgot to put the lid on, the ugly trampoline that nearly took off on one stormy day. She used to like lying out on it in the sunshine until Connor would find her and start jumping up and down to make her get up. The pedal cars, the little bikes with stabilisers, football nets and the endless retrieval of lost balls from next door's garden all still feel like yesterday, her eyes moistening.

Interrupted from her trip down memory lane by the arrival of more guests, Mel jumps up, forcing a smile, hoping that her tears haven't splashed too much mascara down her cheeks. Smoothing down her dress, she welcomes them in. The night swirls around her, Connor and his friends hang out at the top of the garden, someone plays music through a little speaker, and the girls dance around in their own little circle. Connor bought a ton of garden candles, which flicker in the dusk, illuminating their young faces as they drink to their friends' exciting departure.

Plenty of people turn up in the end, and it's nice to catch up with people she hasn't seen for a while. She has soothing conversations with other mothers who share her trepidation about the empty nest and the disbelief that, after all these years, the hard work is finally over. Finding out 'Where did the time go?' is a preoccupation not just for her, but for all the parents whose little ones are suddenly six feet tall and out drinking them down the garden - is reassuring.

She fields off a hundred disappointed enquiries as to whether Aaron is coming, to the point that she's convinced most people only came to see him; he always held a crowd when he made it to the school gates. He's a real 'Local boy done good' these days. However, it's a perfect summer evening. The smell of the BBQ mingles with the music and the sound of laughter, and she wanders happily from group to group, hazily drunk. Going into the kitchen to see if there are any snacks left, she finds Connor's friend, Callum, bumbling about, "Mrs O' Grady!" he roars as he sloppily dishes out drinks into red plastic cups,

"Callum for the 100th time, please don't call me Mrs O'Grady, Connor's dad and I were never married…Plus, it makes me feel old…"

"Sorry, Mrs O'… I mean Connor's Mum, "

"It's Mel," she insists, wondering in her head if she will ever stop just being "Connor's Mum",

"Well, *Mel*, I don't know why Connor's Dad didn't marry you." He stops pouring to consider her, whilst bouncing off the fridge,

"And you're not old. We all joke with Connor about how fit you are…You look lovely tonight." He is drunk enough to blurt it out, but not that drunk that he doesn't go bright red the minute it leaves his mouth. Callum gathers up the haphazardly filled cups while Mel fiddles around with crisps. As he leaves, he proclaims, "He should have put a ring on it!" while spilling half the drinks over the already sticky kitchen floor.

Mel laughs, fetching the mop, wondering for the hundredth time if things might have been different if she'd given in to

Aaron and his parents' wish for them to make it official. He proposed to her several times during his messiest years, but she always felt it was more of a sticking plaster than driven by real romantic desire. Besides, as a child of a marriage break-up, Mel didn't want that mess for Connor. Her parents had not divorced by the time Mel's mum died, but their break-up was hard on her. As a kid, it was all entwined, so that Mel blamed her mum's illness on it and deep down, still believes it's true all these years later.

She redirects her thoughts, fearful that the alcohol will spiral her downwards if she thinks about her mum for a second longer. Instead, she glances into the mirror and acknowledges that she does look kind of lovely tonight.

The following morning, however, she does not feel so lovely. She's not drunk that much since the work Christmas party, and it took her a good few days to get over that. Clearly, a lack of practice makes hangovers ten times worse, she thinks, throwing down some paracetamol with a strong coffee, whilst contemplating the mess from the night before. She'd made a cursory attempt to pick up any BBQ leftovers last night before she collapsed into bed at god knows what time. Connor and his mates were still in full swing, and the trail of bottles this morning indicated that they kept going for some time after all the adults were tucked up in bed. She still woke up annoyingly like clockwork at 7 am.

Pulling her dressing gown tightly around her, she ventures out into the garden. The sky is already blue, set to be another sunny August day, but as she inhales, there is a hint of autumn, that slight chill to the air. As she looks down her garden at the plants, she sees that summer's slowly easing out. Having kids and working in a school means your new year begins in September. After six weeks of solid childcare when Connor was little, she would throw herself a little party when they made it in one piece to the next school year. New shoes and packed lunch boxes, the theme changed every year until he only wanted money for chips. You got used to a new teacher and the increments of change that every school year brings until primary school was over, and he went loping off to high school without a backwards glance, growing up and away from her, which seemed like every day.

She takes a bin bag and a cardboard box to the BBQ area and starts sorting out the rubbish from the recycling. Picking up a Rizla packet with a wry smile, thinking they must have waited all night, desperate for the adults to leave, her eyes alight on a small plastic bag with some weed still inside. She opens it, inhaling the smell that takes her right back to being sixteen and skiving college to drive up to the moors, blasting music out the car speakers, well, until the day they killed the car battery and had to trudge the long, long walk back down to civilisation to get help.

She chucks it in the rubbish, consoling herself again about Connor following in their footsteps to Ibiza, with the fact that at least Aaron knows all the signs to look out for. On second thought, she puts her hand back into the bin bag and slips it into her dressing gown pocket. After all, there are tough times ahead; she doesn't know how she will feel after she drops Connor off at the airport, having been barely separated from him since the day he arrived in the world, red-faced and yelling indignantly.

On that first drive home from the hospital, lorries seemed to loom twice the size, all the cars whizzing by were going far too fast, and Connor seemed far too small to be in a world of such large, dangerous things. She thinks about Aaron making that journey with his newborn again in a few months. He won't be in the back of his dad's Sierra, off his head, this time.

Last week, she went with Janet (against her wishes, but she didn't want to seem rude) to see the new baby of one of the other teachers. Baby Luna was introduced wearing a designer ensemble at just 3 weeks and already owns a curated shelf of Converse, Nikes and tiny pink Ugg boots. As she was dutifully passed round, Mel managed to stop her fussing, lulling her into a peaceful sleep. Chloe, relieved that Luna wasn't spoiling her picture of maternal bliss by crying, was grateful, "You're so good with kids, Mel, the little ones all love you and look, you've got a way with babies. Now that Aaron is "Starting a family", you should have another baby! After all, it'll be weird that Connor has a sibling that's not yours, won't it?" Chloe misses the 'Don't go there' eyes that Janet flashes at her, but Mel didn't and is grateful that at least Janet knows about tact,

"I've not thought about it." Mel lies, changing the subject to inquire how Chloe's stitches are healing.

In the car on the way back, Janet wonders if she should bring it up while the topic is fresh. As a mum herself, she quietly agrees with Chloe that it must be strange to be in that situation. The age gap probably helps Mel get her head around it. She can't imagine that Connor will have much interest in a baby, but fast-forward, and when they are, say, 20 and 38, it wouldn't seem so extreme.

"Has Connor said anything about having a sibling?" Janet enquires. If I make it about Connor, she thinks it might prompt Mel to open her heart. But Mel, wise to Janet's tricks, shrugs her off with a "Not sure" and asks Janet instead for updates on the school expansion plans, a topic she knows Janet will run with all the way home.

Connor could not be persuaded out of bed early on A-level results day. Mel wants to get to school when it opens, but

Connor rolls his eyes and tells her to wake him up later. She knows he's nervous, but less about his academic achievements and more that he wants the new PlayStation his dad promised him.

As she waits, smiling across the car park at Callum's parents, she remembers her A-level results day. She had told her dad she would go with him and didn't come home the night before. She would let her phone run out of battery on purpose so no one could find her. She was perhaps the last one to rock up to the school with Jamie, high or drunk, probably both, to see her father sitting in his battered Land Rover in the car park, probably waiting there since the doors opened, worried that she'd never come home and determined to be there for the occasion. She failed every subject. He lost his temper and told Jamie in no uncertain terms to go home and leave her alone, wanting to blame her failure on his bad influence, even though it was Mel who didn't put the work in. She tried to run away from him, but her dad grabbed her arm to force her into his car. She yelled at him so much that one of the passing teachers came over to ensure everything was okay. Humiliated by causing a scene, Mel said she was just messing about, but her face burned red, and tears threatened to spill down her cheeks. Unconvinced, the teacher hung around to ensure she got into the car under her own steam. As they drove home, she sobbed, "I hate you, I hate you…"

The car door opens, shattering her memory. She can hear Aaron's voice and tries not to feel frustrated that he is stealing her last moments left, right and centre when Connor says,

"I told Dad I wanted you both to be here when I open them."

"Come on then, the suspense is killing us,"

Connor twirls the envelope around teasing, before handing it to her, "You open it, Ma, I can't do it"

Mel's fingers slip into the envelope, "Economics B, History B and Business Studies C. Oh, Connor!" She brushes away the tears, not wanting Aaron to see her cry, while Aaron hollers down the phone, "Nice one, Son!" Connor can't stop grinning. They are good enough grades to get onto the degree course, if he ever wanted to, "I'd better order that PlayStation…" Aaron tells him. Connor wants to talk to his mates, bounding back across the car park and handing Mel his phone to finish the conversation. There is a pause before they both speak simultaneously, "I'm so proud of him," they chorus.

"Bribery will get you everywhere, " Aaron continues,

"How's the house? Are you all ready for the move? I'm sorry I never got a chance to come back and say goodbye to the place…I know we went through some hard times there, Mel, but there were some good times too, weren't there?"

They both fall silent, acknowledging the memories,

"I'm fine, yeah, everything's fine… Did Connor tell you we're meeting your mum and dad for lunch? I haven't seen them for ages, it'll be great to catch up."

"You're so good, Mel, the way you are. You just get on with it, and you don't let anything bother you," Aaron smiles at her.

If only you knew, she thinks.

Splashing some of the money from the proceeds of the house, Joanne and Martin booked a table at an expensive restaurant in the city, telling them to order anything they wanted, which Connor took as read, ordering three courses at an eye-watering cost. Still, they are so incredibly proud of him that they don't care. He was their first grandchild and although Mel knows they are too nice ever to say it, she knows that they are relieved that somehow, despite the extreme odds, Mel and Aaron managed to raise Connor into a polite, educated young man and that they've enjoyed a close relationship with him despite the break up. If they are disappointed that he is following Aaron's footsteps, going off to Ibiza and not university, they keep it politely to themselves.

Joanne, too tactful to mention Maya, splutters on her coffee when Martin, after too much wine, mentions that they are excited about being grandparents again, for the fourth time.

"I hope our Aaron makes a proper job of it this time!"

"Martin!" Joanne tries to stop him, but he continues: "I'm sorry, Melanie, love. I don't mean any disrespect to you. You've done a sterling job, against the odds, with how our Aaron was back then. Connor's a great lad, and we're proud of you, son. But now Aaron is in a good place, I just hope he does better this time."

Joanne, sensitive to Mel, cuts him off by proposing a toast, and they all raise a glass to the future. Mel wishes heartily that she knew what was in store for hers.

Moving day arrives too fast. Aaron has arranged a flight for Connor in a few days, so he's staying with her at Janet's until then. Mel can't believe it's nearly time for him to leave. Thanks to her obsessive organisation, the removal men quickly load everything to go to the storage unit. Sadly, she watches as her worldly goods disappear for god knows how long.

Connor and Callum are loading the car for her with the bits she needs at Janet's. The house seems so empty and echoing, taking her back to when they first looked around. In her mind's eye, she sees Connor toddling about the dining room with toys strewn around the place. He and Aaron sprawled on the sofa watching TV together, then older in his high school uniform sitting at the dining room table doing his homework, all gone in the blink of an eye. She goes back upstairs to ensure the removal men have everything, lingering at his bedroom door, thinking of all the bedtime stories she ever read. Connor comes up the stairs behind her, and they stand together for a minute, staring into the empty room,

"You OK, Mum? The car's packed, Call's gone, I'm gonna meet him for a bit, later if Janet doesn't mind me going out? "

"I'm sure she won't mind as long as you get back at a reasonable hour Con, by reasonable I mean old people reasonable, like 10 pm and don't get so pissed you throw up in her flower bed,"

"That was you, Mum."

"It was *one time!* She poured super-strong gins, and I hadn't eaten anything. I guess we ought to get going then," she says, turning for the stairs. "Yeah, I'll be down in a minute, I just wanna, you know, say goodbye, wait in the car? I'll lock up."

Surprised by his last-minute sentimentality, he is understandably more excited about what is to come than what he is leaving behind. She leaves him to have his moment while she checks the rest of the downstairs. Before Connor can see her, she leans her head on the wall and whispers a thank you, going out the front door for the last time.

Connor throws his bag in the boot and they sit in the car for a minute, "Come on Mum…" Connor nudges her gently, "Time to move on."

ALEXANDRA WILDS

CHAPTER THREE

"Time to move on he said, Jan, as if it's nothing to him…"

After several of her trademark G&Ts, Mel is moaning to Janet, "It's easy for him, moving to Ibiza, starting a new life without a backwards glance."

"He'll miss you," Janet says soothingly, "But he's 18, Mel! You left home at 18 to do the same thing, and I bet you didn't look back either?"

"That was different,"

"Yes, it is because at least you know he's safe with Aaron, and now we have FaceTime!"

"He barely answers the phone to me when we're in the same city." Mel is feeling very sorry for herself. Janet, having raised two boys, has total sympathy for Mel. She knows how insulting it is when they leave home and barely bother to call.

Swirling her lemon around the glass, Mel says, "I remember when Connor was a baby, thinking motherhood was a con. How my life changed so unrecognizably, and Aaron just carried on partying, regardless. I realised that he loved Connor, but not quite as much as I did. Like how mums walk their kids on the inside of a pavement, but dads don't seem to think? I spent 18 years giving up my life to raise my kid right, for him not to give two hoots, and Aaron to get all of the glory." Mel stares hollowly out at Janet's rainy garden,

"I know what you mean, Mel, it's just part of being a parent, though, that letting go "

"But what am I left with?"

"Stretch marks and peeing yourself when you sneeze too hard!" They raise a toast to this grim truth.

Janet offers to drive them to the airport, "I'm worried you might cause an accident on the way home, trying to drive in tears."

"I'm fine!" insists Mel. She isn't.

"Besides, I thought we could go to the Trafford Centre afterwards to take your mind off things. Maybe Selfridges? Touch the expensive handbags?"

"Maybe not try and cuddle one this time though, eh?"

"That alarm was SO loud…"

Janet waits for her in Costa, after totally embarrassing Connor by hugging him for far too long, while insisting loudly that he doesn't do drugs. Mel walks him to the gate, trying to keep a grip on herself,

"You don't need to get upset, Mum."

Connor can tell she is about to cry, "It's only a 3-hour flight away, if I'd chosen, like, Bristol University, I'd be just as far."

"I would've cried then too,"

"I'll FaceTime you, all the time,"

"Will you, though, Con? You don't answer my calls now."

"I don't have my phone on me all the time."

"Connor O'Grady, it's surgically attached to your hand!"

"OK, but I don't always hear it ring."

"Selective hearing!"

"Dad says you can come and visit whenever you want. The house has loads of bedrooms!"

"I'm sure there are lots of hotels nearby."

"I'll probably be home for Christmas."

"Probably? I thought it was definitely?"

"Well, Dad said Christmas and New Year's are a good time to get DJ gigs. Flights can be a nightmare over the holidays, and I'm not sure if I'll be working. You could come to Ibiza instead, spend it with us all?" Mel is so busy thinking about how she will kill Aaron for even suggesting that Connor work all Christmas, that she almost misses the suggestion that she spend Christmas with Aaron and Maya. Bless Connor, he didn't get it, did he?

He grabs her in a bear hug before picking up his bag to go through, "Don't worry, Ma, I'll be fine!" he insists as he goes off with a quick wave, before turning the corner.

She knows that he will be fine, but will she? Selfridges gives scant solace, even the Mulberry bags that always make her sigh with joy (despite the likelihood of ever owning one) aren't doing it for her today. Janet insists they retire to the food court for salvation in sugar instead.

"I think you should buy yourself something nice to cheer yourself up, you deserve a treat from the house sale, something to remember it by, a bag, say."

"Oh God, Janet, you saw the price tags? Even the lesser designers are eye-watering."

"Mel, you never, ever buy yourself anything new!"

"There's nothing wrong with second-hand; it's better for the environment."

"You're addicted to charity shops," Janet shakes her head.

"They're more exciting than normal shops, and you never know what you might find."

"Just because you once found that Joseph jumper in Age Concern for a fiver, doesn't mean you can't buy something new for yourself occasionally! Just think of all the money you'll save, not keeping Connor in crisps,"

"That's true." She insisted that she pay her way while she stays with them, but Janet would only take a small contribution toward food. Mel is a vegetarian anyway, and vegetables are cheap, she says. Pay me in Pimms and Prosecco.

"Just a little something to spark some joy!" Janet twinkles, "Don't start that Marie Kondo'ing thing on me again. After you made me put on my underwear drawer, I didn't have a bra when I needed one."

"You need one every day, Mel."

"I wear a Sports *Bra!*"

"Doesn't count...What if you get run over and a sexy doctor has to strip you down in the ER?"

"Manchester Royal is not Grey Sloan..."

"You never indulge my fantasies," grumbles Janet, leading the way to Lingerie anyway. Mel blinks at all the satin and lace she finds herself amid. Janet rifles through the racks looking for what she thinks Mel should be wearing.

"No, Jesus Jan, I could floss my teeth with that!"

"Melanie McCarthy, unless you make a bit of effort, you will never have sex again."

"Janet!" Mel hisses as the heads of several nearby customers swivel to check her out,

"You know what that doctor said; it's meant to be used." Janet makes a triangle gesture with her hands in case Mel isn't sure what she is referring to.

"Look, Mel, I know you're feeling a bit low right now, I'm not nagging you, but Aaron has started a *whole new life,* and you can too, I know I keep telling you, but it is time you got back out there."

Ultimately, Mel acquiesces, choosing a couple of flimsy-looking underwear sets, mainly to shut Janet up on the subject.

When they get home, Mel excuses herself to her room for a private cry, having held it back admirably all day when it feels like her world has ended. She throws herself blindly on the bed in tears, nearly knocking herself out on a piece of wood. Sitting up, she examines it. Connor has removed the door frame from the old house with all his height markings on it. Mel sobs from her gut. There's so much she has had to say goodbye to in the last few weeks; it's overwhelming. He left a card, telling her not to worry, and that he loves her. She clutches them both to her chest as the tears spill out.

The new school term keeps them both busy, which thankfully keeps Janet off her case about Mel's 'Whole new life!' In contrast, it seems like Connor is throwing himself into his new life with gusto. He always responds to her messages, but sometimes just with a row of emojis to indicate his activities. Sunshine-smiley face-beer-fist bump isn't cutting it. In the end, desperate to know he's actually as "Fine!" as he claims, she takes a deep breath and calls Aaron. He answers cheerily, as always, giving the impression he loves to hear from her, that bloody charm of his.

"Hey, Mel! Great to hear from you! How are you? We're just having lunch by the pool!"

(Of course you are, she thinks through gritted teeth,)

"Connor's here and Maya and her sister, say hi, everyone, it's Mel! In rainy Manchester!" Everyone cheers.

"I won't keep you then, "Mel tries to sound equally upbeat, even though it has been raining for the last three days, and she put on her thermal socks earlier.

" I just wanted to check that Connor's settled in, OK?"

"I do ask him to ring you, Mel." Aaron interjects before he cops a lecture, "Oh no no, he texts me, all the time! "She doesn't want to sound clingy, "Just you know, making sure he's behaving himself, helping out in the house."

"Maya is blown away by how helpful he is! His room is always so tidy, she can't believe he makes his bed every day!"

Mel isn't sure, but she thinks perhaps her throat is closing up. Connor, make his bed every day?

"Great…" She squeaks, "Well, I'll leave you to it then."

"Wait, Mel, I want to talk to you about Christmas,"

Mel pretends not to hear that last part, hanging up the phone swiftly. A couple of minutes later, Connor sends her a flurry of photos of himself floating around an impossibly blue pool on what appears to be an inflatable lemon slice.

'When life gives you lemons, ' says the caption. Mel stems the urge to throw her phone out the window into the gloomy Manchester mist.

Mel and Janet soon establish a routine at home, as they have at work. They get back, change, and then meet in the conservatory for a pre-dinner G&T, comparing classroom notes while Steve cooks dinner for them. Mel offers to cook, but Janet always shoots her down, saying he likes to be helpful around the house. Steve agrees, but then Steve agrees with Janet 99% of the time. Janet jokes that's the secret to a happy marriage, a husband too afraid to disagree. Mel insists she gets takeaway for them all on Friday nights and tries to find things to do on the weekend to give them space. Janet loves to do a Sunday roast and invite the boys and their families or friends, and won't hear of Mel making herself scarce from these occasions, always citing her as part of the family.

These occasions are always chaotic, and thanks to Janet's generous pour, pretty tipsy. Neil, Janet's eldest, has given Janet three grandsons in six years. Janet loves them dearly but secretly hopes they stop there; they are very boisterous boys. His wife, Samya, seems to have endless patience, but the poor woman never gets to eat her dinner, always taking it home to heat up later as she deals with nappies and mashing up veggies, never sitting down the whole day. By contrast, her other son, Jonathan's, wife and daughter, Felicity and Ava, are a solemn pair. Ava is nine and intends to be Prime Minister to save the world from the impending doom of climate change. Ava is a vegan and spends the whole mealtime quoting her environmental heroes, telling everyone how bad beef is for the environment and tutting if anyone dares to say it tastes delicious. She gives Melanie her scant approval for being a vegetarian, but consistently sneers openly at the rest of the family for not saving the world by only eating chickpeas. Felicity and Jonathan are lawyers, drive an electric BMW(they wouldn't dare not), and live in Prestbury. Mel somehow always feels a bit less than in their presence, even though they are always very polite and welcoming.

On Steve's birthday, Janet invites both boys, Steve's brother and his wife, and their son Andrew, who is close in age to her boys, so they grew up more like brothers than cousins, she tells Mel as an introduction, ushering him into the seat next to hers at the table. She doesn't tell Mel that Andrew recently separated from his partner, Cindy. However, it doesn't take Mel long to pick up on the expectant vibes from the table as Janet introduces her as her *single* friend Melanie, their guest, while Mel is house hunting.

Not that Mel is doing any real house hunting; mostly, she is looking on Rightmove at all the large houses in leafy suburbs that she can't, in any way, shape, or form, afford. Unless she wins the lottery, which she gave up doing because she grew tired of being disappointed every week. She lingers longingly over the wide shots of basement kitchens with their accent walls, farmhouse tables & Dual-it accessories, imagining herself drinking coffee from the Gaggia on a Sunday morning. If she narrows the search to the 'reality' filter, it's a depressing bunch of basement flats and poky new builds with views of the inner ring road.

Andrew starts talking to her whilst pouring himself a huge glass of wine, bringing her out of her bifold doors into the garden day dreams, "I thought they were going to put me at the children's table for bad behaviour," he murmurs,

"What have you done to deserve the naughty step?" She checks him out, subtly, not her usual cup of tea, but attractive in a very clean-cut corporate kind of way,

"Not given them that!" he gestures at Neil wrestling a bucking baby into a booster seat.

"They're desperate to be grandparents, and as the lone child, I am their only hope." He takes another huge swig from his glass. "Help me, Obi-Wan Kenobi," she mutters in response. Andrew clinks her glass, appreciative of the reference, and they exchange smiles, none of which Janet misses.

Andrew, it turns out, is the same age as her. She waits, with experience, for the flinch when she tells him she is the mother of an 18-year-old son. To his credit, he doesn't seem put off by it, more amazed that anyone could have dealt with parenthood at such a young age. To be honest, he slurs, having opened a second bottle of red by this point, he doesn't think he'd make a good parent yet. When she tells him about Connor going to live with Aaron in Ibiza, he knows who Aaron is; somewhat more annoyingly, it turns out he used to go to the club nights that kept Aaron AWOL back in the day. She reminds herself that she will not mention Aaron to new people, especially men, who are always so impressed by his career. In contrast, women instinctively understood that being a club DJ didn't always go hand in hand with being a good dad.

When Andrew starts a conversation with Felicity on his other side, Mel takes the chance to size him up. He is smartly dressed, wearing a crisp blue shirt and navy trousers, but it is a formal occasion, even she is wearing a dress. Come to think of it, Janet had insisted she put a dress on, waving away her first choice for something with more cleavage. Mel was half wondering if Janet was trying to use her to lure Jonathan away from Felicity. It's no secret that Janet isn't a fan, but now Mel realises that she is trying to set her up with Andrew. Well played, Janet, thinks Mel, the wine having gone to her head already.

He is attractive, in a professional way, an account executive in finance, he says, dismissing it as too dull to discuss at dinner. He looks like he cares for himself, even if he's drinking heavily for a Sunday lunch that involves a lot of children. She wonders why their relationship broke up; he alludes to having unexpectedly found himself single but offers no further details. It seems impertinent to ask when the wound is still raw. Janet will give her all the details later anyway, she's sure.

She sits back, trying to play it cool and not glance down at his hands too often, which, the more wine she drinks, she seems to find very manly and appealing. There is an expensive watch poking out of his shirt cuff, over a smattering of dark arm hair and he is absently stroking his wine glass which, if she watches too closely, is making her blush. Jesus, Janet is right, it has been far too long. She helps herself to more potatoes to line her stomach; she must be drunker than she thought to be having such inappropriate thoughts at the dinner table.

She offers to help Janet clear the table, standing up too fast, making all the wine rush to her head. Wobbling slightly, she feels his hand on her back to steady her. A slow flush creeps up her face, really having to concentrate on not flinging leftovers over everyone. Luckily, nobody else seems to notice what she feels is obvious. To be fair, everyone else is also quite tipsy by this point, except for pious Felicity and poor frazzled Samya. Conversations are flying at full volume across the table, and the kids are keeping everyone entertained, loudly.

She crashes through the kitchen door, dropping the plates by the sink, leaning on the counter while Janet scrapes them into the bin "Having a nice time? "Janet enquires innocently,

"Don't act like you didn't have a plan all along !"

"Well, you know Jonathan would be my first choice to get you into the family, but unfortunately, there's Felicity, so Andrew will have to do." After perhaps a wine too many, Janet makes this statement loudly, "Shhhh!" Melanie waves to her to keep her voice down, the dining room is only on the other side of the kitchen door, and she does not wish to be in the crosshairs of the ferocious-looking Felicity.

"I think he likes you!" Janet carries on, full volume," I saw him touch your back and you keep staring at him when you think he's not looking, but he caught you, you know, and he was smiling to himself," Janet doesn't miss a thing.

"Shhh, Jan, bloody hell, I'd like to play it at least slightly cool. What happened with his ex?"

"He came back from a business trip to find she'd moved everything out of the flat. He said it came out of the blue, but June (his mother) told me that she didn't think they'd been getting along for a while, that things were frosty at Christmas."

At this moment, Andrew enters the kitchen looking for more wine, even though the stagger in his walk indicates that possibly the last thing he needs is more alcohol. Mel and Janet clam up, but a sixth sense tells him they are talking about him. He looks from one to the other, "What's that about Christmas, Auntie Jan?"

"It was SO COLD & FROSTY!" yells Janet,

"Frosty the snowman!" Mel blurts out the first thing that comes to her mind. Andrew eyes them both glassily before accepting their explanation, leaving with another bottle of wine,

"Frosty the snowman?" Janet starts laughing, which sets Mel off,

"Stop it, I'll wee myself!" which Felicity does manage to catch as she comes into the kitchen with the rest of the dinner plates,

"You really ought to do Kegels, Melanie, "she tuts.

As Mel makes it back to the table, Andrew is merrily onto his third bottle, seeming to forget that his parents and any children are present as he starts to flirt with her, at first touching her arm, then as she flirts back things amp up a notch, he puts his hand onto her leg. Not quite as drunk as him, she removes it but is secretly thrilled,

"You have the most beautiful brown eyes, Melanie. They change colour when you smile, like the autumn leaves," he says, staring intently at her. She thinks they are probably more bloodshot than anything else, but she isn't arguing with perhaps the nicest compliment she's been given in years. As Janet turns down the lights to bring out the birthday cake, Andrew leans over and sort of nuzzles her neck, insisting she put her number in his phone before his parents bundle him into their taxi. Dizzily, she helps Janet and Steve clean up the remnants of the party, hoping he might text her when he gets home. Eventually, she passed out on her bed, half undressed, phone in her hand, thinking of that fuzzy feeling that crept over her when he nibbled her neck.

She wakes up the next morning feeling hungover and guilty that their behaviour may have been a bit much. Much to her relief, Janet admits to only having pretty hazy memories from the main course onwards. She makes them both a strong coffee, doles out the paracetamol, and they drive to school in unusual silence, though Mel is secretly hoping that Janet will bring Andrew up so she can find out more about him, but she doesn't want to come across as too keen. She hates to admit it, but each time her phone buzzes, she finds herself jumping to check it like Pavlov's dog, hating herself instantly for feeling disheartened when it isn't a message from him. She remonstrates with herself straight after. Get a grip Melanie McCarthy you don't need to be chasing after any man. By the end of the school day, she is exhausted by her yo-yoing thoughts. She and Janet have stumbled through the day at half pace, the kids taking advantage of their weakened state, and the classroom is in chaos. After home time, they spend a good hour just tidying up, "For our sins", Janet mutters, drinking another vile staff room coffee to keep her going,

"So, have you heard from Andrew ?"Janet finally asks as they rinse out the paint pots and brushes.

"Err, no, why, have you?" Mel tries and fails to be casual,

"No, but I could text him if you like?"

"And say what? What could you say? I mean, I don't want to look desperate,"(Aware that saying it makes her sound pretty desperate.) This is why she gave up on dating; modern romance, with all its rules and reliance on technology, drives even the sanest person mad. You'd think it'd get easier as you get older, but if anything, it's way more complicated.

"I could say thanks for coming to dinner and stroking Mel's knee during dessert. She's been looking at her phone all day. Please put her out of her misery and ask her out?"

Mel goes as red as the poster paint she is wiping up; nothing gets past Janet. "Oh God, Jan, I'm so sorry, there was a lot of wine flying about!" Realising Janet couldn't see what was happening from where she was sitting, Mel burns up in shame at who else might have seen them. "Who told you?"

"Samya was texting me the updates all night, she could hear your conversation… Then, when she went under the table to retrieve a toy, she noticed *hands*."

"I'm so sorry, Jan, Samya must think I'm a right' flirt,"

"Not at all, she said it was the most excitement she's had in ages. All she does is change nappies and watch CBeebies all day. Vicarious thrills are all that's on offer!"

"I'll text her, apologise." Mel sighs, wishing the ground would swallow her up,

"Soooo, shall I text Andrew?" Janet is keen to push them together. Having just seen herself in the cold light of day, however, Mel says thank you but no and focuses on getting cleaned up so they can go home and she can climb under her duvet and die.

She's just got out of a long, hot shower (a futile attempt to wash away the shame) and into her pyjamas when Steve knocks on her bedroom door. Surprised at the interruption, Janet is out at her choir, (Mel does not know where she gets the energy from, planning on being in bed by 8 pm.) She pulls on her dressing gown and opens the door to find, of all people, Andrew standing there. Silently, she begs God for a lightning strike, "Andrew, err, hi," she mutters, brushing her wet hair down and strangling her waist with the dressing gown cord,

"Melanie, I am so sorry! Uncle Steve, Steve, he just waved me in, he's watching the Golf… I, err, I am so sorry to disturb you, he just said go up." He steps back awkwardly,

"Well, I wouldn't normally be in my pyjamas at, err half six," Mel blusters, (A blatant lie, but you know, preserve any shred of mystique & dignity.)

"To be honest, I was planning on going straight to bed when I got home, "he admits, "I think perhaps I was quite, a bit, err, drunk yesterday. That's why I came round." He shifts uncomfortably,

Oh, great, thinks Mel. Is she getting dumped before they've even been on a date? All while wearing her Tigger dressing gown to boot. In contrast, Andrew looks very suave in a nice charcoal grey suit with a blue tie that brings out the colour of his eyes.

For God's sake, Mel, focus.

"I want to apologise for my behaviour yesterday. I have an awful feeling that I was, god, I can't even say it, and I'm so embarrassed." He looks down, playing with his tie and blushing, which for some reason sends Mel's pulse racing,

"I think I may have misbehaved, Melanie. I was a bit, errm, nervous, I think, to talk to you. You're so lovely, I think I just got a bit carried away,"

So lovely, she'll take that, Mel thinks.

"I'm deeply sorry if I …" He hangs his head,

"It takes two to tango, Andrew. I wasn't an unwilling participant; you'd have known about it otherwise."

She continues before he gets the impression that this was her common garden behaviour,

"I also drank too much wine, and I was nervous, too. Nobody's flirted with me in forever,"

"Really? I can't imagine why not, Melanie," he smiles, relieved.

"It may have something to do with the fact that I'm in my pyjamas by 6 p.m."

"But you look so *attractive* in your Disney dressing gown."

"Good to know." They finally make steady eye contact, and she smiles back at him.

"Anyway, I shan't keep you from your early night." A pity, thinks Mel, things are just warming up.

He continues, "I sincerely apologise again, and I wonder if you might give me a chance to take you out to dinner so I can not behave so badly this time."

"Shame." Mel twinkles, unable to help herself, his eyes are so very blue, "I'd love to."

Janet goes all in, dragging her back to the Trafford Centre to look for something to wear. Andrew has booked a table at a pop-up restaurant that, according to reviews, 'Attracts serious food fans from around the world with its 'Renowned chefs and locally sourced, seasonal menu' which says expensive and achingly cool to her, neither of which is in her remit. Janet seems adamant that it's a posh dress occasion, but Mel firmly steers her from dressing her like she's about to be Prom Queen. Technically, this is Mel's first official date in years; she's somehow been single for far too many years to count now. There was a global pandemic, she likes to point out, for a year, Janet snorts, what's your excuse for the other six? Her last relationship was with Ben, but they never really went on dates. They worked together for a while before starting to see each other as friends outside of work. He was a mature student teacher, on placement from his university at the school, having given up his old job to do something "meaningful" with his life. There were no big romantic moments; it was just a gradual shift from friendship to a relationship, then back to nothing. She would have kept in touch with him after the break-up; she certainly harboured no hard feelings, but Ben didn't seem to want to, citing that as precisely the problem —that her last ex, Aaron, was still so present in her life. Ben would never impress Connor; Aaron's first big remix had just become popular. Poor Ben stood no chance with his earnest, environmental bike riding.

Mel has been living with Janet for nearly two months now. Not that she hasn't enjoyed it; it's been nice—maybe too nice. Janet couldn't be more caring, and her family couldn't be more welcoming. Samya keeps texting her for updates on Andrew, making plans to come round after the date to get a blow-by-blow account (her words). There will be no blowing, Mel insists. Samya begs her to live a little, please, on her behalf.

Thinking about the date with Andrew makes her feel like a teenager again. She fleetingly thinks about her first boyfriend coming to pick her up for the school prom. Well, technically, his dad did, driving them, all dressed up, to the local golf club that hosted the event. Her mum had been diagnosed as terminal by then, and while Mel didn't talk about it, Greenleigh was a small village; everyone always knew everything. He had a corsage for her and a massive bunch of flowers for her mum. She remembers how delighted her mum was that he was so thoughtful. Her face burns up suddenly as she thinks of how badly she treated him when he was nothing but supportive, "Earth to Melanie? "Janet appears in front of her with an armful of ridiculous frocks. "You were miles away!"

Mel snaps back to the present, those old memories, so mixed up and painful that she still can't bring herself, all these years later, to think about any of them. She takes the dresses from Janet with an eye roll. Everything is six inches shorter than she would ever choose, and at least two of them require some sort of strapless bra, a risk she just isn't prepared to take. After much fighting in and out of frocks in the changing rooms, Mel finally agrees to a modern take on a '90s slip dress. It's a silky fabric in a pale gold colour that Janet and the sales assistant (who now knows the whole story and is as eager as Samya for details) say suits her dark hair and skin tone. "With the right shapewear, you'll look amazing…" says the sales assistant, suggesting she try Skims. Mel tries not to be insulted by the suggestion, wishing she didn't live in a world where women were always expected to look picture-perfect.

She gets her retaliation by insisting, to everyone's obvious horror, that she has a cardigan at home that she can wear with it. Still, Janet stands firm, somehow convincing her to buy a pretty kimono jacket, which reminds her of the sort of thing she wore back in the day in Ibiza; it makes her feel young again as she examines herself in the mirror. She draws the line at new shoes, despite Janet pushing her to buy some strappy heels. Mel thinks she'll get away with sandals if it isn't raining. This being Manchester in Autumn, the chance that it will be bucketing down for the next 6 months is a given, but she'll risk it; the thought of wobbling over in heels is much worse.

The hairdressers in the blowdry bar are also wildly excited for her, ("You haven't been out with anyone for seven years?? SEVEN YEARS!! OMIGOD GIRL, you need to GO GET SOME!") Pressing her to have her brows done and, "No offence," her lip waxed and a mani pedi to match the gold dress. She declines the invitation for *other* waxing, wondering how much effort Andrew would've had to put into getting ready. She airs on the side of low maintenance, but he seems like the type who dates glamorous women. She sighs, wondering if this is just a stupid idea.

Mel marches out of there feeling like J Lo, her hair is massive, her brows are arched to perfection, and her fingertips glisten. Poor Steve doesn't know what to say as Janet makes her do an embarrassing twirl in front of him, "You look errr, very nice," he murmurs, unsure of the right thing to say. Janet offers to take her to the restaurant, but Mel firmly declines, not trusting Janet to come and insist she twirl for Andrew too.

In the Uber, Mel takes a few deep breaths, aware that all this hype is blowing the occasion way out of proportion; it's just dinner, no big deal. She secretly suspects that they will soon realise they don't have much in common. For all he seems nice, he exists in a very different social strata to her, he lives in a flat in Parsonage Gardens, (expensive,) does something fancy in finance and his ex girlfriend, Cindy, is a glamorous American who, according to Linkedin, is also some kind of executive and looks like the type who uses one of those desks that is also a treadmill. (Samya sent her a deep dive after she made the mistake of asking what she was like.)

She feels a bit like Cinderella comparatively, but that turned out ok in the end, she reminds herself, getting out of the taxi and dodging the puddles. True to form these days, the exclusive restaurant doesn't look very exclusive at all, housed in an old, dark mill in the Northern Quarter. Mel has to navigate various corridors and staircases to get to it, but it's a whole different story once she's ushered inside.

Soft candlelight gives the room a warm, cosy feel. There are plenty of customers, but no swivelling heads as she imagines in a panic at the door. Andrew is waiting at the bar, and everyone smiles as he looks at her. Getting up, he kisses her on the cheek, whispering, "Where's your dressing gown? Seriously, you look amazing, Melanie!"

Mel rockets from intense trepidation to it being the best date ever, her mood fuelled by some overpriced, high-octane cocktails. Andrew is charming and easy-going, never dwelling on any subject that might accentuate their differences. Instead, he asks her many questions and tells her funny stories from his travels. His job involves many business trips, which are not the exciting jaunts she envisaged, or so he says. Mel, who has barely been abroad since her time in Ibiza, apart from a few city breaks for some pretty hideous hen dos, thinks going to Milan just for the day sounds incredible, but isn't going to highlight her lack of experience by saying as much. She consciously tries not to talk too much about Connor. Other people's kids are boring unless you both have kids and are comparing notes on how annoying they are. However, he doesn't ask about him much, and if anything, he is more interested in Aaron (surprise, surprise). He is like the ghost of all her past, present and probably future relationships.

The food is fantastic; you don't choose (how fancy!) They just bring you dishes to try, and every crumb is delicious. They wind up the night with incredible coffee, some artisanal liqueurs, and chocolates before Andrew orders them an Uber; they are one of the last to leave. True to his promise, aside from that kiss on the cheek, he is on his best behaviour anddoesn't go anywhere near her. Conversely, it is making her move closer and closer to him, hoping that he might at least like, touch her arm, anything, but he doesn't. He won't hear of her splitting the bill. When Mel glances down at the figure on the bottom of the receipt, she is gobsmacked and relieved. He also leaves a generous tip.

"I'll take you home first," he directs the driver firmly. She is a little disappointed that he doesn't discuss going anywhere or to his place. Abstinence makes the heart grow fonder? All too soon, they pull up outside Janet's house. Mel swears she sees the curtains twitch as Andrew hops out to walk her to the door,

"Thank you for a lovely evening, Melanie."

"Mel..." she tells him for the 10th time, the only time her parents have ever called her Melanie, "Thank you so much; it was amazing."

"I hope I've redeemed myself for my behaviour on Sunday?" "You've been the perfect gentleman." Too bloody perfect, she thinks, tilting her head and pouting as a hint that all is forgiven and that he is now more than welcome to kiss her. She feels quite drunk and doesn't even care if Janet is watching. He leans down and kisses her chastely on the cheek again, "Good night, Melanie."

As he drives away, she allows herself a little frustrated stomp before Janet opens the front door with a raised eyebrow, "Don't ask!" Mel says, going sulkily up to bed, knowing Janet is eager for details but unsure what there is to tell.

Of course, she then can't sleep, replaying the whole night repeatedly, looking for the clues as to whether she can call it a success. Conversation flowed, tick. He complimented her outfit, told her several times, and even said that she looked gorgeous, tick. However, there was no real flirting, and most telling of all, there was no mention of another date. She tosses and turns, checking her phone in case he sends a follow-up text, eventually falling asleep in the early hours, after watching endless Friends repeats and wondering why on earth life never behaves like a sitcom.

Janet has invited Samya and Neil for lunch the next day, and Jonathan and Felicity are busy running a marathon for charity (of course, they are). While the men and kids are out in the garden, (Janet has tasked Steve with building the boys a play fort to keep them out of her hair.) The men discuss two-by-four while Samya demands all the details. Mel, who felt sure she'd hear from Andrew after the date, has spent all day moping like a teenager. She dissects the evening again for Samya's benefit, hoping she might pick up on some nugget she and Janet have perhaps overlooked on their previous ten reruns. Still, Samya declares herself thoroughly disappointed that there is no salacious gossip. However, she does provide some further gossip on his ex-girlfriend, Cindy, whom she met a few times at family gatherings. From what she remembers, Cindy's parents are quite prominent in the church in America and were increasingly frustrated with the lack of a ring, given that they had moved in together the previous year. When Cindy had tried to push Andrew into proposing, he said he wouldn't be forced into marrying her just to please her parents,

"A commitment phobe, Mel, you're better off out of it…" Samya shrugs,

"I wasn't looking to put a ring on it…" Mel sighs.

"I am!" huffs Janet, who wants Mel officially in the family, wondering if she should have a quiet word with Andrew.

"It's fine, honestly, it isn't like I'm massively into him or anything; besides, I've got more important things to do."

"What's more important than getting some action after a seven-year drought? "Samya asks, incredulously.

By the time he messages her, she has entirely convinced herself that she isn't bothered. Realistically, can she see herself fitting into his life? They are probably just too different. However, when she sees his name flash up and snatches up her phone, she knows it's true—the lady does protest too much. "Thank you for a great evening. Would you like to do it again sometime?"

She goes to reply, but a shred of dignity surfaces; she's waited to hear from him, and if she'd been advising a friend, she'd tell them to be equally cool, although all the 'rules' around communication are the reason she can't be bothered with dating. Besides, she needs to put in some time on RightMove today, such as looking at houses that she can afford, instead of daydreaming about dual aspects and open fires. She puts her phone down and carries on sorting out her washing, but it starts ringing,Connor.

"Hey, Ma!"It was his first phone call; most communication was usually emojis, scattered with the occasional voice note.

"Hey Con, is everything okay? "She tries not to sound suspicious. "Yeah, Dad said he's been trying to get hold of you, but you never answer his calls."

"Sorry, I've been busy, you know, with school and house hunting and stuff," Mel lies smoothly,

"Have you found a house then?"

"Err, no, not one we can afford anyway... How are you ? What have you been up to?"

"Yeah, good. I've been with Dad in the studio just like watching what he does, and I've got a job on a weekend at Cafe Samba, just collecting glasses, and they're gonna train me on the bar, and maybe eventually I'll be able to play a set there...It's been pretty quiet in the past few weeks, but Dad says it will pick up again in December. That's why I'm ringing. Dad wants to know if you want to come out here for Christmas? He's gonna sort out the flight, but they get booked quickly..." This is the exact reason she's been dodging Aaron's phone calls; he's left her several messages telling her how welcome she is. Not to be rude, but the idea of sharing her Christmas with him and Maya just makes her feel more inadequate than she already feels.

"I just don't know Con, I mean, if I find a house,"

"You're not gonna be moving house on Christmas day, Mum! It'll be fun! What are you gonna do if you don't come? Spend it with Janet and Steve in the cold? Or you could come and stay in the sunshine? Dad's letting me drive the Jeep. We can, like, drive to all the places you used to go?"

It's his last comment that finally makes up her mind. Lately, she can't somehow shake the feeling that she will never be able to move forward with her new life unless she faces up to some of the ghosts from her past. "Well, thank him for the very nice offer, but I can book my flights and tell him to double-check with Maya that she's cool. I don't want to intrude,"

"Maya is way cool, Mum, she won't mind at all, they're going to stay with her family on Boxing Day for a few days anyway, so we can just chill out here, in the pool all Christmas!! I don't think I'll ever come back to Manchester!" he says without thinking,

Somewhat strangled, Mel replies, "I don't blame you, Connor."

Pretty sure she had said the same thing to all her friends when she sporadically reported back in from Ibiza herself,

"Ma, I didn't like, mean *never*, hey, maybe you should move out here too? Anyway, I'd better go, I'll tell Dad you're coming, 'miss ya Mum!"

"Love you, Con. Be careful in that Jeep, ok? "

He puts the phone down, and she takes some deep breaths. Sometimes, she misses him so much that it feels like a physical wrench. He'll always be her baby, and she wonders if that ever changes.

Guilty thoughts creep in about how her dad must have felt when she disappeared to Ibiza without a backwards glance. She never rang him, just sent the occasional text to let him know she was still alive; she never answered any of his calls. He must have been so worried. Now here she is, in her dad's shoes, and she feels so much guilt, but it's an uncomfortable truth that she can do nothing about now. She thinks again that she must tell Kath that they've moved house. She'll get Connor to send her a postcard.

To distract herself from thinking about the problems from her past, she turns her attention back to Andrew, it's been nearly an hour, not exactly playing it cool but better than nothing. She crafts a reply, "I'd love to (Is love a bit strong?) She isn't sure, so she changes it to, 'That would be nice' Does nice sound a bit lame? 'Hey Andy, that would be fun? That sounds cool?' She dithers so long that bloody AI pipes up. No, I don't need your help, do I? It'd probably do a better job.

Aware that Andrew could be watching 'Mel is typing ' and wondering if she's writing him a 3,000-word essay; she goes with, 'That would be great, it's my treat this time.' Then she panics, she doesn't have his budget, " Probably won't be anywhere award-winning lol," She adds on,

He immediately replies, "It's the company I'm interested in, not the food" With a grin, she replies, "Friday?"

"Great, let me know when and where."

Settling on a casual 'Will do', she immediately starts to freak out over where she can take him that will give his expensive, artisan taster menu a run for its money,

"JANET!"

After much debate, a FaceTime with Samya, some random suggestions from AI of 'Great date ideas' and scouring all the local events, Mel comes up with a shortlist, her personal favourite being the one that both Janet and Samya think is the absolute worst. As it's mid-October, all the Halloween events are starting, and they are holding an open-air cinema event at Southern Cemetery. It's a horror film, of course, bring your picnic, umbrella, and blankets. Mel loves horror films and has done so since she was a teenager. She used to try to outdo her then-boyfriend by finding the scariest films for them to watch together. She still jumps out of her seat like the next person at a good scare, but she can sit through the creepiest of movies without sleeping with the lights on for the next month.

Southern Cemetery, made famous by The Smiths' song, is a rambling maze of dramatic Victorian graves. She used to walk Connor around it in his pram when he wouldn't go down for a nap, pointing out the resting places of Manchester's great and glorious as they trundled around. Maybe it was a bit morbid, but Mel found it interesting to look at the lives of people gone by, plus it was always quiet enough for Connor to fall asleep. Janet protests that Mel can come up with something better,

"What if he hates horror films?"

"Then we're not meant to be," Mel asserts. Of course, she can't resist the text "Meet me at the cemetery gates." She wonders if he will know what she's talking about and, if he does or doesn't, whether that will be a sign. A sign, she laughs at herself. Does dating at any age make you act like you are somehow in a Hallmark Christmas movie?

He sends back a question mark. Disappointed that he isn't a Smiths fan but reminding herself that opposites can attract, she spells out the address and time. She reminds him to wrap up warm and that all food and beverages will be provided. Thankfully, due to the nature of the occasion and the already baltic temperatures, (Manchester mostly jumps from its paltry summer straight to winter,) she doesn't have to have any hot dates with the blow-dry bar this time. Janet rolls her eyes as Mel plonks a woolly hat on her head on the way out. This is much more her style, if she's honest. She may not look a million dollars, but she has spent what feels like it on the food from the fancy local deli, deftly packed by Janet into her vintage wicker picnic basket, with local craft beers to drink and a pile of picnic blankets that she imagines they might snuggle under as the night progresses.

Arriving at the cemetery early, she watches the eclectic crowd going in; it doesn't take her long to spot him arriving; he hovers awkwardly, looking around him. They aren't the oldest there, but he's probably the smartest in his formal grey wool overcoat and scarf. He looks heartily relieved to see her, nervously kissing her lightly on both cheeks, insisting that he take the basket and bags from her. Mel smiles. It's nice to be looked after for a change.

"I wondered what you had in store when you told me to meet you here," he looks around, confused by a group of steampunks milling about in their finery,

"I bet you think I'm a real weirdo." Mel wonders too late if perhaps she should have listened to Janet and Samya (and everyone else she'd asked for advice)

"I looked it up, did you know it's in a Smiths song? "

"Meet me at the cemetery gates?"

"Oh, right, I get it now." He grimaces,

"I thought everyone from Manchester loves The Smiths?" she teases, "Are you a big Smiths fan then? I was more into clubbing, to be honest, I told you, didn't I? I used to go to Aaron's night at Sankeys,"

Mel cuts him off before Aaron's ghost can join them in the already haunted location,

"I don't dance around with gladioli, but surely you can't live here without listening to them? They're like Manchester music royalty." She stops herself from joking about 'The Queen is dead', he won't get that one either.

"Though, for the record, I'm not a Manc, I'm a white rose," She tells him,

"Wow, now you tell me, so I'm on a date with a shoe-gazing, gore-loving Yorkshire woman in a creepy cemetery in the pitch dark. Should I be worried?" He laughs, reaching out for her hand; at least he has a sense of humour about the event. Mel enjoys the warmth of his hand in hers as they file through the famous gates and onto the lawn, which serves as the open-air cinema. Andrew is relieved they aren't sitting amongst the graves, although up the path behind them, they can see the shadowy shapes of stone angels in the gloom.

"I looked up the trailer for the film, and it looks terrifying."

"Oh, good, you haven't seen it before?"

"No, to be honest, horror films aren't my thing."

Mel freezes from lying out the picnic blankets. What was she thinking? Janet was right; she should have checked.

"Oh, we can do something else, if you don't want to watch it?" She blusters,

"No, not at all, I don't *mind* them, this is all very... cool!" He waves at the crowd settling down around them, "Not something I'd ever think to do. It's good to get out of your comfort zone, isn't it? Thank you for inviting me. Have you seen it before then?"

"Yes, and you're right, it is terrifying,"

"Well, you can tell me when to shut my eyes."

She suggests they eat before the film starts, "Depending on whether the sight of blood puts you off your food?"

" Not something anyone has ever asked me before", he clinks her bottle," Thanks for the lovely picnic."

While they nibble on mini pies and posh pastries, Mel digs for details about his past relationships. She would rather not be a rebound fling if she could help it,

"So not the sort of date you went on with your last girlfriend?" She asks casually,

His face immediately goes rigid at the mention of her, "Not in a million years she would more than likely consider this blasphemy, she's American, heavy on the Christianity. They have extreme feelings on lots of things us Brits do that Jesus would disapprove of."

"Oh, she's American?" Like she didn't know,

"I'm sure Janet will fill you in," he abruptly closes the subject. Sensing a shift in his mood, she changes the topic to his work. He's been away that week, so they talk about that instead until the film starts. Poor Andrew is trying his best not to appear scared, but after about the 10th jump, scattering crisps and beer again, she moves closer, telling him to feel free to hide his face in her shoulder and tell him when to look away. Mel tries to appear casual as he circles her waist with his arms, leans his head on her shoulder to watch, and buries his face in her hair when it gets terrifying.

At that point, Mel starts to lose all focus on the film, hyper-conscious of his thigh touching hers, his warm breath on her neck whenever he leans in. She lightly rests her hand on his leg when the film gets scary; in return, he rests his hand on her thigh. Enjoying the sensation, Mel tries not to react but wonders if, as things progress, will she just spontaneously combust; it's been so long? She takes a large swig of beer. She supposes this is what you get when you don't date anyone for years.

The film comes to its bone-chilling conclusion. The relief on Andrew's face is obvious. Mel is disappointed when he jumps straight up; she could've happily sat there snuggled up to him all night,

"You don't want to go for a look around the cemetery,

then?" she half-jokes. Andy Rourke and Matt Busby are here somewhere, and Tony Wilson."

"[Manchester] 'City for the record, plus I don't think I'll ever sleep with the light off again as it is, thanks Melanie."

"Mel," she reminds him, again,

"How about we go somewhere with all the lights on for a nightcap?" He suggests, shouldering all the bags.

Mel suddenly decides her top priority needs to be moving out of Janet's. If she lived alone, she would have invited him back there for a "Coffee" even though no one their age drinks coffee after 6 pm anymore. They decide to go to Didsbury, where there are plenty of bars to get a late drink, so they walk down Barlow Moor Road. To pass the time, they swap their best Manchester stories. He's been in the queue at Sainsbury's behind Shaun Ryder. She offers that Connor once played in a park with Ryan Giggs' kids, and years ago, she'd once served pizza to Howard Donald, who signed a napkin for her; she still has it somewhere. Andrew used to play football with Nick Grimshaw, and of course, they'd both seen various Corrie and Emmerdale stars in the bars. Andrew admits that there are sometimes paparazzi outside his apartment block, but he isn't sure who the pouting girls are that they are snapping.

At the bar, warm and full of a glamorous friday night crowd, Mel, self-conscious about her clothes, keeps her coat on (Acquiescing that she really should have listened to Janet), quickly pulling off her hat, though, hoping her hair is passable. Andrew, who only wears a plain jumper over a shirt and jeans, somehow looks perfectly in place. Wealthy people have this aura that can't be replicated, even if you wear all the gear. She watches him navigate the crowd; it's an innate confidence that everything is always alright, never having sleepless nights about the winter gas bill or being inventive with tuna and pasta again. In her heart, she knows that whatever this is between them will probably never amount to a serious relationship; their worlds are too far apart. He sets down the drinks, then toasts her, "To a most unusual but enjoyable evening!"

"See? Horror films aren't horrible…"

He looks at her with a smile hovering on his lips. "Honestly? I stopped concentrating on the film when you cuddled up and stroked my leg."

Mel's pulse starts to quicken. It's so easy, or perhaps she's just easy.

"I was just trying to distract you from that scene where he got the chainsaw and…"

"Can we please never talk about that again?" Andrew groans, "Touching your leg?" Mel desperately tries to remember how to flirt, "That gruesome murder…You can talk about, and touch, my leg anytime, for the record,"

"Well, thank you, that's a very generous invitation." Emboldened by the red wine, on top of the craft beers, she rests her hand on his thigh, and before she knows it, his head moves towards her and his lips meet hers. He may have only gone in for a kiss but Mel, enjoying it far too much to let him stop, presses her lips into his and finds her hands pushing further up his thighs, momentarily forgetting where they are, before a sense of dignity kicks in and they draw apart, "Back to mine?" He murmurs. Silently thanking Janet for pressuring her into buying those flimsy pants (that she only wore tonight to reassure herself), Mel murmurs back a yes, safe in the knowledge that at least her underwear is up to the occasion. They only make it out of Uber before they start kissing wildly like teenagers, so caught up in the moment, Mel scarcely pays attention to the swanky apartment block he leads her into. A silent lift whisks them, fumbling, up to the upper floors where it deposits them into a quiet hallway. Giggling Mel follows him through the door into the poshest flat she's ever been in.

It wouldn't have been her taste in a million years, but she can't help but be slightly in awe. Ultra modern & minimalist, not a scrap of clutter anywhere, just sleek black surfaces with discreet appliances and a jaw-dropping view of the city through the large windows. Mel looks out at the Manchester skyline, twinkling ahead of her, the momentum of passion temporarily forgotten. She steps to the window and is entranced. "Some view!" She says, returning to reality with a bump, this place is far from her comfort zone.

"Not as nice as this one," he says, turning her round so her back is pressed up against the glass, kissing her again. It feels good, great even, but something about the wealthy apartment has broken the spell; she's out of her depth. This is a world she's never inhabited, and a man who is very different from anyone she's ever dated feels uneasy. Nervous giggles bubble up, and suddenly, she can no longer stem them. Stopping, he steps back from her, frowning, "Is my kissing funny?"

"No, no, sorry, I just..."

He steps away into the kitchen. Mel wants to kick herself for ruining the moment. He opens the vast black fridge,

"Can I get you something to drink?"

Suddenly feeling sober, Mel asks for a glass of water. Silence falls as he gets her a chilled water from his fancy fridge. She turns back to look at the city lights, trying to decide on her next move. Sex suddenly seems like the last thing she wants to do. She remonstrates with the fired-up Mel of earlier. What were you thinking? You don't know him well enough, yet. Now she feels awkward, babbling about everything she can see out the window just to break the silence. He sets their drinks down next to the long, low sofa, kicking off his shoes and sitting down. If he pats the seat next to him, she thinks I'll run out the door. He doesn't, making polite small talk. The mood is as cold as her water. He seems to get that the moment has passed, and once he finishes his drink, he offers to call her a ride home. Should she apologise, she wonders, as they go back down in the same lift they had been groping in an hour earlier. For what? She argues with herself; she is allowed to change her mind. She mutters to him as she climbs into the Uber, "I just, I got nervous."

Andrew says he completely understands, that they got a bit carried away earlier, and he should never have suggested that they go there. He kisses her lightly, telling her to message him when she's home. Her face burns. She feels like such an idiot. Although she likes Andrew, or what she knows of him, she isn't ready. Relieved that Janet is already asleep, she creeps into bed feeling disheartened.

The next morning, she wakes up cringing, but at least with no regrets. She might have felt worse this morning if she had gone there, but then again, would she? Perhaps she might have been smirking to herself all day with a twinkle in her eye, like you used to when you had some bona fide fun. She rolls over in the empty bed, face planting the spare pillow with a sigh, wondering what will happen now.

Pulling herself together, she decides it's time she stops distracting herself with Andrew and starts sorting her life out. She needs to take her property search seriously. Being at Janet's is so easy. After 18 years of being the head of the household, juggling bills, and doing all the food shopping and DIY, she's probably enjoying having no responsibilities, a bit too much. It's a bit like being a child again, although her childhood wasn't this blissful. Her parents had never seemed happy together. Mel always felt an underlying tension that she could never quite grasp, and when she was a young teenager, her dad left them to live with Kath. Things got better for a while anyway, but it was never carefree; it wasn't long after that her Mum got sick.

Downstairs, making a strong coffee, she fends off Janet's enquiries about the date with vague answers, trying to ignore Janet's raised eyebrows that are desperate for details. She takes her coffee to go, deciding she'll take the tram into the city, with a plan to trawl the estate agents in the areas she'd like to live in, then, more realistically, the places she can afford.

Raised in an old stone mill cottage with wonky floors, low beams and open fires in every room, Mel is struggling to reconcile living in a boxy flat. When she'd lived with her dad and Kath, it was in a remote, ramshackle farmhouse up on the moors, which had the most amazing views that, of course, she took for granted.

Manchester is so expensive these days, she sighs, staring frustratedly at the window of another estate agent. The price of some of the flats is eye-watering. She peers at one that looks familiar. It's in the same block as Andrew's in Parsonage Gardens, but the price tag is about five times what she can afford to spend. She checks her phone. No word from him, just more messages from Samya pestering her for dirty details.

Whether she likes it or not, she knows she needs to realign her property expectations and widen her search area to less desirable areas; perhaps she can find something in the next up-and-coming district. I mean who'd have known twenty years ago that 'Levy would have been gentrified?

New Islington is the place to be, the estate agents keep telling her. 'Vibrant' is the buzzword they keep throwing at her, but as it's already up and came. It's out of Mel's budget anyway; besides, she remembers when it was just plain old Ancoats and nobody in their right mind wanted to live there. If she moves further from school, she'll face a tedious commute. Sitting in traffic on Trinity Way every day holds zero appeal. She doesn't earn enough to afford a substantial mortgage, even though she has some money from the house sale to use as a deposit. It seems to her like single and low-income people are increasingly getting pushed off the property ladder. On top of interest rates going up, the cost of living crisis and talk of another recession, Mel feels a wave of despair wash over her as she looks in the windows. How does anyone afford to rent anywhere, either? The prices are eye-watering, and she's heard of people offering over the asking because it's so competitive.

She tries not to think of the white washed farmhouse with its distant sea views and turquoise swimming pool that Aaron managed to buy. Looking over the depressing choices, she becomes consumed by fury. She's the one who slogged it out on the school run every day for 7 years, making endless packed lunches, watching Fireman Sam on repeat until she could scream if she heard the word Pontypandy again. She was the one who washed the sick out of the sheets at 2 am, organised every birthday party, and cleared up the reindeer food in the cold on Christmas Eve so Connor would think Santa had been. Yet she's the one who'll be living in Stockport in a high rise with a lift that smells of wee. Connor will never want to come home and visit because it's so depressing. She will die alone, and there won't even be a dog to eat her, because she's heard the horror stories about the size of vet bills, so she can't afford to get a pet. When did necessities like homes, food, and pets become luxury items? How are everyday people supposed to live?

Hot tears spill down her cheeks, and she hurries away from the estate agent's window before anyone can ask her, politely, to move along. She finds herself wandering in an area she doesn't know, half blinded by the tears that won't stop coming, caught up in a surge of frustration at Aaron happily starting all over again when, try as she might, she can't find anything much to look forward to. It doesn't feel fair. Out of the blue, she hears her Dad's voice in her head. Mel had repeatedly protested that it wasn't fair that she was forced to live with him and Kath and adhere to their rules. He'd looked her in the eye and told her sternly, "Life isn't fair, Melanie, and if you think it is, you are going to be very disappointed."

He was right, life isn't fair, and she is very disappointed. Her phone starts to ring in her bag, breaking her from her misery. She answers it without thinking,

"Hi Melanie? I just wanted to say thank you again for an interesting night." Oh God, it's Andrew, taking a deep breath, she tries to sound upbeat,

" I'm glad you enjoyed it," she stutters,

"Are you ok, Melanie?"

"I'm FINE!"

"Are you sure? You sound upset?" Men do pick their moments to be intuitive,

"Just err, out house hunting. These prices are enough to bring you to tears." She says, not untruthfully,

"I know, I came to see you at Janet's, to apologise. I feel terrible about last night. I pushed things too far, too fast. I'm sorry."

A group of lads walk by, yelling at each other, music blasting from their phones, they push past Mel without a second glance,

"Where are you?"

Mel stopped and looked around, none of it was familiar "I don't know, "she sniffed, "I'm a bit lost...Castlefield somewhere, I think,"

"Ping me your location, I'm leaving Janet's now anyway, I can come and get you. If you want me to?"

"It's fine, I'm alright, you don't have to..." she trails off. She really wants someone to take her away from all this right now. Andrew sweeps up 20 minutes later in his shiny black Audi with its personalised plates. She hasn't thought about the make-up she's wept down her cheeks, until she sees him staring at her concerned. She climbs into the car, grateful for the instant comfort from the heated leather seats,

"I've got mascara all down my face, haven't I?"

She pulled down the mirror in front of her with a grimace. He indicates a packet of wet wipes in the glove compartment, and she tries to make herself look presentable, wondering what on earth he must be thinking of her right now.

"Where to' love?" he asks playfully,

"Oh, I don't know. I'm supposed to be going to some estate agents, organising viewings, but to be honest, after a couple, it's a bit depressing."

" I can drop you back at Janet's?"

"You've just come from there. I'm sure you've got things to do. Would you drop me at a tram stop somewhere?"

"I came to Janet's to see if I could take you out for lunch to make it up to you for last night. I'm not making the best impression, am I? This is my second apology to you, and I've only known you for a few weeks."

"And as I said last time, it takes two to tango, it's not all on you, you know, we were both a bit drunk, again."

"Can we start over, do you think? "He looks so forlorn that it tugs at her heartstrings,

"Hello, nice to meet you, I'm Melanie McCarthy," She offers him her hand, "Andrew Johnson, at your service."

After that, they slip, somehow, into a relationship. Janet declares herself cupid, thrilled to see them both happy. Despite her initial reaction to Andrew's flat, Mel soon gets used to staying in the swanky apartment, especially fond of the huge bathroom with its jacuzzi bathtub. I mean, who could resist? The large windows extend into the bedroom, so you can lie in bed and look out at the twinkling city lights, soon getting over her fears. They are very different people, but they both enjoy nice food, wandering round the Northern Quarter on a Saturday and lying in bed on a Sunday morning with the newspapers. Andrew passes her the magazines, and they do the crossword together. He always makes her feel appreciated, and it all feels very mature, even if Mel doesn't.

Every time she stays over at his, she feels like she's having a night at a 5-star hotel. The only downside is that it's making her house search seem even more depressing. Andrew offers to accompany her to viewings, but she can't bear for him to see the shoe boxes in her budget.

December arrives quickly, the city is aglow with festive lights. Andrew was very disappointed when she told him she'd be away for Christmas, voicing his surprise on several occasions that she'd be staying with Aaron and Maya. Mel is conflicted herself; she misses Connor so much, but the thought of spending all that time with Aaron and Maya is making her anxious. Now with Andrew in the picture, it would've been nice to see him over Christmas, but then again, now she is seeing Andrew, it might not be so bad spending time with Aaron. She flies to Ibiza on the 23rd and will return on the 29th. Andrew keeps suggesting that they go away somewhere for New Year's Eve. Mel worries that after leaving Connor, she may not be in the mood for more celebrations.

Somehow, she can't articulate this to Andrew without sounding ungrateful; he seems determined to arrange something. Beginning to sense a slight chip on his shoulder about her staying with Aaron, she gives in, saying she'd love to, then he tells her it will be a secret. Mel is not a fan of secrets, so much was kept from her as a child, but she acquiesces out of guilt. She just hopes it doesn't involve too much activity; by the sounds, she will not get much R & R in Ibiza. Every message she gets from Connor includes a link to something they will see and do, most of which involve going out when she usually goes to bed. Andrew drives her to the airport, despite her insistence that she can easily take the Metro. He's been a bit, how would she put it? *Clingy* in the last week, and she isn't quite sure how to handle it.

"Have you told Aaron about us? " He fishes. Not again, Mel thinks, she isn't sure she can handle another man with an Aaron-shaped chip on his shoulder. "It's nothing to do with him, but he'll be pleased for me. Connor will be too, it's just, you know, Drew. (She's trialling this nickname, so far, he seems accepting.) It's still very early days,"

"I am serious about you, though, Melanie." He squeezes her hand." You're not like anyone I've ever met."

What, poor you mean? Thinks Mel, wondering if she could technically be classified as his bit of rough. He's never made her feel less than, yet she's acutely aware of the disparity in their wealth. He kisses her at the gate, telling her he can't wait to see her next week for their New Year's getaway, but to be honest, she is too thrilled to be going back to Ibiza to give anything else a second thought.

CHAPTER FOUR

As the plane taxies down the runway, Mel's stomach lurches excitedly. It was strange to travel without Connor, not that they'd had many holidays abroad, but watching the excited kids on the plane made her feel nostalgic. That's the thing with being a parent: in the moment, you're so busy trying to keep your kid alive and on the straight and narrow that you don't necessarily get to enjoy the things you're doing. Only years later, when the chubby little hand no longer grabs yours, you realise having two free hands isn't all it's cracked up to be. Sometimes she aches for Connor to be that round-faced toddler again on the beach, happily playing in the sand and splashing in the sea. Where did the time go?

Letting out a huge sigh, she startles the couple next to her, who take it as a fear of flying and quietly offer her an array of medication. Mel takes a mint instead and tries to quell her nerves by rewinding her thoughts to her first trip to Ibiza. Her best friend's aunt and uncle ran a bar on the Sunset strip and offered Siobhan a summer job before she went to university. After her terrible breakup (technically, breakups), Mel had begged her to take her along. Siobhan had always planned on coming home in September, but after the last few years, Mel was over her old life. As far as she was concerned, there was nothing left for her in Greenleigh; it was over with Jamie, Chris was never speaking to her again, she'd burned all her bridges with his family,(who she had loved) and she hated living at the ramshackle farmhouse with her Dad and Kath. She packed up all her belongings when she left, not wanting her Dad to go through her stuff once she was gone, and she'd thrown it all in the bin without a second glance, determined she was done with that part of her life; there was no going back. It was time to leave her miserable past behind and start a new life.

She remembers that feeling when they'd first stepped off the plane and the heat hit them. She'd never been further than Scarborough on holiday. She and Siobhan did a crazy dance on the aeroplane steps (of course, they'd been drinking at the airport and on the plane) and everyone behind them cheered. As they stood outside the airport waiting for Jackie to pick them up, marvelling at the blueness of the sky and all the palm trees, for the first time in years, Mel felt free from her grief. She was determined that all the sorrow and heartbreak wouldn't come with her on this leg of her journey.

If only she'd known then where that path would take her. Staring blankly at the screen on the seat in front of her, she replays the night she first saw Aaron, playing a set in the bar they were working in. As he bobbed around, beaming, dancing behind the decks, she found him so attractive that she could barely look at him, but plenty of other girls in the bar weren't so shy. She felt sure he wouldn't notice her in a 100 years. As it turned out, he had a DJ slot at the bar most nights. Still, Kev formally introduced them, he warned Aaron to steer clear ("These girls are family, not to be joining your queue of holiday hookups," the exact words he used.) Mel had not been too happy about the stern warning, but Kev was right; there were always plenty of women around Aaron, and she didn't want to be just another one of those girls; she was still reeling, hard, from what had happened with Jamie.

The flight is only two and a half hours long, but after she lingered on memory lane and flicked through a magazine, the plane circled to Ibiza airport. Mel cranes out the window at the little island below, and her stomach flips. She can't wait to see Connor. Grabbing her bag from the carousel, she jogs toward the gate. When she sees Connor in the distance, her heart lurches. He looks older; he has vestiges of facial hair, yet his baby face is still evident. She knows he'll be embarrassed, but she can't help hugging him for far longer than she needs to,

"Alright Mum, it's not been that long!" He shrugs her off as gently as possible,

"I swear you've grown again and your hair,"

"Yeah, growing it."

He leads her out to the car park as Mel looks around to get her bearings. It's so much more built up than the first time she came here, obviously, but the huge palm trees are still there, swaying gently in the breeze. She nods her head at them, "It's good to see you again."

It feels warmer than Manchester, but it's winter here too, so she probably won't be wearing flip-flops on this trip. She inhales. The smell remains the same: brine and beer. She hesitates at the Jeep, driving with Connor makes her nervous, let alone on the wrong side of the road. Aaron insisted on buying him lessons for his 17th birthday, but Mel felt 27 was too young. Connor could barely operate the dishwasher, and yet he would be legally able to drive a car? Annoyingly for her, she wasn't ready, he passed his test first time, begging her to insure him on her (seen better days) Ford Focus. She prayed aloud the first time he went out alone, following his whereabouts mile by mile on the app, which was her non-negotiable for borrowing her car. When he came back in, casually swinging the car keys, she'd never been more relieved; honestly, it hadn't got much easier, "I could drive?" She offers,

"On the other side of the road!" He scoffs,

"Err, yes, this isn't my first time here, remember?"

"Dad said you'd want to drive," he laughs

God, she hates Aaron for knowing her too well,

"Fine, you drive. I'll get a better look at the scenery from the passenger seat."(Whilst putting her foot on an imaginary brake pedal the whole way.) The road looks familiar, then unfamiliar as they snake out of town and turn onto the road up the coast. Of course, it's more built up than she remembers, but occasionally the buildings stop and the sea appears, a bit dull today, but it's still breathtaking, especially to someone who has spent most of their life living in the middle of the country. Thinking of the murky, misty Manchester she left this morning, she doesn't wonder that Connor wants to stay out here.

As they drive on, Mel wonders what life might have been like if she and Aaron had moved back there, as they had always talked about. Would they have stayed together then? How different their lives might have turned out.It's quiet on the road. She's forgotten what it's like to live without a million cars; they even see a man with a donkey, which makes her smile and want to cry simultaneously. Eventually, Connor turns onto a rough track, bumping up a hill through bare fields before turning off again and pulling up to the house. As she exits the car, Mel looks back down the hill behind them to the sea stretching out in the distance. She tries not to think of the last flat she'd been to view, where the view from the lounge was of a wall.

"Dad and Maya are still out, getting stuff in for Christmas day, but they said just to make yourself at home." Mel relaxes slightly as Connor leads her round the back of the house, passing the pool, which, with its turquoise tiles, still looks inviting even on a dull day. He takes her through into the house, Mel tries not to be envious and fails. Everything is beautifully styled, very Ibiza boho, all moroccan lanterns and vintage rugs. Every room smells divine, with a sort of spicy orange and greenhouse tomato scent. It's beautiful," she can't help but let out a sigh, which Connor thankfully doesn't notice. Big silver bowls full of fruit litter all the tables. Connor picks out a peach and offers her one, before eating his in a couple of bites. At home, she had to resort to bribery to get him to eat any kind of fruit, if only she'd known that the answer was to strew it artfully about the house.Thankfully, her room is next to Connor's on the ground floor.

"Dad and Maya are upstairs, with the baby's room. I helped paint it. Do you want to see it?"

"Err, I might just have a quick shower first, feel a bit grubby from the flight." She says, One thing at a time. It's weird enough being in Aaron's house, where he lives with his wife. She knows there will be emotional fallout from the baby situation, but she'll cross that bridge when the time comes.

"Sure, there's a bathroom down there and a toilet in here," He opens a door to reveal another tasteful space. Even the toilet is like something out of an interiors advert.

Her bedroom is also like a magazine shoot, there are fresh flowers, divine-smelling candles and a neat pile of expensive-looking towels folded neatly on the low bed. When Connor leaves her to it, she quickly takes some photos and sends them to Janet and Samya, who set up a WhatsApp group to get the Ibiza lowdown. She then remembers Andrew, having promised to let him know when she landed. She fires off a quick " I'm here!" hoping he won't notice the delay. He responds with 'Miss you all ready'. She sighs, having been on her own for so long; being accountable was strange. Honestly, she wasn't sure she liked it all that much.

Getting out of the delightful, rainfall shower, she hears voices coming from the kitchen, scurrying back to her room to make herself look decent. She'd spent time picking out the most boho things in her wardrobe, but now, looking at the array of floaty tops, they just look a bit lame. She pulls on some flares instead, a vintage-looking t-shirt and the kimono jacket. It's the perfect temperature in the house, of course, with under-floor heating, so she stays barefoot, hoping it will make her seem more laid-back. Her stomach is tossing butterflies around like it's hurricane season however. Tousling her hair for a casual effect, she takes a deep breath and trots down the hall to the kitchen, where Maya unpacks her sustainable shopping bag into the orange Smeg fridge. "Melanie! It's so great to see you!!" She steps in for a huge hug, her neat bump squashed between them. Mel reminds herself to keep smiling,

"Thank you so much for coming! Connor has been looking forward to it!" Mel is doubtful Connor would ever express such a sentiment out loud, but takes the compliment gracefully,

"Thank you so much for inviting me, the house is gorgeous."

Maya shrugs with the innate confidence of the stylish: "It still needs work, but Connor has been helping me decorate. He's so helpful. I hope this one turns out to be as nice as his brother."

"Oh, it's a boy!! I didn't know you knew." She is thrown a little at the thought of it being another boy, what if he looks like Connor?" Her heart lurches,

"It's practical to know, huh?" Maya continues, unaware of Mel's turmoil, "So you can plan? It will be surprising enough to have the baby on the outside." She pats her bump soothingly, a picture of maternal bliss, it would seem, not for Maya the indignity of haemorrhoids or varicose veins and due to all that yoga, she'll probably snap back to her bendy self a few hours after giving birth. Mel is still putting cream on her stretch marks eighteen years later.

She starts to feel panicky. Why on earth did she let Connor talk her into staying here? It's a *terrible* idea; she doesn't know how she's going to get through the next 10 minutes, let alone a week. She needs to get a hotel immediately. Then Aaron appears, gathering her in a huge hug also. People are a bit touchy-feely in this house for her liking,

"Mel's!! You made it!! Good flight? Did she drive here?" he asks Connor, who is helping himself to more bloody fruit as they all stand around the kitchen island,

How could she also have forgotten that they love ganging up on her? "No, but she did suggest it, so I think technically you owe me the 20 pesos, "

Maya interrupts, "Leave her alone, you two idiots! Connor, why don't you take Mel to see the horses and give them their dinner while we cook? Ari is going to make some fresh pasta? Will that be ok, Mel?" For some reason, it bugs her that Maya calls him Ari. She pronounces it 'R-reee' with her sexy Spanish accent, conveniently forgetting that she is trying to shorten Andrew's name.

"Sounds good," Mel mutters, scurrying out the door behind Connor. They walk past the pool, "It's heated, so you can go in anytime. Did you bring swim stuff?" She did, but wearing it while anyone else is in the house is not happening,

 "Umm, I'm not sure," Mel blusters,

"I'm sure Maya'll lend you something,"

Imagining Maya probably only owns tiny crochet bikinis, Mel changes the subject quickly. She follows Connor across the yard to an outbuilding next to a field, where two horses come trotting towards them. Connor always wanted a dog; he begged her for years, but Mel, having grown up with many animals, was practical enough to know that it was a lot of extra work she didn't have time for and money they couldn't afford. They had goldfish named after the Simpsons for years. Bart died several times, but Connor never knew it wasn't the same fish. Connor brings out some hay from the shed and looks at their water trough: "This is Lola, and this is Celeste." He rubs their noses. The earthy smell of the hay takes her back to living at Kath's. She'd had two donkeys whom Mel used to whisper her problems to.

"Look at you, Connor, I've seen you eat two pieces of fruit without being forced, and now you're a horsey type." Mel can't help herself. She feels a little jealous.

He shrugs, "Dad's been teaching me to ride, can you ride a horse? You can ride right down to the beach from here. We could do that one day?"

"The only thing you ride in Manchester is the Metro, Connor."

"Yeah, but you grew up in the country, there were loads of animals at your Dad's."

They had only been to see her Dad and Kath a handful of times before her Dad died. Connor, too young to pick up on the tension between them, was just excited by all the animals that wandered in and out of the house. There was always a baby something he could cuddle, a kid, kitten or a duckling, "Actually I used to ride, a long time ago though, I was 7 or 8 I think." When her parents were still together, she used to have riding lessons on Saturday mornings. Stroking Lola's soft, probing nose, she recalls her parents cheering her on at the County show, where she'd taken part in the kids' Gymkhana, a dusty rosette had stayed pinned up on the kitchen noticeboard for years afterwards, proudly gathering dust,

"Do you think it's like riding a bike? You never forget?" Connor asks,

"I'm up for finding out." Just don't suggest I borrow any jodhpurs from Maya.

Dinner isn't as awkward as she was worrying about, although, since when did Aaron become a master chef with his freshly made pasta and pesto? (Both of which are annoyingly delicious.) Her phone starts ringing in the middle of eating. Andrew, of course. Apologising, she turns it to silent, not wanting to seem rude. Even Connor, who is perpetually browsing, appears happy to put his phone away at the table.

Afterwards, Aaron lights the fire in the lounge, and they bicker gently over what film to watch, with everyone vetoing all the horror films on Mel's watch list, settling on the latest Netflix release, a romantic comedy. Sitting here with your ex and his beautiful new wife is neither romantic nor funny, she thinks somewhat morosely. Not following the film, she surreptitiously looks at Aaron, all clean cut and glowing as he sits at ease on the other vast, squashy sofa with Maya's feet resting in his lap. He looks younger now than he did in his hard partying years, how far he's come from blowing all his money on Coke every weekend on a 48-hour partying bender. If only she could say the same about herself. She feels like she's going backwards, especially living with Janet. Her phone vibrates. Andrew, again,

"Sorry, I said to…Janet, I'd ring her. I'll just nip out,"

"We'll pause?"

"No, I'll be quick, carry on, sorry."

She slips out to sit on the chairs by the pool as she calls him back, simultaneously annoyed and flattered by his attention, "Hi, sorry I couldn't answer earlier, we were eating," She babbles, feeling weird but not knowing quite why,

"Hi, it's fine, I just need to check a couple of things with you. How was the flight? Are you having a good time? It must be nice to see your son. "All good so far, yes, it is nice. What do you need to know? It's just we're all watching a film so…"

"Oh, right. I just wanted to check when you need to be back after the New Year. Do you have any other holiday plans, I mean?"

(Was that a dig? Mel ignores it if so)

"Why? Are we off on a round- the -world cruise?"

"Not this time, Melanie, but never say never!"

How many times does she have to say that it's just Mel?

"No, nothing until I'm back at work, on the fifth, why?"

"It's a surprise!"

She still hasn't had the heart to tell him she is not a massive fan of surprises.

The next day is Christmas eve, and despite all Mel's offers of help, Maya tells them to go off and enjoy themselves, Aaron too.

Mel protests she's happy pottering about the house, but Maya insists they leave her to wrap gifts and tidy up, as if anything is out of place. She packed them off after the healthiest breakfast Mel had eaten in years. More fruit, of course, and tofu scrambled egg (who knew?) with sourdough made by Maya, Mel is trying hard not to be envious.

"Where do you want to go? Ibiza is your oyster!" Having spent at least 15 years sleeping until the afternoon, Aaron is now an annoyingly chirpy morning person. He's already been for a run by the time Mel gets up. They get to the car and she debates if she should get in the front or back, when Connor climbs into the back as if he's still a child,

"Where do you want to go? "Aaron enquires, "Connor, we can show you where you were made."

Mel chokes back a laugh as Connor's face puckers up. Putting his fingers in his ears, he begs, "Never, EVER mention that again!"

It's a clear, sunny day, hard to reconcile with Christmas Eve, not that there's been a picture postcard white Christmas in England for a long time, probably since she left the wilds of Yorkshire, where snow often meant snowed in.

" Kev and Jackie might be around? I'll call them, they'll be so pleased to see you. Do you want to drive up to the flat for old times' sake? I haven't been up there for years or down to,"

Connor interrupts, "I don't want to ditch you, Mum, but if you guys are just gonna talk about old times all day, I might meet some... *friends*? Louis and Jorge are around today."

"Might Maggie be there ?" Aaron raises his eyebrow in the rearview mirror,

"Err, dunno," is all they get from Connor,

"Maggie? "Mouths, Mel, this is the first she's heard the name. Aaron pulls a smooching face, Connor bats him on the back of the head, "She's just a mate." He's blushing, though,

"It's fine by me Connor, if your dad doesn't mind being stuck with me, but I can amuse myself if you've got stuff to do?" she says to Aaron, well aware that it's been a long time since they've spent any time together without Connor as a buffer. He shrugs to signal he's fine with it, and they pull into a parking space.

Looking out to sea across the bay at all the boats, the view is much the same as she remembers, but the strip is twice as crowded with buildings and new bars. She and Aaron both worked at a beachside bar on Sunset Strip called, imaginatively, Beach bar. It wasn't a huge place like Cafe Mambo, but Siobhan's uncle and aunt had moved out there in the 90s, after getting into the house music scene. After travelling back and forth for a few summers, they snapped up the little bar when it came up for sale, and it's been going strong ever since, despite San Antonio going through many changes since then. It would be really nice to see them both after all this time; they were a big part of her inventing her new life.

Siobhan had gone home after their summer adventures to start University. She'd got her degree and a good job, married someone from her office, and eventually moved back to Greenleigh after she had her eldest daughter. Mel kept in touch until then, but after Siobhan was back in the village, Me l couldn't handle hearing about life back home. Her communication became more sporadic, until it was just a text on her birthday and a Christmas card. She's not even written those this year, distracted by house hunting, Ibiza and Andrew. Remembering him, she snaps a few pictures of the view and sends them with a quick message saying she is sightseeing for the day. She doesn't mention that it's with Aaron. However, she sends the same photos to Janet, admitting that it feels strange. Janet replies, "You need this, make the most of it." Janet is very big on Mel getting "Closure" from Aaron, so she can move on and settle down, hopefully with Andrew.

Mel thinks it will take more than a few days to unpack all her excess baggage.

As she watches Connor and Aaron on the beach together, she knows she must make peace with the ridiculous irony of their current circumstances. Whoever said that history repeats itself couldn't be more accurate. She'd left home at eighteen for the White Island, and now her own son, made here, is doing the same thing, working in the same bars his father used to and wanting to do the same job. Janet also likes to say that if you don't learn your lessons in life, they just keep coming back on repeat, and you'll keep going round in a circle until you do. What is the lesson here? She ponders, wandering away down the strip, letting all the memories flood back.

She and Siobhan thought they were so cool when they told everyone they were going to work out in Ibiza. In reality, when they got here, there were a thousand kids like them, working hard in bars, putting up with drunk customers until the early hours, then joining them at the late-night club scene, which started back in the day at Amnesia and by then, all over the island. It was possible to keep clubbing 24 7 and they frequently did. Mel shudders at the thought of staying up all night now, but it had been so easy back then. Ibiza had eventually put its foot down, curtailing hours and noise, and Mel didn't blame them. It must have been such a beautiful island before the party crew blew it up in the '80s. The beach bar used to close at 2 am, and after cleaning up, they could make it to a club by 4. The sun would rise in summer as they made their way to the party. Siobhan's Uncle Kevin lent them a scooter, but it got stolen after one of them left the keys in it. Mel remembers they would fly all over the island on it, never wearing helmets, shaking her head at her past reckless self. She would shamelessly follow Aaron about on his DJ circuit. He would play a slot at the beach bar most nights, then pack up his stuff, helped by his mate 'Tall Tony', to play at varying other clubs and bars around the island until all hours. Mel notes to ask Aaron what happened to Tony, wondering if any crew are still living it large on the island.

Looking back, it seems embarrassing. She followed Aaron around like a love-sick puppy until they finally got into an actual conversation that wasn't "Alright? Yeah, you? Yeah."

While he was DJ'ing and she was behind the bar, she didn't notice anything else but his head bobbing up and down; she thought he was the coolest guy she'd ever met.

"You said that about Jamie," Siobhan had reminded her, not unkindly but just to give her a reality check, " Look at how that turned out…"

"Aaron is nothing like Jamie," is all she would counter. Siobhan had disagreed. When you'd met one charmer, you'd met them all. When Aaron finally turned his charm on Mel, Siobhan gave it a week, tops, new holidaymakers would be arriving at the weekend, and Aaron wasn't interested in anything serious. Still, as it turned out, they were a good match. Once Siobhan left (begging Mel to come home with her, knowing full well what trouble was ahead), Mel was free to party as hard as Aaron, which suited her demons very well; they were more a match made in hell than heaven. In her mind's eye, Mel sees her 18-year-old self dancing down the boardwalk ahead of her. She gives her a nod, we've come a long way, she acknowledges, but there are still plenty of painful memories tucked away that also need exorcizing.

Aaron and Connor catch her up, "Whatever happened to Tall Tony?" Aaron laughs," Of all the memories, you're thinking about Tall Tony? He eventually went back to Epsom; he's something big in IT. We keep in touch. I saw him when I played at Glastonbury; he came with Paul Ashby. Everyone's on Instagram. If you ever get into this century, there are some mad videos. I'll show you later."

Mel snorts. She has no wish to see herself from back then, praying to God that Connor hasn't seen any of them either. She swore off social media after years of chasing down Aaron's whereabouts by stalking him online. She has no desire to start it back up now. Connor shuffles awkwardly, "If you don't mind, I'm gonna meet my mates."

"Yes, of course, go, do you want us to pick you up later? "

"I've got some Christmas shopping to do, I can probably get a lift with someone." Mel gave him instructions earlier to get something nice for Maya and his Dad, then gave him the Euros to pay for it, then some suggestions, when he claimed to be clueless.

"I'll ring you when we're done, see where you are?" Aaron suggests, while Mel says quickly,

"Don't get in the car with anyone drinking!"

Connor rolls his eyes,"' Course not! Have a nice trip down memory lane." He wanders away on his phone, and they watch him until he disappears. Mel shifts on the balls of her feet. They've not been alone together like this for years, it's nerve-wracking.

"You want a Coffee? We can get takeaways and wander? Then head to the beach bar for lunch?"

They stroll back towards town to find a coffee shop, Aaron seems to know everyone as they walk up the street, Mel is still lost in her memories,

"Thanks for inviting me out here." she says after he presents her with a Coffee, (he has Matcha, of course). They lean on the harbour wall, the familiar sound of boats clanking in their moorings, the salty smell of the sea mixed with engine oil,

"Thanks for coming, Mel. I wasn't sure if you would, but I knew you'd hate a Christmas without Connor…I know it's been hard for you, leaving the house, him moving here"

"He told me yesterday that he doesn't think he'll come home. Not that I blame him at all."

Mel can't look at Aaron; she can feel tears behind her eyes. She doesn't want him to feel guilty, well aware of how fortunate Connor is to have this opportunity to do something so exciting with his life, "Somehow I'd forgotten how beautiful it is out here. Manchester seems so busy and built up in comparison."

"Out of season, summer is still mental."

"I don't know how we did it?"

"Drugs and alcohol!" He shakes his head, "It still happens, obviously, but these are very different times, thank god, I know you worry, but I *swear*, I won't let Connor make any of our mistakes, he's a sensible kid, we did well, *you* did well. I'm so proud of him, he's doing great. " Mel bites her lip. He always could read her mind. She does trust him now, finally. He notices her wobbly lip and smoothly changes the subject, "How's the house hunting going?"

Mel sighed. One thing she didn't need to do was lie to Aaron, especially as Connor wasn't here to worry.

"Awful, honestly. Property prices have skyrocketed, especially in the more desirable areas. Would you believe even Levenshulme is out of my budget?! We were so lucky buying back then, well, thanks to your mum and dad."

"They've finally booked a cruise. Dad says mum won't stop buying outfits. She says you're always welcome to go round, you know, she misses you and Connor. They're coming out after the baby's born,"

"A boy! Maya told me,"

Aaron turns to her,

"Honestly, is it weird for you, Mels? "

She pauses, fiddling with her coffee cup,

"I'm not sure I'd say it's *weird*… I mean in the sense Connor will have a brother that's nothing to do with me, yeah, that feels a bit strange, but I'm just really happy for you all,"

" I know you didn't want him to be an only child like you…If I hadn't been so unreliable, we might have, I'm sorry."

Aaron is welling up himself, he's very open these days, Maya has been good for him, Mel smiles reassuringly,

"He was fine, Aaron. He had all his cousins and plenty of friends, hell, we were kids ourselves when you think about it,"

"I can't believe we were his age, out here unsupervised, madness! I won't let him do anything stupid, Mel, I promise, you don't have to worry. I want you to enjoy your freedom. You deserve it. Do you have any plans?" Mel shakes her head, choking up.

"I haven't a clue yet, to be honest. It means a lot, though, what you just said,"

" I'm really glad we've been able to stay friends," he says sincerely,

"Whoah, I wouldn't go *that* far. I mean, I might send you a Christmas card next year."

"No Mel, seriously, you've always been so cool. I was a selfish arsehole when you needed me most and I'm just really grateful you let me be in Connor's life when I didn't deserve it, "

After he finally decided to sort himself out, Aaron went to A.A. and N.A., which meant he did a lot of dissecting and apologising, all of which she was happy to hear and use to find her own path to forgiveness.You can't co-parent successfully if you harbour grudges, and Mel knew she had to let go of any resentment.

"Aaron, we don't need to do the whole amends thing again. We're good, honestly. I'm really proud of you. Let's go to the beach bar before we both start crying."

They wander by the closed bar fronts, trading memories of this wild night, that DJ, and all the colourful people they had met. Aaron shows her some of the old photos online. The pair of them pop up here and there, looking impossibly young, arms around a big gang of mates whose faces are familiar but mostly whose names escape her. They were bonded by living life to the full and motivated by having the most fun.

What would young Melanie think of her now? Fun seems like a rare commodity these days. It's nice being with Andrew, but is it fun? Honestly, not like it used to be. Do people who are nearly 40 still have fun, though, or are they just too tired?

By the time they get to the bar, Mel is feeling pretty wobbly. It's a lot; all these memories are flooding back in. She's spent her whole life trying not to remember how she ended up here, and it all feels too adjacent currently for her liking.

Kev and Jackie are thrilled to see her. They won't let her pay for lunch, and they keep feeding her drinks, even though she knows day drinking is a fast track to being in bed by 7 p.m. Jackie shows her pictures of Siobhan and her kids, two girls, who attend the same tiny primary school where they went to school. Siobhan looks happy, grown-up, like a proper woman. Mel looks down at her scruffy Vans and wonders at what point she will ever feel like an adult.

Before they leave, because she is a little bit drunk, Mel ducks behind the bar, looking over at the DJ box, which is still in the same place, Aaron sees her and wanders behind the booth, pretending to spin the turntables, raising his hands in the air like he used to do to her across the crowded bar. She would do it back, across the sea of dancing people, her heart leaping, for a second, she swears she can smell the dry ice. She raises her arms in response, and as they smile at each other, she knows that she is finally ok with the twists and turns of their past because of Connor. If she had never met Aaron, then there would be no Connor. No matter what her life brings her in the future, Connor will always be her greatest achievement. Because Aaron is right, against all odds, they raised him properly, and he is a good boy. Oh God, she's crying again, just a little bit. She's had too many gins.

The rest of the holiday speeds by, and despite her initial reservations, she enjoys every minute. She floats around the pool on the lemon inflatable on Christmas Day with Maya's gorgeous family, who welcome her as warmly as they do Connor. They ride the horses on the beach, not like riding a bike, but it's a lovely day, even if her bum hurts for ages afterwards. They go to a bar to watch Connor DJ a brief set while they cheer him on, much to his total embarrassment. She meets his new friends and Maggie, who seems very sweet. Her parents own a boutique hotel in Portinatx, so she's very much part of the cool Ibiza tribe. Maggie watches Connor do his set with a look on her face that Mel remembers only too well. Just be careful, she prays, thinking she must ask Aaron to have that conversation with him. Mel stands in the baby's bedroom with Maya for ages, telling funny parenting stories about Connor, who is embarrassed afterwards. She even becomes a bit broody as she admires all the beautiful baby things in the nursery.

She finally remembers to ring Kath to wish her a happy Christmas, but there's no answer, so they drunkenly sing her a carol, leaving her a message with her new address and details. She makes a mental note to try again when she gets home. Andrew constantly keeps in touch, which is endearing, if slightly cloying. He refuses to tell her anything about their New Year's plans. She tries to find the right moment to tell Connor about him, knowing she should say something, in case she is off radar over New Year, but somehow she can't. She doesn't know how she feels about their relationship yet, and until she does, she doesn't want to make a big deal about it.

They all take her to the airport, where there are big hugs all around. She promises to come back and meet the baby in Spring. She holds Connor tight, letting him know it's okay if he wants to stay and make a life there. Of course, she cries on the plane, but she feels different as she leaves—lighter, like she's banished some ghosts, leaving them to watch the sun going down from the Cafe De Mar.

Andrew had offered to pick her up from the airport several times. She told him it wasn't necessary, as it's an evening flight, she just wants to go home and sleep off a week of far too much wine, some seriously late nights and the sadness of saying goodbye to Connor, so she can't quite believe it when she spots him waiting at arrivals. When she sees him in the distance, she wants to swerve back and hide around a corner, but she forces a smile onto her face, despite her irritation.

"Andrew! What a surprise! I told you I'd get an Uber!" He kisses her on the cheek, taking her bag. He looks strangely serious,

"I know, it's just well, I hate to have to tell you this, Melanie, but there's been some...news,"

Her mouth goes instantly dry. She's just texted Connor to tell him she's landed, and he replied with an obligatory thumbs-up, so, oh god, not Janet?

"What's happened?" Her heart starts to race.

"Janet got a phone call. I'm afraid your stepmother has passed away." So relieved that it isn't Janet, Mel takes a few seconds to digest the information. She never considers Kath to be her stepmother.

"You mean Kath?"

Looking at her as if she is in shock, he leads her over to a bench, sits her down and takes her hand,

"Janet rang me to ask what she thought she should do? If to

ring you in Ibiza, but we decided not to ruin the rest of your trip, I hope that was the right decision," he searches her eyes,

"What happened?" Her stomach goes into a free fall,

"I don't know all the details, but Janet spoke to Chris? Oldsworth? "

"Chris Oldswick?" Mel hears her voice go up an awkward octave. Oh God, what fresh hell is this? Why is he somehow in the mix?

"Oh, you know him? He's her neighbour."

"His parents own the farm next door. How on earth did he end up ringing Janet?" The last Mel heard was that he'd gone to Australia to work, with his little brother Josh, who, Mel thinks, won't actually be so little anymore.

"He's been trying to get hold of you since it happened, but couldn't find an up-to-date number for you. Then it turned out that you left a voicemail on her house phone, while he was there at her house, I think Jan said," Mel's heart sank to join her stomach,

"Oh God, he must've thought we were such idiots, we sang 'We wish you a Merry Christmas'." Mel curls back into the bench in horror, imagining the look on Chris's face as he listened to them blathering on, her and Connor were pretty pissed when she finally thought to ring,

"Why didn't he pick up the phone and stop us?"

"I think he said he couldn't find the actual handset. Janet got the impression the house is a bit of a mess."

"It was a hoarder's paradise twenty years ago. When did she die?"

"Last week. I think Chris was the one who found her." Mel dips her head between her knees while Andrew rubs her back, "Shall we go? I can take you back to Jan's, or you can come to mine if you don't want to be alone, it must be such a shock."

Mel lets Andrew steer her into the car, not knowing what to think or say, "This Chris is taking care of all the livestock, but he really needs to talk to you about that, and he's passed your details along to her solicitor apparently."

"The solicitor?" Probably Ken Braithwaite, who'd dealt with her parents' affairs,

"Has she any other family? If not, I guess that makes you her next of kin?"

Mel shrugs, "I don't know, I never met any of them. I didn't have much to do with her. Oh God, Andrew, I never rang to check up on her. I mean, I just sort of ignored her after my Dad died." Guilt crawls over her,

"Hey, hey, it's ok. Even if you did stay in touch, there's nothing you could've done. Do you think she might have left you the house?"

"Oh God, I hope not, she used to let goats live in the lounge," she smiles weakly,

"I'll bet a farmhouse with land in that part of Yorkshire is worth quite a bit, we'll have to look,"

"Andrew! I *really* don't want the farmhouse; she's probably left it to some animal charity. I don't want to think about all that right now anyway, poor Kath."

She feels so guilty. She can't stop picturing Kath alone with the animals wandering around her. Andrew pulls the car out of the airport car park. "Do you want to come to mine?"

"Thanks, but do you mind if I go back to Janet's?" She needs a hug, a large G&T, and to find out what Chris Oldswick had to say. Andrew leaves her with Janet pouring an industrial-sized drink, but not before gently reminding her that they are leaving the day after tomorrow, which Mel can't even acknowledge right now. She shuts the door on him, possibly too firmly, then collapses into Janet's arms. Poor Steve is ushered off to bed, and they sit by the fire. Mel feels fuzzy-headed from the shock / the enormous G&T, but makes Janet relay the conversation with Chris, word for word,

"Well, he asked for you, of course, he explained that he got this number from a voice message you'd left Kath and that he urgently needs to speak to you... I told him that you were in Ibiza until today, I think he muttered something like 'Of course she is' then he asked if he could have your mobile number but I said that I would pass his number on to you, I mean, he could've been anybody...He was quite impatient, I explained that we're close friends and that I'd give you a message as soon as possible, "she falters a little, "He said 'Tell her thanks for the off key Christmas medley but Kath died last week and we've been trying to get hold of you ever since. Braithwaite's solicitors need to talk to you. You need to talk to the Coop about the funeral, and there's a menagerie of animals that you need to come and take care of, but then he hung up abruptly.Sorry, Mel, this must be a lot to take in. I didn't know what to do for the best, so I rang Andrew and we both agreed it could wait a day to save the end of your holiday from being ruined. I hope that was the right thing to do?"

Mel shrugs, totally overwhelmed by everything she suddenly needs to think about, "I don't suppose another day matters at this point."

"Do you know him, this Chris…Oldswick?" Janet probes, he hadn't seemed particularly friendly for an old friend.

"I do, he's not exactly one of my biggest fans,"

"I got the impression that was the case,"

Mel takes a long swig of her gin and sighs, "Remember I told you about the farmer's son? That was Chris. We've known each other since toddler group. We grew up as mates, and then we went out together in high school. First love and all that. Then it ended horribly, and we've never spoken since. He hasn't forgiven me, and quite honestly, Jan, I don't blame him." She sighs.

She knows Janet's mind is ticking over at the thought of Mel's first love reappearing and what on earth she could possibly have done to still be unforgiven 20 years later, but Mel has no intention of reliving that terrible part of her past right now. The gin has kicked in, and she gets up unsteadily and excuses herself to bed.

She wakes up disoriented, half expecting to be in her boutique bedroom in Ibiza, not lying in the grey December light amongst the half-open boxes containing her life. It takes a minute for the events of yesterday to fully come back to her. Her stomach was swirling dangerously as she acknowledged that she would have to speak to Chris Oldswick today, let alone make funeral arrangements, and what on earth did he mean by taking care of the animals? How is she supposed to do that?

Tempting as it is to put her head under the pillow and ignore the day, she also needs to get organised for this mini break with Andrew, which frankly is the very last thing she wants to do right now with this on her shoulders. All Andrew will tell her is that she needs to pack for cold weather, long walks & formal dinners, all of which sound far too much like hard work. With a reluctant sigh, she gets up to get coffee.

Chris's number is pinned on the kitchen noticeboard. As she waits for the coffee machine to do its thing, she imagines what a grown-up Chris might be like. The last time she had been in Greenleigh was for her father's funeral. She had prepared herself to see him there, but his mum had explained that he was working out in Australia with Josh, his younger brother, politely passing on their condolences. At the time, Mel was relieved that she didn't have to face him; the day was fraught enough, and she was well aware she was already being judged by the whole village for a whole back catalogue of misdemeanours.

Chris had always been tall and skinny, with sandy hair and the sort of colouring that indicates he spent most of his life outside. He was out working on the farm as soon as he could walk, driving the tractor as soon as his feet reached the pedals. He was always serious for his age, but underneath his earthy exterior, he was actually the sweetest, most thoughtful boy she had ever met. He had completely doted on her until she cruelly broke his heart.

Clearly, he's back living on the farm, then. She wonders if his parents are still living there or even alive. Siobhan probably would've told her if anything happened to them, she reasons, but it's been a long time since she's spoken to Siobhan, too. She wonders how long he's been back. Was he married? Did that Sarah Hinchliffe finally get her claws into him? Eugh, Mel hopes not, she used to throw such daggers at Mel when she saw them together. Are there little Oldswicks? Must be by now. He was always an old soul, wanting to settle down and keep the farm in the family for generations to come. She's absolutely dreading making the call, but she can't help being curious about him. Her Mum had thought it was lovely that they were a couple because she said they always used to play together at playgroup, his mum had photos of them as Joseph and Mary in the school nativity.

Racking her brains, she tries to remember if Kath ever mentioned any other family. Honestly, she knows very little about the woman that her Dad lived with for all those years. Although it isn't quite the same situation, she's glad Connor gets along so well with Maya. She ought to ring and tell him the news; he'd always been so intrigued by Kath as a kid and would ask when they would visit, but she constantly fobbed him off with excuses. After her Dad died, she only ever saw Kath again at the funeral, and she had never been back since, glad to finally have a reason to leave her past in Greenleigh forever. It was far easier to write off those years when the memories weren't waiting around every corner.

In the two years that Mel lived with her dad and Kath, she had been intent on not having any kind of relationship with Kath, but to her credit, she seemed quite content not to interfere. She was always busy; she worked in, Mel tries to recall, something to do with livestock feed, then there were all the animals to look after, and when she wasn't doing that, she'd made an art studio in one of the outbuildings where she would go to paint. As Mel remembers it, it was something to do with painting that crossed her and her dad's path. Did she used to teach an art class? She vaguely remembers that her dad used the art studio too, not that she took any interest. She only went back to their house when she needed to. She spent most of her days next door at the Oldswicks, then staying out with Jamie until that ended, then she shipped out to Ibiza and didn't look back.

It takes another coffee, a long shower, some unpacking and repacking, a round of washing and a fat slice of Christmas cake that Janet insists she eat, (if only to stop her from eating it), for Mel to finally take herself out to the conservatory, take a few deep breaths and with a shaky hand, dial Chris' number. It rings for a while to the point where she hopes she might have a lucky escape and the voicemail will kick in, but then he answers it, gruffly, "Hi Chris? It's Mel..anie... Melanie McCarthy," she says, fiddling with the marzipan off the cake.

"...Finally," his voice is deeper but still achingly familiar. Clearly, he is not exactly thrilled to be talking to her, though.

"I'm sorry I couldn't speak sooner. I was in Ibiza," she stammers. "Do they not have phones there?" God, he is cold.

"I've been trying to contact you urgently."

"I know, and I'm sorry, and I'm sorry to hear about Kath,"

His voice softens slightly, "She was a good friend, part of the family really." For a second, he sounds more like the Chris she knew way back when,

"How are your folks? And the farm?"Mel tries to break the ice, "This isn't a social call Mel," he spits witheringly, "You need to get up here and sort the place out. Braithwaite's solicitors want to talk to you urgently, they're closed until next week but Ken said to give you his home number, have you got a pen?" he reads it out before she can say anything, continuing at rapid pace,

"They've taken Kath to the Coop funeral home, but you need to talk to them **as soon as possible** about the funeral. I've fed the animals this morning, but they get fed twice daily, so they'll want feeding again tonight, and the goats need mucking out. They're all so used to her being around that they're upset and confused. We've got the keys up at the farm, so come pick them up when you arrive."

"Err, I wasn't, umm, planning on coming today," her head reeling from his insistent demands,

"Well, I suppose I could see them again tonight, "he sighs heavily, "But I do have other things going on, and we have been looking after them for a week already. What time can you be here tomorrow?"

Mel pauses, knowing how well her next comment will be received, "The thing is, I'm going away tomorrow, I have plans for the New Year," She cringes, realising how that sounds, he must think she's still some 24-hour party person,

"You've just come back from Ibiza," he states coolly,

"I know, but this trip was sort of sprung on me!" Why is she explaining herself to him?

"Kath dying was sort of sprung on me!" It seems he is still determined to hate her,

"I appreciate that, Chris, and all that you've been doing. Have the solicitors tried to find any of her family?"

"You are her only family, Mel," he lashes out at her,

"We aren't really family," Mel regrets saying it the minute it leaves her lips. There is a palpable silence,

"You never thought so, Mel, but Kath did. You need to talk to Ken, but as far as I know, she left you everything, so perhaps your next jaunt can wait, because you've got responsibilities here that can't." With that, he hangs up the phone.

Mel shuts her eyes, trying to blink away the pool of tears building up behind her eyelids. Although she hated hearing it, every point he made was valid; still, there was no need to be so mean. However, she remembers now, all too well, how horrible he'd been towards her after she broke his heart. But also, she didn't know that Kath would die and leave Mel everything to sort out, did she? It isn't her fault that she has other plans, luxury hotel and haute cuisine-type plans (she's presuming). If she's honest, however, she knows it isn't fair to expect him to keep looking after the animals (She hates that they are upset too) and the house for free, maybe she can offer to pay him to look after them for the next few days? She quickly dismisses the idea; she isn't going to give Christopher Oldswick the satisfaction of asking him for any more help, if he wants to sulk about something that happened twenty years ago, that's his problem.

Swallowing her frustration, she dials the number he gave her and waits for Ken Braithwaite to pick up the phone. His is another voice from the past she didn't particularly want ever to hear again. The last time she'd talked to him was about her mum's will. Relieved to have finally tracked her down, though, he explains it would be best if she could come and see him in person, as soon as possible, so that they can talk through Kath's affairs. He was free tomorrow. Instead of explaining the whole holiday situation again, she just says she'll let him know by the end of the day. Before she can hang up, he impresses the need for her to talk to the funeral home as soon as possible, too. Mel looks down at the dissected Christmas cake on her lap. Could this day get worse? They were very nice and understanding, but asked that she come by and see them as soon as possible, as they prefer to talk in person. She puts the phone down, squeezing her knuckles, trying to ignore the rising panic building up in her chest as she stares blankly out at the grey garden.

Andrew answers instantly, full of concern. While trying not to reveal that Chris is an ex-boyfriend who still holds a long-standing grudge against her, she breaks it to him as gently as she can, saying she is sorry, but she can't go away with him. There is a long pause before Andrew replies, incredulous, "You're telling me you're going to turn down a trip to Paris to go and feed some animals in the back of beyond?"

"Paris?" Mel gasps, she's dreamt her whole life of climbing to the top of the Eiffel Tower. The closest she's ever been is binge watching Emily in Paris, she wasn't watching it (solely) for chef Gabriel but for all the glimpses of pavement cafes, chic boutiques and beautiful boulevards,

"Surprise!" he mutters darkly,

"Oh, Andrew, I didn't know you were planning Paris!" Mel is taken aback, Paris! At New Year! That must've been expensive, she thinks, guilt heaping on her from every which way,

"You told me it was your dream holiday," he says frostily. Understandably so, but she can't take another man with a chip on his shoulder today.

"It's not just the animals Andrew, I told you, I need to go and see the solicitor and the undertaker, they've already waited a week and the whole village thinks I'm awful as it is, it just, it feels selfish to be honest, to go off on a holiday while poor Kath is waiting to be buried," her voice wobbles, all the stress of the last few phone calls suddenly overwhelms her. She bursts into tears, the guilt she's been holding at bay wracks out of her in huge sobs. Although annoyed, Andrew is not a total monster, "There, there, " he soothes, "Of course I understand. I'll cancel it now, don't worry about it. We can book another trip when this is all sorted out. I'll pack some things and come and get you, and we can drive over to Yorkshire this afternoon if you want."

His suggestion brings her back from the brink, there is no way in hell she is taking Andrew to the farmhouse, for one, she can't imagine that he would step foot in the door once he sees the state of it, (which from her conversation with Ken Braithwaite, is pretty perilous). For two, she is not rocking up at the Oldswick's in Andrew's brand new Audi, he'd have an absolute fit trying to take it up the lane, which was full of potholes 10 years ago and can't possibly have improved. Thirdly, as if she needs a third reason, there is no way in hell she wants Andrew anywhere near the good people of Greenleigh, who seemingly have the memories of elephants. She knows he isn't going to like it, but she tells him, thanks, but no thanks. He says he understands. From the tone of his voice, he doesn't, but that's the least of her worries right now.

By the time she finally gets off the phone, her ear is burning and her head throbs from the stress and the crying. Janet, who has been hovering all morning, pulling sympathetic faces, comes into the room,

"Well, that sounded like total hell. Are you OK? Too early for Gin?"

There is no such thing in Janet's book. Especially over the festive period. Mel buries her face in her hands, "Better not, I've got to head off to Greenleigh today for a few days."

"Oh! What about Paris?"

"JANET!!! You knew? You could have given me a heads up!"

Janet grimaces sheepishly, "Andrew asked me what I thought.

I'm so sorry, Mel. Is there anything we can do? Could Steve and I go up there and help out so you can still go with Andrew?"

God love Janet, but she would whip out the antibacterial wipes at the first sign of dirt. She would immediately wither and die if she ever went inside the farmhouse, where the floor was always covered in muddy footprints, animal hair, and quite often manure. You went barefoot at your peril. "Thanks, Jan, that's a very kind offer, but I need to just go and get it sorted. I'm hoping it'll only take a few days to work out what needs to be done, so I should be back for school starting."

"You can ask for some bereavement leave, if not, Peter will totally understand, I can drag in some help from somewhere, don't worry about that. Are you sure you'll be ok though, going on your own?"

I'll have to be, thinks Mel, going upstairs sadly to unpack her dresses and dig out her wellies and woollies.

CHAPTER FIVE

Typing the address into her phone (not that she needs directions), a huge wave of guilt crashes over her again. Greenleigh is less than a two-hour drive away, yet in her head, she's banished it to the ends of the earth. The afternoon light is already fading by the time she finally sets off, but she's hoping that if she puts her foot down, she can get there before Chris goes back to lock the animals up. She can at least derive some satisfaction in proving him wrong about her, not that she cares one bit what he thinks.

On the drive, she calls Connor to break the news, asking him to tell Aaron. Connor is pragmatic: "Well, she was an old lady, Mum." Mel tries to work out how old was, ashamed that she doesn't know, her dad was only in his 60's when he died, which seems so young now in the scheme of things, only 20 odd years older than her now, a sombre thought, "Not that old Connor," she corrects him. In that teenage way that death seems like something they'll never have to think about, he asks very practical questions and is hysterical with laughter when she tells him she will go and stay there for a few days to sort out the animals, "Watch out, Dr.Dolittle!" he snorts. She tells him she'll let him know about the funeral as soon as possible, and he can decide what to do once there is a date. It'll be a whole village affair, that's the Greenleigh way. There's no escaping the reality that she will have to see everyone from her past again.

Her heart sinks, realising that she will probably have to consult with the Oldswicks about a lot of things. The thought makes her very uneasy. They had been family to her, so supportive when her Mum died, and yet...Mel's skin starts to prickle with anxiety at the reality of what and who is in front of her.

As the miles count down, the countryside of her childhood starts to become achingly familiar, even in the heathery dusk, she recognises the contours of the valleys etched in near darkness. She knows this place. There are more wind turbines dotted here and there now, and some fancy houses where only cows used to stand, but as she passes The Fox House (scene of many a drunken debacle) and the road winds up the brow of the hill, her heart gives a jolt as the familiar view opens up below her.

The warm, glowing lights from farms and villages dot across the valley below her. Beyond that, in the inky night, distant towns and further away, cities glitter, sending their glow up into the darkness. Mel finds herself welling up as the solemn television mast, always a beacon of home, winks back at her from way across the moors. As she takes the one winding road to Greenleigh, she flounders in a wave of emotion that she can't quite put her finger on, nerves, nostalgia, or is it that she is just coming home?

A bit last minute, she tips the rear view mirror to review her reflection, setting off in such a hurry she'd not given much thought to her appearance. Her holiday in Ibiza had been hectic, with more late nights and drinking than she had experienced in a while, and she was exhausted. Coupled with the shock of this situation, Mel does not exactly feel at her best right now. She makes a note to at least apply mascara before she sees anybody.

By the time the sign for Greenleigh looms out of a hedgerow, her stomach is choppy with anxiety. To get to the farmhouse, you have to drive through the village and back up out towards the moors. The street lights are on, and Christmas lights twinkle in all the windows. It was always a picture postcard at this time of year, even more so when they got snow. Unchanged for as long as she's known, the Christmas tree stands in the memorial square, its blinking star pulsating like a lighthouse, the same beat for as long as she can remember. At primary school, they sang carols around it, and everyone would cheer when 'Santa' pushed the button and the village lit up around them. She had always taken Connor to the light switch on at Albert square, but even with its celebrity guests and dramatic light shows, it never shared the same atmosphere as standing here on those toe-stomping winter nights, singing about Rudolph, so excited to see Santa, even if it was just for the chocolate he gave out as you got older after you'd realised Santa was Alice Fretwell's Grandad.

Driving slowly, she rounds the corner past The White Horse pub. She still almost can't look at it. Then up by the village primary school, which only held about 60 kids, so everybody grew up knowing everybody, turning down past where the Chip shop used to be, where they used to hang about outside, eating chips, bits and gravy. The village is an uneven jumble of slate roofs and lamp-lit ginnels, leading you up worn stone steps to the top road, where she had lived in a tiny terrace cottage with her mum. Tucked amongst the cluster of stone cottages is Nelson's shop, still looking exactly the same. She pulls in, suddenly thinking that there probably won't be anything much at Kath's, not that she feels like eating anything right now. Janet, of course, has given her a bag of bits in takeaway boxes to keep her going, but at the very least, after the day she's having, wine.

Squinting in the car interior lights, she daubs on some mascara before she slowly gets out of the car, casting her eyes round the quiet street whilst tidying her hair and wishing she was wearing something a bit less Christmas break (down) and had thought to put on a few more layers. It was so much warmer living in a city, she'd forgotten it got this cold, tucking her hands in her jacket as she crosses the road, wondering if Kath's house is still only heated by fires and the Aga and if it's been kept on.

Mel pauses before she pushes open the door. Once Mr. Nelson knows she's back, the whole of Greenleigh will know in record time. As ever, the bell rings over her head as she slides in the door. She moves swiftly, keeping her head down as she stealthily gathers some basics, lurking behind the shelves as much as possible, wondering how much wine she can get away with in one purchase.

"Sorry to hear about Kathleen, Melanie," Mr. Nelson shouts from behind the counter. Of course, he never misses a trick; they used to say a flea didn't bite in Greenleigh without him hearing about it.

He continues before she can say anything, "Heard they had to drag you home from some party in Ibiza." Clearly, the rumours were already flying, she frowns, imagining Chris telling everyone at the bar at The 'Horse, just like old times, and she's only been back five minutes. God give me strength, she mutters in her head,

"Not quite, Mr. Nelson. I was visiting my son, who lives there. I came here as soon as possible," Mel tries to keep her voice calm, or the gossip will include that she is still a hysterical mess.

"Like mother, like son, is it? I remember you going out there to do your clubbing… I hope your son calls you more than you ever did your dad!" Mr. Nelson was always a bit of a disapproving grinch, old school in his ways. Mel wouldn't be surprised if he still doesn't take card payments.

"Not that you ever came to see him after you got back either,"

She'd not exactly forgotten how unforgiving Greenleigh is, but it still hurts, as the truth tends to. She curls her fist tightly round her bottle of Merlot, "If you remember, Mr. Nelson, he wasn't exactly thrilled about my choices." She hurries out of the shop, before he can insult her further, letting the door bang behind her, clutching two bottles of wine (any more and he'd be adding 'Still got drinking problem' to the Chinese whispers).

Night has descended well as she bumps up the rough road uphill. Turning to go up the single-lane track that leads to Kath's and Old Holme Farm, she is surprised by a large sign at the turning. Her ancient Ford Focus is not made for country roads, but it seems this part of the ancient cart track has been somehow smoothed over, a strange sensation but welcome.

She's forgotten how pitch-black it is at night without the city streetlights. It never gets this dark in Manchester, even in the dead of night. She goes at a crawl so as not to veer into any ditches. Kath's farmhouse looms up first. There are no lights on anywhere, so she doesn't stop. It looks pretty creepy in the darkness, and a sudden chill runs up her spine.

Squinting into the gloom, she takes the next turn up towards the Oldswicks' farm, but confusingly, there are new buildings in the field before you get to the gate. They are log cabins with a new, separate entrance. The lights are on in a couple of them, a Christmas tree glowing cosily through a window, and fairy lights twinkle along their roofs; they look so welcoming compared to Kath's place. Have the Oldswicks sold off some land? She wonders, surprised, even more so at the gate when she sees a sign for a farm shop. Things do change, and she reminds herself, even out here in the land that time forgot.

Holme End Farm stands as it has for nearly two hundred years. 1838 carved into the stone lintel over the front door. Made of weathered local stone, the house stands on one side in a courtyard cluster of barns and outbuildings.

When she used to come here with Chris, it was a working dairy farm, everything revolved around cows but as she slowly parks up in the yard, she can't see any farm machinery or evidence of live stock, just Mr. Oldswick's ancient Land Rover, (that Chris also drove from when he was tall enough to reach the pedals). She sniffs, not a hint of strangely sweet manure in the air, and the yard is weirdly tidy. The smart-looking farm shop is advertised in what used to be the milking parlour, and it looks like the barn's also been converted. Mel looks around, discombobulated; the gentrification that has hounded her in Manchester has somehow also reached this corner of Yorkshire.

As she gets out of the car, it feels weird not to be greeted by the smell and barked at by the plethora of farm dogs that followed at Chris' dad's heels. When she would try making a fuss of them, he would tell her off, gruffly insisting that they were working animals, even though she saw him pat them lovingly when he thought no one was looking.

Aware of how hard her heart is pounding, she meanders toward the back door they always used, pushing against many memories that threaten to overwhelm her. On top of the dread of seeing Chris, who is still holding a grudge. Why on earth didn't she think to change out of her ancient leggings and Connor's old hoodie? She straightens her clothes whilst taking some deep breaths in an attempt to quell her apprehension.

Scared that anyone inside is watching her dither through the kitchen window. She knocks on the ancient wooden door, timidly. After a few attempts, she gets no response. In the end, she tentatively tries the door; it's open, as always. No one ever knocks at any of the farms in the valley; you would just go in with a shout. Even after all these years, it's a very familiar feeling stepping onto the worn flagstones of the hallway floor.

Mel stops, taking in the scene, the collection of old coats hanging by the door, pet bowls and muddy boots littering the passageway, the smell unchanged, wood smoke and engine oil, animals and apple pie. She shouts a rather weak hello down the stone-walled corridor, instantly greeted by a flurry of activity: dogs come running at her, and Mrs.Oldswick comes out of the kitchen to greet her.

It must be all the fresh air, but she doesn't look any older than when Mel last saw her, over ten years ago, and she thought then how little she'd changed. A small, wiry woman whose husband, then both sons, dwarfed her, sweeps Mel into her arms as if she had only seen her last week. Her strong arms, as ever, comforting, "You haven't changed a bit, Melanie love, has she?" She asks her husband as they go through into the kitchen, where time has also stood, mostly, still; the cluttered pine table still sits in the middle of the room surrounded by mismatched wooden chairs, the kitchen shelves groan with every type of crockery, random farm equipment lies next to kitchen appliances but there is one obvious change, a shiny, duck egg blue Aga stands where the rusty range used to be. Mel gravitates toward it to warm up, taken aback at how instantly she feels at home.

Mr. Oldswick looks up from fixing something at the kitchen table. "No lass, not a bit," he nods at her, looking up only briefly before carrying on tinkering, as if he, too, had only seen her yesterday. She hovers in the doorway, but Mrs. Oldswick ushers her in, moving a cat off an armchair by the fire, and waves Mel to sit.

"We didn't think you could get here yet. Chris's already fed all the animals on his way out, and he'll stop in to let the dogs out on his way up home, I'd imagine. "

"There's no need! I'll take it from here!" Mel barks sharply,

Mrs.Oldswick shakes her head, "You're not going to be able to avoid each other, Mel…We've another key somewhere, I'll dig it out while the kettle boils."

Mel feels her shoulders relax for the first time that day, knowing Chris is out. However, she's slightly aggrieved that she missed getting there in time to do the evening jobs. At first, she turns down the offer of a drink; she doesn't think she's quite ready to be back in this kitchen with its million memories. However, now that it transpires that the animals are fed and put to bed, nothing is waiting for her at Kath's but the cold and dark. She leans towards the crackling fire, it's just sinking in that she will have to sleep there, alone and by the sounds of it, it isn't pretty. She backtracks on the offer of a tea from the ever-present pot.

"If I'd known you were coming today, I'd have got Chris to leave the lights on and light the fire, we leave the Aga on for the animals so it's not freezing, but still, I'd have had a bit of a fettle for you, love."

"It's fine, you've done more than enough already. I'm grateful for you keeping an eye on the place."

She thinks, too late, that she should have brought a thank you gift and makes a note to do so; they were always so nice to her, even after everything.

"Couldn't let the animals starve," interjects Mr. Oldswick, "Kept telling her to get rid of a few, mind, but she wouldn't turn a stray away, too soft that woman," his voice breaks a little, "She'll be missed."

Mrs. Oldswick agrees," She was never the same after your dad died; they reckon she died of a broken heart." She murmurs softly,

"At least they're back together now."

This hits Mel like a ton of bricks; she clenches every inch of herself not to burst into tears, feeling suddenly overwhelmed and tremendously guilty. Mrs. Oldswick gives her a knowing sideways glance, pouring the tea from what Mel can tell is the same enormous brown teapot from her childhood. "Still take two sugars?" she asks. Mel nods even though she doesn't drink tea anymore, let alone with two whole sugars. Overcome by their kindness, none of which she feels she deserves, she stares into the roaring fire, not quite trusting herself to speak, sipping her sweet tea while Mrs.Oldswick goes looking for the spare set of keys. A clatter down the corridor makes her guts jump into her mouth; she swallows, her throat tight, a tall figure ducks under the low kitchen door, and her heart speeds up. A man enters the room, she almost gasps out loud, but it isn't Chris, holy hell, it's little Josh, all grown up. He stops in his tracks when he sees Mel sitting there,

"I wondered whose car that was! Bloody hell! 'Melsbells!! I thought I'd stepped back in time for a minute then, seeing you sitting there, like old times, you don't look any different!"

"Told you love," says Mrs. Oldswick kindly,

"Well, you do, Joshy," Mel retorts, using his childhood name back at him, whilst simultaneously trying to process that this grown man in front of her is the little boy who followed her and Chris around everywhere. He must be nearly 30 now, she reminds herself. It's weird to see the young face she knew so well, but he's morphed into a grown man, though. A large man like his dad and his brother, similar looking to Chris, but with darker hair. Where Chris was serious, though Josh was always a joker,

"Well, well, Melanie McCarthy, back in town...This'll put the cat right amongst the pigeons," he bellows, laughing, "Have you seen my brother yet?"

Mel shakes her head, embarrassed by the obvious connotation that it's going to be somewhat awkward,

He laughs, "Man, I have to be there to see that, after all this time, that wound, it's still deep, you know Mels. When they were talking about you in the pub last week, he said..."

A sharp look from his mum swiftly silences Josh. "I'm sorry about Kath," he changes tack, pouring himself a brew, sprawling out in the chair opposite, and upending the poor cat again. Mel can't, but also can, believe she was being talked about down the pub before she'd even arrived,

"So, Mel, I take it you haven't been to the house yet?" She doesn't like his concerned tone,

"No, she hasn't! "interrupts his mum. I think you should go down with her, Josh. Light the fire. It'll be freezing otherwise, and err, you can show her what to do with all the animals."

"Great, then Chris won't have to come by anymore," Mel asserts, "I can take it from here."

"Oh, I didn't realise you've become a livestock expert, Mels," Josh slugs his tea, giving her a wolfish grin, "I heard that you've been partying it up in Ibiza for the last twenty years."

Mr. Nelson and his bloody rumour mill, "I work at a school in Manchester, actually,"

"Well, dealing with kids is bound to be helpful when you're

trying to round up Kath's Zoo. Honestly, Mels, I've never met a worse-behaved bunch of animals."

"You should probably talk to Dixon, the vet, half of 'em are on their last legs anyway, be kinder to put them down," Mr. Oldswick mutters darkly, not looking up from his task.

"How many animals are there exactly?" It starts to sink in that there is maybe more to this than putting a few feed bowls out. They all suck in their teeth, Josh starts,

"Well there's all the goats...5 or 6?"

"5? 4 sheep,"

"One's only got 3 legs, so you've got to be careful he doesn't fall over and get stuck on his back," Josh interjects. Mel hopes that's a joke, but he carries on without laughing,

"The three dogs...Arlo, Skippy and what's the sort of blind one called?"

"Milly? Then there's the chickens and some ducks,"

"Wow..." says Mel faintly, after losing count at the sheep,

"There are cats...A lot of cats, I think one had kittens that Kath was going to re-home,"

"And the donkeys, of course, but they're no bother," Finishes off Mrs.Oldswick," They just need fresh hay, mucking out, and I think one of them is on medicine from' vet,"

"As I said, you want to call Dixon, you can't re-home 'em, they're too used to Kath's ways, you remember, most of them live in the bloody kitchen."

Mel slurps all the sugar out of the bottom of her cup as the blood drains from her face. Rather unwillingly, she gets up. "Well, Josh, if you don't mind introducing me," she says. It's now, she thinks, or she just gets back in her car and drives straight back to the city without stopping to pass go.

Josh folds his long legs into the Focus, chattering ten to the dozen. As they pass the cabins, Mel thinks to ask, "We had to diversify, Mels, there's no money in dairy anymore. Chris was adamant that we weren't losing the farm; we're fourth-generation Oldswicks at Holme End, don't forget. You know how much it means to him."

Old memories surface,

" I'd forgotten about Nana Betty...That amazing apple pie with the cream she churned herself." Memories of her and Chris in the stone larder behind the kitchen, sneaking slices of warm pie off the plate and dipping it straight into the big bowl of yellow cream, blobbing it on each other's noses, kissing the crumbs off each other's faces, tasting of cinnamon and buttery pastry.

She had been so happy then, before her Mum died."Chris got this idea to start the farm shop, do events and maybe holiday lets," Josh was oblivious to her dizzying trip down memory lane,

" So we went off to Oz to earn some dollars to pay for all the changes. We worked out in the mines for about six years, on and off, real hard yakka, squeeze my guns Mel, look, I'm a beast!" he flexes his beefy arms at her. Mel laughs. He's still the same stupid kid.

"When we came back, we built the cabins with the money

we'd made from scratch... Chris is a total tyrant, I'm sure you can imagine, but he's done a great job; now we rent them out as holiday lets. They're really popular. When they took off, we opened the farm shop, and now we host weddings and other events in the barn; it keeps us afloat, and we might even make some decent money this year. He has grand plans to build a wood-fired sauna, and we've made a start on a swimming pond behind the cabins; guests love that. Mind the big hole if you cut across in the dark! Dad has some special breed sheep to keep him happy...It beats the constant smell of manure!" he laughs while Mel adjusts to this seismic turn of events for Holme End farm.

Chris used to hate even going into town; it must've killed him to spend six years away from his beloved land. Mel must grudgingly admit that she admires his dedication to keeping the farm afloat.

She pulls up next to a dilapidated looking truck, "Not sure if it's still running but if you want to save the suspension in this thing, you could get it going again," He starts laughing to himself, "You should err, ring Brooks, I'm sure for you, they'll send *someone* out,"

"Why's that funny?" Mel remembers Phill Brooks, another no-nonsense local,

"You'll see!" He bounds up the path and rattles the front door open, "Key's a bit stiff, I don't think Kath ever used it."

"We only used the back door, and it was never locked, obviously." Mel inches behind him up the dark path. She can barely see in front of her until Josh switches the lights on and Mel steps through the door and into another time warp, except with more stuff, a lot more stuff. There is stuff everywhere. She doesn't quite know where to look, and then the smell hits her.

It's so familiar, it's overwhelming how quickly she swirls back in time to living here as a teenager. She has to resist the impulse again to back out the door, get in her car and hightail it out of there.

Two dogs come wandering towards her. Both look disappointed when they realise she isn't Kath. Her breath catches in her throat. It breaks Mel's heart to imagine how much they must miss her, but there is no time to dwell on that now as she follows Josh, giving her instructions ten to the dozen, through to the kitchen, trying not to trip over the magazines and bags of animal feed that litter the corridor.

As he flips the switch, six pairs of eyes blink from varying chairs and baskets and a little Jack Russell limps towards her hopefully, sniffs her, then makes her way back to her basket with a disgruntled flop, "That's Milly, she can't see too well, this one's Arlo, (a black and white collie,) He's a worker, he should, in theory, round up the goats and sheep for you at night but I think he's only used to Kath's signals, he doesn't listen to me. The spaniel is Skippy; he's supposed to be a working dog, but Kath could never train him. However, she was too soft to get rid of him. He chases the chickens, you have to keep an eye on him, but those two don't need a lead."

Bending down, he scratches Milly on the head, "Milly's no bother, well, except she's pretty much blind, so don't let her get out of the gate, we get a lot more traffic up the track now 'cos of the farm shop. I have no idea about the cats..." Half of them slink suspiciously out of the cat flap at the sight of her, but in one basket, there are three kittens cuddled up together. If Mel weren't in an increasingly state of horror at the chaos, everywhere, she'd drop down and fuss over them, I mean, who doesn't love kittens? But her eyes are darting over the animals to the mess the kitchen is in.

Josh continues, "All the cat and dog feed is in the pantry. You might need to stock up. The cats will chase the mice off it. Chris has been feeding 'em for the past few days, so I don't know. I've been staying at my girlfriend's."

"Ooooh Joshy's got a girlfriend" God, Mel, she catches herself, stop talking to him like he's still eight years old,

"I know, get me, you might remember her. Her sister was in yours and Chris's year, Lindsey Mellor? Her little sister, Lacey, remember?"

Mel would never forget the Mellor girls; there was also an older sister, Caz, who was the school bully.

"She's a total babe, she lives in Leeds now," he says with that recognisable, dreamy look of a man in lust, "She works for Asda, in the offices."

He is miles away, smirking, leaving Mel with no doubt how he spent his Christmas, "Err, the other feed is in the building out back, it's not locked, you'll know what's for who by the bags, the water bowls will need checking for ice, it's been brassic this week. Chris lets the chooks and ducks out when it's quiet, but they will try to come inside, so be warned. I think the TV works, but I'm pretty sure Chris said there's no WIFI. I mean, who lives like that? The wood store is still by the back door."

Mel shudders, remembering, "Is it still full of a century of cobwebs?"

"And the world's biggest spiders, I swear one the other day was bigger than a rat, err, are you alright Mels? You look a bit pale?"

Pale is an understatement, Mel thinks dizzily, leaning over the kitchen table. The enormity of the impending task sinks in with the speed of an arrow. She feels completely swamped, but is also determined that her panic doesn't get back to Chris. Forcing a bright smile, she mutters she's fine, hoping Josh doesn't notice that she is holding onto a chair like she is bracing for a collision.

Josh kindly lopes out the back door with the log basket and Mel plonks herself down, looking around the kitchen. The increase in stuff aside, it's the same as she remembers it from when she very first used to come and stay here.From the age of 11, it was agreed, not by her, however, that she would come and stay every Friday night after school. She would get the school bus back, walking as slowly as she could up the lane, mostly behind Chris, who, at that age, was not going to talk to a girl unless he had to, despite them knowing each other for years. She hated going, begging her Mum every week, then sulking while she was there, mainly hiding out in the barn. It must have been pretty difficult for her Dad and Kath, too, she thinks remorsefully.

She'd wanted to be a vet back then and was only happy when she could spend time with the animals. The house was basic back then, you would always see your breath on a morning until the fire got up, no change there. She moves toward the ancient Aga while Josh lays the fire,

Warming her hands on the iron surface, she mutters, "I don't know how anyone lives without central heating."

"You've gone 'nesh Mels, now you're a city girl. Don't you remember the fun of scraping ice off the inside of the windows in winter so you could see if it had snowed?"

Mel considers what she threw in her suitcase earlier; she'll have to wear every item in it to prevent her from freezing to death overnight.

"Are you sure you're gonna be ok, Mel? Mum would put you up, you know, if you don't want to stay down here on your own? The cabins are all booked for New Year, but you could have Chris's old room; he's living in the one he's finishing off now."

Mel thinks about it, temptingly, for a split second, but she doesn't think she could handle being in his bedroom again, nor does she imagine that he would want her to be. Her determination kicks in. She will show him no weakness.

"I'll be FINE! I lived here for years, remember?! I just need to, you know, get *reoriented,* that's all," She tells herself, as much as him,

"I'm playing darts tonight at the 'Horse, so I've got to get going or I'd help you settle in …Oooh, you can come with, if you like? Can you imagine?!" He starts laughing to himself,

"What's so funny?" Mel quizzes,

"You know Greenleigh Mel, it has a long, *long* memory, you'd cause a right commotion, especially if Chris is there and/" he laughs again, shaking his head,

"Well, thanks for the invitation, I think, but I'll pass,"

"Another time, though, yeah? You have to!! Everyone will be so stoked to have you back… Now, are you sure you'll be OK? Don't be creeped out, Kath died out in the yard, you know, so you don't have to think about her body in the house,"

"JOSH! Shut up, will you!" Mel does not want to know about the actual, you know, details, right now anyway,

"Sorry, I'm just trying to help," he pulls on his beanie hat,

"Thanks for the lowdown and the fire," she practically sits in it to warm herself up.

"Errr, will you see Chris later? You can tell him he doesn't need to come by anymore, I'll be fine," She hopes she sounds convincing.Shrugging, he adds, "It's your call, Mel! You can't dodge each other forever, you know, Greenleigh's a small place, remember! Look, take my number in case you need anything… Just don't go booty calling me at 3 am, yeah? I know what you're like, 'Bells." Chuckling, he waves goodbye, pulling the heavy front door, asserting that she has to come to the White Horse with him on New Year's Eve.

The mention of New Year makes her reach for her phone, but there are no messages from Andrew. Warming herself by the growing fire, she rings Janet, but it won't connect. Frowning at the screen, she sees that there is no phone signal. Back in the day, you used to have to go all the way down the hill, but surely in this day and age, technology has improved? Or maybe not.

She gets no joy anywhere downstairs; slight panic starts to set in. She gathers herself to go up the stairs. It isn't a big house, but there are long corridors that she always found a bit creepy back then; she can't even persuade the dogs to come with her now that they've all settled down by the fire. Cautiously, she goes up the staircase, jumping out of her skin when a black cat shoots out of one of the bedrooms and barrels past her. Buckets litter the corridor to catch the rain through the leaky roof, and plaster crumbles as she brushes by. Tentatively, she edges towards the bathroom. When she lived here, she would do anything not to go in there, especially at night. The old metal bath stained with iron from the taps, which always looked a bit like blood stains to her. Mel had happily watched a thousand horror movies as a teenager. It was one of hers and Chris' favourite things to do, always trying to outdo each other with creepier films, none of them ever bothered her until the minute she got in the shower, then all she could ever think of was Psycho. She decides against opening the door, feeling anxious enough as it is. Kath's bedroom door is also closed; she'll save that for the light of day, too.

She tries the box room door, but it won't open because of all the stuff stacked inside. Panic builds in increments; she is never going to get this place sorted in the few days she'd imagined.Her old bedroom is right at the end of the corridor. Pushing open the door, she wonders what manner of junk she'll find lurking in there. Flipping on the light, Mel is stunned to see that her old duvet cover is still on the bed and the very few things she left are still on the shelves. A-level textbooks and trinkets are coated with what looks like several years' worth of dust. It's surreal, as if she's in a dream, or a nightmare.She backs away, hurrying back downstairs, chalky plaster swirling around her feet.

She'll have to go outside to check for a signal; she must bring her bags in from the car anyway. The dogs follow her out, including Milly. How does someone walk a blind dog, she wonders, catching her by the collar and putting her on a lead before she disappears into the dark, the last thing she needs is to lose any animals. She can only imagine what Chris would have to say about that.

A crescent moon hangs gracefully overhead. Looking up, she's blown away by the number of stars she can see. The light pollution in Manchester means you seldom see anything but the neon glow from all the street lights. She remembers lying out in the fields on summer nights with Chris, who knew all the constellations. She spots Orion and smiles to herself. Her breath forms clouds in the air, she dashes to the car to look for more clothes, pulling on her bobble hat gratefully as her earlobes begin to sting. As her eyes finally adjust to the darkness, she takes in her surroundings, glad that she can see all the lights from the log cabins up the field. Before they were built, there were no other properties in sight. Old Holme Farm is tucked a bit further away over the hill. She makes out the hen coop and hears the goats bleating around in the barn. Walking up to the end of the garden, waggling her phone in vain, she sees the donkey shelter. She wonders how long donkeys live and if they could be the same two Kath owned when she left for Ibiza.

Weirdly, after trying all sorts and almost considering a drive back to civilisation, it turns out that if she climbs onto the flat bed of Kath's pick-up truck, she can just about get a phone signal. Her phone beeps to life as she tries to make herself comfy on the freezing cold metal. There are messages from Janet, Andrew, and Aaron, who had heard about Kath from Connor. She leaves messages for Ken Braithwaite and the undertaker, then rings Janet, who bombards her with a hundred questions, completely intrigued by Mel's mysterious history. So far, Mel has declined to share any details with Janet, but Janet is determined to break her.

Having the very real excuse of losing feeling in her fingers, she rings off, psyching herself up to ring Andrew, wondering what mood he'll be in; the last thing she can handle is any more guilt on her shoulders. Much to her relief, Andrew just seems concerned that she is ok, reiterating that he is happy to come and help her, "Why don't I come up so we can spend New Year's eve together? I can look for some local accommodation if the house isn't guest-friendly. Are there any hotels or holiday rentals nearby? There must be something?" Mel looks over at the log cabins, but she is very unwilling to mix the two worlds.

"Not that I know of, it's been a while since I lived here, remember? I mean, everywhere's probably booked up at this late stage anyway."

"I'll find somewhere, I don't want you to be alone in that house for New Year's eve."

Mel can't help but wonder if it's he who doesn't want to be alone, she opens her mouth to mention Josh's pub offer but closes it again, the less he knows about her history the better, "I'm fine honestly Andrew, don't worry, I mean I'm seeing the solicitor and going to the funeral home tomorrow, so I should know more about how long I'll be here by then. I'll ring you after that."

By now, she can't feel her toes either, even the dogs are whining to go in, so after sending Aaron and Connor a quick text, she takes her things back to the house. Dumping it all on the worn stone flags, she startles the cats, the kittens come wobbling toward her. Welcome of the distraction, Mel sits down in the big armchair by the fire, sinking into the worn springs, her Dad used to sit here. She closes her eyes and pictures him, her hand tightening on the threadbare arm of the chair. The sea of regret starts lapping at her feet. To distract herself, she picks up the three kittens. Intrigued by the strings on her hoodie, they play with the ends until they get tired, curling up clumsily. They all go to sleep on her knee. Imagining that she'll never be able to sleep a wink that night, it all feels way too weird, she sits watching the fire flicker, making a mental list of the million things she has to do in the next few days.

Arlo settles by her feet, and a few cats come by for a curious look. She doesn't remember closing her eyes, but the exhaustion from Ibiza and all the events of the day somehow catches up with her. She falls sound asleep sat in the chair, and when she opens her bleary eyes, it's morning, technically, her phone says 4.22 am. It's still pitch black outside, and the fire has turned to glowing embers; she can see her breath faintly. One kitten is still nestled in her lap, but as soon as she shifts position, stiff from sleeping upright, the others wind around her ankles, expecting food. She desperately needs a wee and coffee. What she wouldn't do for a Starbucks Latte right now.

Rifling through her bag for warm clothes, she slings her dressing gown round her shoulders and the bag of weed she found after the party falls out onto the floor. She leaves it on the kitchen table, thinking it might be exactly what she needs to take the edge off this crazy week; she has no idea how to even start the task ahead. There is no coffee in the cupboards, but she finds some dusty tea bags, scouring the mug first for at least five minutes whilst scribbling a list on the back of an envelope. She has to go into town to see the undertakers, so she'll go to a big Asda and buy all the cleaning products they stock, especially if Andrew is insisting on coming. She's going to need a lot of bin bags. She writes SKIP on the list and underlines it. Does Kath even own a Hoover? Poking about, she unearths a clunky upright that she could've sworn is the same one they had back in the day, she adds Hoover to the list with PET HAIR next to it. If anyone with allergies came here, they would keel over in seconds. Every time you move, dog hair drifts across the stone floor like tumbleweed.

Her stomach rumbles, she's not eaten anything since a biscuit with her brew at the Oldswick's. Casting a narrow eye at the fridge door, she wonders if anyone has thought to empty its contents. With trepidation, she opens it, only to reel back from the funk, shutting it firmly again, her appetite duly subsiding. RUBBER GLOVES, she writes, DISINFECTANT, BLEACH. For lack of anything else to do at 5 am, having fed the indoor menagerie, she drags the wheelie bin up to the house, cranks up the crackly FM radio and sets to work on the kitchen. The sooner she gets done, the sooner she can go home.

It doesn't get light until almost eight, but she makes good progress, despite working with limited resources. It was fair to say that cleaning had never been that high on Kath's priority list. Mel keeps the kettle boiling on the Aga, using her shampoo for soap when she runs out. Tying her scarf over her nose (what is that smell?), she sweeps everything from the fridge into an old feed bag, dumping it swiftly outside. Milly starts whining at the door, clipped firmly to a lead, she takes her outside.

The sun is streaking across the big sky in vivid orange and reds. Mel remembers the rule of thumb from growing up: the prettier the sunrise, the chuffing colder it is outside. Watching her breath float away, she loses herself in the view, which is more beautiful than she ever remembered. They don't call Yorkshire God's own country without good reason. Frost glitters all the fields, and the distant moors float dreamily amongst the pastel clouds. If she looks down the valley past the cabins, there is barely a man-made structure on the whole horizon, and it's so quiet, well, save for the goats who are bleating indignantly to be let out. Putting Milly back inside, she sets about feeding the rest of the animals. Pulling open the shed door, she tries to discern whose feed is whose, but it's all in big tubs, looking inside the buckets at the varying shades of brown kibble doesn't help. Whether she likes it or not, she already has a dozen questions. She shoots Josh an SOS text, leaving her phone on the truck bed to await a reply. While she waits, she decides to let the goats and sheep out. (Open the gate, then the barn door, Josh instructed her last night, they'll just run into the field, he made it all sound pretty easy.)

Swinging the door open confidently, she is instantly

stampeded by animals, losing her balance on the icy pebbles and banging her knee hard as she lands amongst the, thankfully frozen, goat poo. The slippery ground means she struggles getting up again, as she realises, frustratingly, that not one animal has trotted obediently into the field as promised. Instead, they are happily gallivanting over the garden, nibbling on the plants. She panics, should they be eating those? One of the goats starts to butt the chicken coop, sending the hens into a clucking frenzy. After awkwardly getting back on her feet, she implores Arlo to round them up, but he just sits watching her; she could swear he's enjoying the chaos. What commands would Kath have used? "Fetch! Round them up, Arlo!" She tries everything, but he remains steadfastly unconvinced.

With no other option, she sets about chasing them into the field herself. After half an hour of feeling like she's being pranked, she's forced to admit defeat. If she gets one in the field, as soon as she opens the gate, the first one escapes. With still no word from Josh, she makes sure they can't get out onto the road and steals herself to go over the fields up to Holme End, praying she comes across Mr. Oldswick. She is pretty sure he'll round them up with a single look.

CHAPTER SIX

The stunning sunrise has given way to a picture-perfect winter day; it's freezing, but the sky is blue, and it's satisfyingly crisp underfoot. Mel feels unexpectedly cheerful as she crosses the fields, buoyed by the stunning views, not a drive-thru McDonald's or block of executive flats in sight. Arlo and Skippy trot beside her as she cuts through the fields, like she always used to, except now she has to skirt round the bottom of the log cabins, past the half built swimming pond, where a beautiful dry stone wall rises one side, another skill Chris had acquired from when he was a kid. From this angle, she can see that each cabin has floor-to-ceiling windows around the back, with a large deck overlooking the far-reaching valley views. Is that a vintage bathtub she can see through one of the big windows? She sighs, wondering what she wouldn't do to have a hot bath right now and with that view, too. A touch begrudgingly, she admits that Chris seems to have done an impressive job.

Set farther back from the others, one cabin is still being finished, intrigued; she intends to go for a closer look, when both dogs take off toward it at pace, and she notices there is someone around the far side, sorting out timbers. He looks up as the dogs barrel into him, and she realises far too late that it's Chris. Freezing abruptly, she almost trips over her feet, his profile is still so overwhelmingly familiar despite the lapse in time. Unready, however, to have another unpleasant conversation with him, she panics, turning firmly the other way as he squares his shoulders and starts studiously looking at the wood in his hand. She shouts feebly over her shoulder to the dogs, but the traitorous pair stay at Chris' feet. Irked by him making no attempt to send them back to her, she carries on, more shaken than she expected to be by the sight of her past catching up with her twenty years later.

Sidling into the yard, making sure he isn't following, she lets herself straight into the house. Mrs. Oldswick is cooking; something's already in the oven; the smell of warm pastry makes her stomach rumble loudly. Mrs. Oldswick ("Call me Sheila, you're not 16 anymore, love") insists that she has some toast and tells her to get a brew. Mel, who had given up sugar years ago, finds herself heaping it in the cup, stirring nervously, needing the blood sugar boost after seeing Chris. She still feels guilty about what happened between them; she realises this with a jolt, but she has no intention of dragging up the past by trying to apologise for it, not at this very moment anyway. One thing she can be sure of is that the cat won't stay in the bag in Greenleigh for long, but if she keeps her head down and stays off radar, she can be in and out of their lives with no repercussions this time.

A thought she will come to laugh at later, hollowly.

"I've just got a few questions about the animals, I wasn't sure whose food is whose and err, I can't get the goats or the sheep into the field so I wondered if Mr. Oldswick, ("Call him Jim for god's sake,") would pop by and show me what to do?"

"Didn't you pass our Chris out there? I thought he was out working on the cabin…" She gives Mel a hard stare; nothing gets past her, "Chris designed them all by himself, you know, Mel."

"Josh told me, they're gorgeous."

"Aren't they?" She says proudly, "They're very popular."

"He err, he looked really busy, with some wood, he didn't say anything and I, errr, I didn't want to bother him,"

"He's still sulking over you more like, idiot, ignore him, he'll give you a hand if you ask him."

"If Jim could maybe just explain the food..." Mel isn't ready for a big reunion today. She hasn't even got mascara on. She didn't think this through at all. Of course, he's still sulking. She doesn't even blame him, to be honest.

"Christopher's been looking after them mostly, so he'd know Mel."

"He's done enough, I don't want to interrupt him. Is Josh about?"

Sheila dusts her hands off on her pinny, "Mel, love, it was a long time ago, you were just kids, now you're grown-ups, you both need to get over it and move on...We all know what happened with Jamie Hirst was unfortunate, but..."

Despite the twenty-year distance between events, at the sound of Jamie's name, Mel dies instantly inside, her stomach swirling with shame as Sheila carries on, "We all knew what you'd gone through, it wasn't surprising you went, a bit...Off the rails love. Hurt people *hurt people*. It was a long time ago, Melanie, everyone's over it."

"Everyone except Chris," Josh tsks, having come into the kitchen behind them. He swipes a slice of Mel's toast and continues, "Us lot might have forgiven you, but nobodies exactly forgotten it though, I was telling everyone last night that I'd seen you and it's the first thing anyone ever brings up when they hear your name, even people who've never met you."

"JOSH!" Sheila splutters.

Begrudgingly, Mel takes two cups of tea out of the kitchen and dawdles over toward where Chris is working, both dogs sitting obediently at his feet. Barely able to meet his eyes, she passes him the cup of tea and stands back, staring into her mug. It's hard to reconcile this grown man with the boy of her memories. Like Josh, he is all muscle, thanks to their time in Australia and the manual labour on the farm. He's become a not unpleasant hybrid of Yorkshire farmer and Aussie surfer, his hair longer and blonder where it flips out messily from under his grey beanie hat. There are lines across his forehead and around his grey-blue eyes (currently looking anywhere but at her). His face has been weathered from the Aussie sun, and he has a rough beard that takes the edge off his boyish features. She remembers when he first started shaving those wispy hairs from his top lip; she used to tease him mercilessly about it. His face is so familiar, yet he's twenty years older; it feels confusing, yet he's still so Chris, out here in the fields first thing, with the dogs, his hands dirty, in his lopsided, woolly hat, old checked shirt, scuffed-up jeans, and battered work boots.

He's been a stranger to her all these years, virtually, save the odd picture she's seen on social media here and there, and that was a while ago. He was never the type to bother looking at a phone; he's been too busy. Mel is in awe of all he's done to save the farm, but she isn't surprised, his DNA is in the dirt of Holme End.

She thinks too late about the state she's probably in after a night sleeping in a chair, wondering if it's as weird for him, looking at her, after all this time. Josh might have proclaimed that she hadn't changed a bit, but Mel is suddenly conscious of how she has aged. She isn't the skinny, bad bottle blonde with a nose piercing that she was back then. They were just kids, really, Connor's age, when they last saw each other in person; now she's the mother of a child that age, it's a bit mind-bending.

His flinty eyes give nothing away, and he gives her a tight smile when he catches her stare, but only because he is too polite not to. He quickly looks back down at the dogs at his feet. It's way more emotional than she imagined; they have such a heavy history. He doesn't say anything, though, and it's starting to feel awkward.

"I err, just wanted to thank you for everything you've been doing. I appreciate you helping me out, especially now I know how much work is involved."

"I didn't do it for you, I did it for Kath, she loved those animals." Reaching down, he pats both the dogs,

She clenches her empty fist. "Well, I'm grateful nonetheless, but I do have a few questions,"

" I imagine you didn't come across much livestock in Ibiza." Ouch.

He puts down his mug, picks up the wood he was measuring and practically turns his back on her. Mel cringes. This is excruciating,

"I let them out of the barn but they won't go into the field and I don't know what to tell Arlo to get him to help, also I don't know which food belongs to who, so if you could just help me with those things, I'll get out of your hair, for good."

Josh appears loping over the field, much to Mel's immense relief, "Mum told me I was to wait in the kitchen, but I escaped! I've been dying to see the reunion of the century since we heard you were coming back…"

He stares at them both expectantly, when no one speaks, he carries on,"I invited Mel to come to the 'Horse with us tomorrow night, we could all go together! Imagine!" Josh seems giddy at the thought,

"Josh!" Chris shoots him a warning look,

"Come on, Bro, there's been no decent scandal for *months,* well, I suppose your fight on Christmas eve was pretty gossip worthy,"

"It wasn't a fight!" Chris turns back to Mel, "It wasn't a fight," he repeats, agitated.

"All right, chill out, bro! Mel's I just saw your text. Do you want me to come help you catch those bloody goats? If I stay here, he'll only make me help him in his labour camp,"

"Thanks, Josh. I'd appreciate a friendly face." She throws a pointed glance at Chris,

"No worries, you know you were always my favourite of all Chris' girlfriends, nobody likes *Marlowe,* that's his current squeeze, sorry 'Bro but you know how I feel... She's from *'Lahndan'*, she's far too city for him, but she's got him by the,"

"Josh!" Chris's face is thunderous, a look she remembers only too well,

"You know I was gutted when you stopped coming over after, *you know*...I think, Mels, you were probably my very first crush, you used to wear those short denim shorts, and I used to think about you when,"

"JOSH!" Mel and Chris chorus.

The dogs have zero intention of following Mel, and Chris murmurs he'll bring them over later. She explains that she's got to go see Ken Braithwaite and then sort out the funeral, so if he could just put them in the house, if he doesn't mind. As she turns to follow Josh up the field, Chris asks her suddenly if she's going alone. She nods, "I could come with you, Mel, if you don't want to go by yourself," he offers.

Taken aback, after his earlier rudeness, she stutters that she'll be fine, thanks, and sets off after Josh. The last thing she needs today is more eggshells to tread around. She is desperate to know about this Marlowe; however, she'll probe Josh later, although the last thing she wants is for him to tell Chris that she's interested in his love life, which she isn't, obviously.

It still takes nearly an hour for both of them to corral all the animals into the field, after which they let the chickens and ducks into their runs. Josh explains to her again how to feed them all. Checking the time, Mel realises she's going to be late for Ken if she doesn't get a move on. She leaves Josh at the house (he says he's happy to do some tidying up in exchange for asylum from Chris). Throwing on a clean jumper and sponging the worst of the goat crap from her jeans, she sets off, scraping her car out the rocky yard, thinking using the truck might be a good call.

Relieved to not have to go to the solicitor's offices and relive the reading of her Mum's will (as it turned out she left nothing but debt), driving up instead to the large bungalow where Ken lives. This side of Greenleigh is now the posh bit, another hard-up farmer having sold off some parcels of land, and a small estate of large houses appeared, making the village suddenly very desirable whilst contentiously pushing up all the surrounding house prices.

Ken is much greyer since the last time she saw him, but as he invites her in, he insists that she hasn't changed a bit. Mel, who at the time was sporting multiple piercings, had yellow peroxide blonde hair and a penchant for aggressive eyeliner. She hopes to god she has changed a lot since then, but doesn't like to be rude as she is making time to see her at his home. He ushers her into his study and sits down behind his desk, pulling out a great wad of papers,

"I'm very sorry about Kath's passing, Melanie, you're so young to have suffered all this loss."(Thanks for reminding me, Mr. B.)

"Now, have you been to the house?" Mel nods, and he pulls a sympathetic grimace, "Right, well, you can imagine how difficult it is to find all the relevant documents. There are several we still desperately need. Christopher has been wonderful, a godsend when we couldn't get hold of you; the number Kath had in her book was no longer in service. Anyway, we have the things needed to register the death, so the funeral should be straightforward, although the cost will fall on you for now, I'm afraid."

It's the least she could do, thinks Mel, "It appears there are no other immediate family, she was also orphaned young herself, as you know, with no siblings, "Mel nods at what she feels are the pertinent places, not wanting to admit the truth that she didn't know much about Kath's past, which as it turns out, is a lot like her own,

"The will is fairly specific, Melanie. Kath has left the house to be divided by you and your son. Provided we can locate all the relevant documents, etc, there should be no issues; the contents are yours to dispose of as you see fit. There are the animals, no specific provision is made for them, so you can decide what you do with them all, re-home them I suppose or have them, you know…" He makes a swiping motion across his neck, Mel shudders at the thought, her heart is starting to race as the responsibilities mount up,

"As for the house, well, you can see it's in a terrible state of disrepair, so your best bet is to put the house into an auction, get rid of it quickly. With the land it'll be a popular lot if a developer thinks he can get planning on it, which is debatable but it's not listed, so probably they'll knock the house down, you could easily get a few houses on that acreage."

While he rambles on, it sinks in that she might now have enough money to move her up the property ladder and into something with a garden, maybe even in a nice area and Connor, provided he doesn't blow it all on vinyl, could maybe put down a deposit on a place in Ibiza. While Ken continues, "As for other assets, well, I'd be very interested if you could find any of your Dad's paperwork, I'm sure Kath won't have thrown it away and, well, it might be, useful." She stops listening and is miles away, in her dream kitchen. Perhaps she would also have enough money to return to college and retrain as something, is it too late to be a Vet nurse?

Ken coughs, "As I was saying, we desperately need to find those other details, so if you could let me know as soon as you find anything, and we can get all the ball rolling."

Shaking her hand, he tells her not to worry, that everything should be sorted out in a few months. That brings her back to earth a bit; she has no intention of staying in Greenleigh for one second longer than necessary, hoping to wrap this up in the next few days. As she walks out to her car, she looks up the road at The Briars, where Siobhan lives and thinks about popping in; it's been such a long time, though, and she's the one who dropped off the radar.

It would have to wait until another day anyway, she's due at the funeral home. Her phone starts beeping with a flurry of messages as she gets a signal, and en route, she rings Connor with the news. As she relays the news he starts hollering with excitement, and she hears Maggie's voice in the background. She doesn't say anything, after all, she knows exactly what she was doing at his age. Why do they have to grow up? She ruminates on where the years have gone as she drives the familiar road into town.

Mr. Parker, the undertaker, is very polite and understanding. No, she does not want to see Kath, but thank you. After her Mum died, people were adamant that she should go and see her at the funeral home. Perhaps they thought it would help her process her death, but at the time, she was outraged. She had watched her Mum lose her hair, her weight and the will to live slide away from her. Mel saw that every day, why on earth would she want to see her now? The memories were bad enough. Chris, however, had gone in there for her with his mum to take in the clothes that Mel had picked out for her to be buried in, while Mel cried in the car outside.

He asked if she knew Kath's wishes, but she didn't. Mr. Parker took everything in his stride, however, suggesting a service in the village church, then a cremation and perhaps a plaque to go with her father's in the churchyard.

After her Mum died, she would often go up to the little churchyard, and Chris would sometimes accompany her. He would wait on the wall under the Yew tree while she took flowers and obsessively tidied her grave. A lurch of terrible guilt hits her like a truck as she imagines the years of weeds that must be curling around it now. She knows she should go there, but every bone in her body resists. She has spent the last twenty years trying not to think about her Mum, but now, being back here, it's proving impossible and painful.

"Will that be suitable, the 9th?" Mr.Parker looks at her concerned. Mel doesn't want to sound like she's in a hurry, but that's 10 days away, "Is there nothing sooner?"

"I'm afraid not."

Mel hands everything she can get away with to Mr. Parker. She has so much on her plate already, she can feel the stress building up. She has to concede that, realistically, it will take her at least 10 days to clear the house and make arrangements for the animals, shelving thoughts about what those might entail. She'll have to talk to the head teacher about missing the first week of term and just dig in. This will be the last ten days she's ever going to spend in Greenleigh, she reasons with herself, pulling into the Asda car park with a list as long as her arm.

By the time she gets back to the house, laden with enough cleaning products to disinfect a small country, it's getting dark, and the lights in the farmhouse are all on. It looks cosy, from a distance anyway. Josh is outside putting the goats and the sheep back into the barn. He waves as she bumps the Focus into the yard, trying to ignore the suspicious thud that indicates she just hit a rock with her exhaust. Josh helps her in with all the bags. Amazed, she looks around the kitchen to see that most of the junk is gone,

"Josh!! It looks incredible! I can't believe it, you didn't have to do all this!" It looks relatively habitable, or it will once she throws bleach at every available surface.

"I got by with a little help from my friend…" Josh picks up the baggy from the table and waves it at her, "Nice weed that Mels, you sly dog, hope you don't mind I helped myself to a cheeky one or two. I couldn't face going home today, bloody Marlowe's come up to stay for the New Year. She does my absolute head in, so I thought I'd just make myself useful here instead."

Mel rifles in a bag and gets them both a beer; this is her chance to dig for details. As she potters round feeding the dogs and cats, she asks as casually as she can, "So, err, how long has Chris been going out with her?"

Rolling his eyes Josh says, "Too long, seriously, I thought he'd have realised she was a dick months ago but I guess his dick hasn't realised yet!" he clinks his bottle at Mel, laughing at his joke, he's a bit wasted,

"She was a bridesmaid at a wedding we did, the bridal party stayed in one of the cabins. They were a frickin' nightmare, city people have no clue. She was all over Chris from the get-go; he stood no chance, bless 'im. She's an "Influencer". I still don't get what that means, but to be fair, she does get us a lot of bookings, but her London friends are as silly as she is, trying to walk in heels over the cattle grid. I mean, she's fit, I get it, but she spends all day here taking selfies and pictures of Chris working in the fields with his top off... She hashtags Chris on all her photos - 'FarmersDoItBetter'. He's very popular amongst her followers. Do you want to see? If I can get a signal up here?"

Mel hopes he can't actually, but it would seem churlish not to look. Marlowe's page is full of beautifully curated photos, most of which feature her in a neutral palette, lounging against matching neutral backgrounds. She also clearly travels a lot to 'Gram worthy destinations. She is stunningly pretty and very stylish. Mel's stomach starts to clench. Here and there are varying pictures of Chris, who always took a good photo. He looks artfully dishevelled in one as if he's just got out of her bed, eugh, and then surprisingly sexy in another, leaning on a dry stone wall. There's one of him sitting in the Land

Rover with a dog beside him, wistfully staring out at the stunning view. There's even one with his top off, walking in the wildflower meadow, which she stares at a little too long. He has *a lot* of likes.

Mel feels her face start to flush with irritation; the Chris she knew would never be into this.

"I'm surprised he…" She manages to squeak, feeling very uncomfortable all of a sudden,

"He doesn't look at it, couldn't care less, you know Chris. If anyone takes the piss, he just says it's good for business, which it has been, to be fair. Seriously, though, I don't know what he's thinking with her. I think he was just single for so long. I mean, yeah, out in Oz it was hard to meet women; at least I tried on our off time, though. It's quite a standing joke that he's never got over you breaking his heart, 'Bells,"

Mel's face flushes. Being back here is proving to be an enormous smorgasbord of guilt. She drains her beer, popping open another one on the edge of the table.

"Mum and I just think he was just getting desperate, you know Chris, he's a soppy get at heart and let's face it, he was kind of born an old man wanting a wife and a brood of kids, remember? He says he sees a future with her, which is batshit crazy because she is not farmer's wife material and he wouldn't last five minutes in London. He goes down there to see her, but he's always 'right relieved to get back…Anyway, she's staying here for a couple of nights, so I'm gonna hide out here 'til she's gone, if you don't mind?"

"If you help me clean up the rest of the house, you are more than welcome. Thanks for helping out, there's so much to do," She sighs heavily, sitting herself down in front of the fire, putting the kittens up on her knee, "Do you know what these three are called?"

"That one's Kim, the tabby one's Kourtney and the little one is Khloe."

"Seriously?"

"Yeh, all the K's, honestly Kath loved the Kardashians."

"You're winding me up!!"

Josh laughs, "What about you, Mel? Are you married or 'owt? I know you've got like a grown-up son, which seems crazy 'cos you just look the same to me, but that's about all anyone knows about you these days on the great Greenleigh grapevine…"

She tells him all about Connor and Aaron. Obviously, he is excited when he finds out who Aaron is, demanding she take him to Ibiza for a VIP clubbing experience. Happy to have pleasant company, rather than facing tough decisions, unpleasant memories and all the hard work. Mel opens more beers, Josh finds some club classics on the radio, cranks it up, and starts dancing, dragging her to her feet. The dogs jump around barking, and the cats watch curiously from their various perches. He opens the back door to smoke. He is shouting through funny stories from the weddings they've held at the farm, making her howl with laughter, tipsily she decides sod it, she'll roll a joint too and is just licking the papers together when a shadow obscures the light and she looks up to see Chris appear through the front door, taking in the somewhat mad scene with obvious disdain.

Hastily, she puts the papers down, trying to disguise the weed whilst also reaching for the radio to turn it down. In her rush, she knocks her beer over, which, somehow, rolls off the table and manages to splash all over Chris' leg on its way down, before then smashing on the flagstones, scattering all the animals. Mel doesn't trust herself to speak, nervous giggles forming in her throat. Scrambling to pick up the broken glass before the dogs go near it, she offers him a cloth, which he tersely turns down. His face says he's beyond annoyed, just like old times, Mel thinks, as she tries not to appear too drunk.

Josh comes crashing in from the other door, equally wasted, "Hey, Bro, what're you doing here? Where's Marloooowe?"

"Mum's been looking for you all day, Josh. You promised to help her clean the cabins."

"Shit I did, didn't I? Blame Mel, she's a bad influence with her wild ways, she's been plying me with drugs and alcohol all night. She won't let me leave." Josh smirks woozily,

"Not true!" Mel interjects swiftly, even though the evidence is pretty damning," I didn't make him!" She looks to Josh to back her up, but he is too out of it to notice her frantic eye signals.

"Hey Bro, did you know Mel's ex is Aaron O'Grady?" Chris looks blank,

"The DJ, you know that remix with/"

"Never heard of him. Look, Mum sent me to get you, so come on." He turns to leave, nodding at Josh to follow,

"Well, MelsBells, I bid you adieu, thanks for the craic! Will we see you at the pub tomorrow night? Everyone's coming, Chris will be there with Marlowe, won't you, bro? "

Dying under Chris' painful scrutiny and thoroughly vexed by Marlowe's curated life, she blurts out, "Actually my boyfriend's coming up tomorrow to stay and I'm not sure what he's got planned, probably something exciting knowing him. I mean, we were supposed to be in Paris to see in the New Year, under the Eiffel tower, but maybe we'll pop by for a drink."

Stick that on your Instagram.

(FYI, they would absolutely not be popping in for a drink, knowing that it will take five minutes for someone to bring up every indiscretion from her past.)

She has to hold onto the dogs to stop them from following Chris.

"Errr bro, have you pissed yourself?" She hears Josh ask as the door closes.

Once they disappear into the night, she goes to the yard to get reception to call Andrew and confirm his plan to come and stay. She finds at least three missed calls from him and several text messages, including one from Siobhan, who said she'd run into Mrs. Oldswick, who told her Mel was back and that she'd love to see her while she was home. Mel thinks she'll save that phone call until she is less tipsy. Making herself comfy on the flatbed, she rings Andrew and tries to sound normal,

"DREW!!!"

"Have you been drinking, Melanie?" he asks straight away. Guess she hasn't hidden it that well, then.

"Nooooo, well, just a few beers, that's all!" She needs to eat some food to soak up the alcohol, but all she'd stupidly bought from Asda was bleach and Budweiser.

"I've been calling you all day, trying to sort out a hotel for tomorrow."

"Ohhh, great. Have you found somewhere?"

"There aren't a lot of options nearby, but I did find these nice log cabins. "

"Oh...really?" Mel grimaces, looking over at them,

"But they're all booked up,"

She sighs with relief. How awkward would that have been? "So I'm sorry. I guess we'll have to leave it?" He says tersely,

"No! NO! You can come and stay at the house!!" She is not going to lose face in front of Chris Oldswick and the marvellous Marlowe,

"But you said it isn't habitable? And there are all my allergies?" he enquires cautiously,

"Well, it is a bit rough, but I've done loads of cleaning and clearing out today." She is exaggerating a bit. Could you maybe bring a blow-up bed, though, a warm duvet, and some fleece blankets 'cos it gets pretty cold at night?"

"You're making it sound very appealing,"

"I hate to think of you all alone," Mel wheedles.

"Ok, I'll pop to my parents first, they'll have all those things, I'm sure. I'll be with you mid-afternoon?"

"Perfect!" Mel proclaims while calculating how to remove every pet hair from the house in under 24 hours.

She spends another night in the armchair next to the fire, with her feet up on a pouffe, wrapped in her dressing gown under the sleeping bag that she's glad she thought to bring from Janet's. With several kittens to keep her lap warm, Arlo on her feet, and several beers in her, she falls surprisingly sound asleep again (Country air?), but it's another early start as Milly starts yapping to go out at 4.30 am.

As soon as she moves, a plethora of cats wind around her feet wanting breakfast. She still can't work out how many there are in total. As they run to their food bowls, she wonders what on earth she's going to do with them all, there must be an animal shelter nearby for the cats and the dogs, not that she wants to do that to any of them, but what will she do with the donkeys and the goats or sheep? She should ring the vet; perhaps he might know someone to rehome them? Would putting the older ones to sleep be the kindest thing? She doesn't think she could ever make that decision; she is already getting fond of them, even the seemingly stupid sheep.

As if Skippy knows what she is thinking he pads over to her and drops his chin on her lap, she scratches his head, wondering if Janet might mind a few dogs in the house until she gets her own place, (and the Kardashian kittens, maybe?) but what would she do with them all day while she's at work? Manchester is not exactly brimming with wide open spaces for them to run around in, and there are too many cars to have cats like these, used to wandering the land.

As it's officially New Year's eve day, she excuses herself from thinking about any of it; besides, with Andrew coming up this afternoon, she must focus on some serious cleaning. She decides that if she can just clear the sitting room, they can sleep in there and use the downstairs bathroom, meaning he never needs to set foot upstairs. She fires up the ancient Hoover, scattering cats, but most of the pet hair just wafts in its noisy wake, so she gives up and returns to the kitchen to throw some cleaning products around instead. The wooden kitchen units are probably at least 50 years old, but other than needing a coat of paint, they are more solid than the Ikea kitchen she put in the old house. Some serious bleach lifted all the stains off the worktops. In the back of a cupboard, where she is stashing all the crap off the shelves, she found a lovely vintage tea set that she put out on the ancient pine Welsh dresser.

Between hers and Josh's efforts, it looks almost habitable now. Sitting at the scrubbed table with her third cup of tea of the morning, she sees herself sitting there on a peaceful Sunday, flicking lazily through a magazine like she's always dreaming about. The view from the window is stunning, and the peace and quiet, after years of Manchester traffic, is like a tonic.

Hang on, she catches herself, she doesn't want to come back to Greenleigh in a million years, nor can she afford this house in another million. Shaking herself from the unexpected fantasy, she sees the rest of the animals. It's another fresh but sunny morning, and she hums merrily as she sets about feeding everyone. The donkeys trot up to her, and she scratches their ears while they eat their hay. The chickens spill out, furiously clucking. She checks whether their sleeping quarters need cleaning, finding an egg nestled amongst the straw. Excited, she takes a photo to show Janet. Before she opens the barn door, she tries again to appeal to Arlo, but he remains stubbornly unhelpful. Instead, she lets them out slowly, doing her best to stop them from going wide by prancing up and down and waving her arms, which does the trick. With satisfaction, she shuts the gate to the field, catching a movement out of the corner of her eye.

Up at the cabins, she spots Chris standing out on the steps, clearly watching her do her crazy dance. He raises his mug in greeting. Mel isn't sure from this distance, but she's sure he's smirking. Mortified, she is about to pretend she hasn't seen him when the cabin door opens behind him and an ethereal blonde slides out, putting her arms round him from behind and kissing his neck. Mel can't help but stare. They look like a pair of models in a Ralph Lauren campaign.

Banging herself on the gate in a swift about turn, she goes to clean the barn. As she shovels, she ponders why it bothers her so much to see him with someone else; she doesn't exactly have any claim on him. So distracted by this uncomfortable train of thought, she doesn't notice something in the yard which upends the wheelbarrow, sending goat poo flying everywhere. Whatever it is, it's metal and suspiciously resembles a car part.

Embarrassed even further, she peeks up at the cabins, but thankfully, Chris and Marlowe have disappeared back inside. She must remember to send Andrew a message about leaving the Audi in the school car park and ask him for his dinner requests, thinking she'll have time to shoot back to the supermarket to get some provisions before he gets here.

Now that the kitchen is so much improved, she goes in to tackle the sitting room, which remains completely untouched. It looks as if Kath has just popped out. Her glasses are on the table, next to an open magazine.

Overcome with sadness, she sits down in Kath's armchair, gripping onto both arms. She can't stop torturing herself about what it must have been like, hoping Kath wasn't in any pain, imagining Arlo and Skippy, confused, nudging Kath to get up. She wondered how long she had lain there until Chris found her. Unable to stop them, fat tears pour out of her, soaking her cheeks. Reaching out for Kath's cardigan on the back of the chair, she holds it to her face, absorbing some comfort from the familiar scent of their washing powder, mixed with farm life.

She feels so ashamed that she never bothered to stay in touch. What a terrible example she has set for Connor. Imagine if Aaron died and he just completely ignored Maya afterwards? That would be on her, god, she's an awful person. Claustrophobia overwhelms her, her chest tightening. She gets up swiftly, grabs her bag, and jumps into her car; she'll go do the shopping to get out of her head.

She doesn't get very far down the track before a troubling series of loud bangs indicates that the metal thing in the yard was part of her exhaust. Cursing, she drives slowly to the main road with what is left of it skittering behind her. She needs to get to the supermarket, but it's eight hilly miles into town, and she doesn't want to end up stranded, and she certainly doesn't want to have to ask the Oldswicks for more help.

She remembers Josh mentioning Brooks Motors and wonders if anyone might be there today, she can try and if not perhaps she'll just leave the car parked there anyway, for when they do open. Then she'll pop into Nelsons for some bits and walk back, whilst calling Andrew to ask him to pick up some food en route. She lets out a long breath, feeling pleased that for once she has a plan and everything should go accordingly.

CHAPTER SEVEN

As she drives up toward the garage, she sees the open doors and pulls up, relieved. There's no one out front, but there's a car on the ramp and the radio belts out Rock FM.Mel hums along as she stands awkwardly waiting for someone to come out, a door opens in the back; she is expecting Phill Brooks, who'd fixed her Mum's beaten up Fiesta more times than she can remember, when out strolls Jamie Hirst; beefier, more tattooed and sporting a sort of man bun that she wants to hate but looks annoyingly good on him. There are a few grey streaks in his dark hair and chiselled lines on his face, and yet somehow, and of course he would be; he is more attractive for it. Like Chris, he's filled out from a skinny boy into a man's body, a great body, she thinks, trying not to stare at his bulging, tattooed biceps under a tight black t-shirt that shows off his muscular chest a bit too well. She looks down, he's still wearing those sexy Blundstone biker boots, they'd had a matching pair for a while, they would often keep them on, only them.

Mel's palms suddenly go very sweaty as visions of all the very bad things she used to do with him come flooding back to her. She clenches her fists, digging her nails into her palms to stop the treacherous thoughts in their tracks. No wonder bloody Josh mentioned Brooks Motors and laughed,someone could've bloody given her a heads up that Jamie was back in town. Now she knows why Josh kept inviting her to the pub; he knew exactly how much drama it would create if they were reunited publicly, after all these years, at the scene of the crime.

Jamie, polishing something intently with an oily rag, doesn't notice her at first. This is a good job because, as all the X-rated memories deluge her mind, she isn't sure she can comprehensively string a sentence together. He looks up and, after realising who she is, a bemused smile creeps onto his perfect lips (Stop it, Mel, concentrate!) He tips his head slowly to one side in appraisal, that same old look of unmistakable lust emanating from his eyes,

"Well, well," he drawls, "If it isn't the return of the Mac."

Of course, she's wondered about Jamie over the years, but the end of their relationship was so messy and painful that it was also easier to add him to the memories of Greenleigh that she keeps firmly locked away. Their awful break-up was one of the major reasons she went to Ibiza, well, that and seeing the utter hatred on Chris's face every time they crossed paths. Last she heard, though, Jamie had gone off to work in Leeds. He didn't show up at her Dad's funeral, not that she blamed him; her Dad had no time for him (and she hated herself for scanning the crowd for him). If she thought about ever seeing him again, she imagined she'd have a slew of cutting comments to throw at him, payback for all the pain he caused her, but, at this moment, it's all she can do to stop her muscle memory from batting her eyelashes.

He walks right up to her, a little too close for comfort, smiling that suggestive smile of his, she watches his eyes travel her over, too late she remembers the crying fit and that she's been shovelling goat crap for two days in these very same clothes,

"I heard you were back in town, Mac, but I wasn't expecting you to come and see *me*, given the last time we spoke, you said if you saw me again in a 1000 years, it would be too soon." She did say that, but he's teasing her. His big brown eyes don't drop the eye contact, and she looks away fast for fear of falling straight back under his spell again. Her common sense is beseeching her to keep it professional; she's here about her car, remember. Squaring her shoulders, she manages to mutter, "The exhaust needs looking at."

Walking briskly behind the car, to get out of his powerful tractor beam, she surreptitiously checks her face in the wing mirror, she didn't put any mascara on this morning so there are no tear marks at least, but then as she hasn't put any makeup on this morning, she looks exactly as if she's barely slept in days. While he gets down to look under the car, she tries to sort her hair out, and he gets up, catching her in the act.

"Looks like a right mess,"

"Yeah, well I've been sleeping in a chair in Kath's house for two nights 'cos I'm too scared to go upstairs in the dark... I *still* keep thinking of being murdered whenever I go in that bathroom, so I haven't washed it since Sunday!" She bursts out,

"I meant your exhaust, it's missing a bracket, and the box is dented...You could never look a mess Mac, Josh told everyone at the pub you are quite the Milf and he's not wrong."

Mel thinks she might kill Josh next time she sees him. She pulls an indignant face despite feeling secretly a bit flattered,

"Do you want me to come...with you... In the shower? "he raises an eyebrow,

Mel who rarely blushes, is the approximate shade of a raspberry and she isn't entirely sure if it's the Milf comment, her mortification at the misunderstanding about her hair or the thought of showering with Jamie.

"Not *come* in the shower," he takes a beat, "Not come *into* the shower with you. I mean, I could sit outside and keep a lookout for any suspicious looking men with knives, if you want? You must be pretty lonely up there, Kath's zoo aside,"

Professional! her brain yells while her body is ready in the shower, washing his tattooed torso. She bites the inside of her cheek to stay focused. "Can you fix it today?" She manages to squeak, quite unbelievable to her, that after all these years and everything he put her through, that he can drop one comment and her mind is throwing off her clothes with indecent haste,

"Not today, babe, need to get parts ordered and it's New Year's Eve, so it won't be 'til the day after tomorrow, maybe the day after that. You're not in Kansas anymore Dorothy," he winks, *winks,* who even winks in this day and age? Isn't it classed as sexual harassment now days? But damn it, it makes her insides lurch,

"If I drive it as it is?"

"You won't get very far, and you might need a whole new exhaust then. What about Kath's truck? It might need a jump start, but I did the MOT not that long ago, it might be older, but that truck can still go some, " he arches an eyebrow.

Everything he always said seemed like a double entendre,

"I can run you back to the farm with a battery, and we can get the truck going if you like. I've got my bike."

Of course, he's still riding his motorbike. Jamie was the original rebel without a cause but there is no way she is getting on the back of his bike, wrapping her arms tightly around him like she used to love, leaning her head against his shoulder blade, smelling his leathers as his hair blows in the wind from under his helmet and her thighs pressed up against him. Mel's face goes hot; she needs to get a grip, quickly.

"Thanks, but I'm off to see Siobhan now, actually, and my

boyfriend, Andrew, is coming up this afternoon so he can help me with the truck. Thanks for the offer, though. Umm, can you ring me when the car's done?"

"I'll need your number then." He gets out his mobile and keys in Mac, his pet name for her. "Will you be bringing your *boyfriend* to the pub tonight? The Backroom Boys are playing,"

"Jesus, they're still going?"

"Yeah, the use of *boys* is getting pretty wide of the mark!"

"Errr, I'm not sure they'd be Andrew's cup of tea and besides, if you, me and Chris are all in the pub, let's be honest, nobody'll be watching the band." Why is she bringing up Chris? Just shut up and leave Mel.

"Chris is going down tonight, is he? I wish he'd piss off permanently to London with his stuck up girlfriend, he was such a prick on Christmas Eve, I swear, he still hates me you know, still thinks I took advantage of you."

So the fight Josh was talking about was Chris and Jamie, fighting over her, still, what the hell?

"You didn't, we *didn't*... We were both just drunk; it was so long ago."

"You know Greenleigh has the memory of an elephant, Mac. It's good to see you, though, lass. I'm glad you're not still holding a grudge like bloody Oldswick,"

"It doesn't mean I've forgiven you, Jay." He isn't getting away scot free after he broke her heart so badly, no matter how many years ago it was.

"Melanie Mac, I do know I was a total dick to you. Believe it or not, I have thought about it over the years and it's one of my biggest regrets, 'cos you were having a hard time and you didn't deserve what I did to you.Is there any way you can find it in your heart to forgive me?" He is smiling *that* smile at her the whole damn time,

"I'll think about it..." and try not to think about all the other things,

"Don't think about it too long, the offer expires at the end of the year," he pushes her arm lightly and she tries to ignore the automatic thrill that shoots through her, her body is a total traitor,

"It's good to know that you're still an idiot after all this time,"

He shrugs, laughing, "How long are you in town or rather... How long is your *boyfriend* in town? Let me take you out for a drink to say sorry, not to the 'Horse, well, unless you want to be talked about for another twenty years. Hey, we could go out somewhere on the bike like old times? We could go up' the falls?"

She would absolutely not be riding to Folly Falls with Jamie. On hot days, they used to skinny dip up there, until one time they got caught jumping off the rocks naked. Jamie laughs, "Remember that day those walkers came over the top, that man's face, I swear, he was so mad he went purple."

"Yeah 'cos you stood on the rocks swinging your / shouting there's nothing to be ashamed of, god made us this way!"

Before it all went wrong, Jamie was a lot of fun, and that was exactly what she had needed right then.

She makes herself leave the garage, congratulating herself for successfully managing not to commit to spending any extracurricular time with him, for now at least. He says he will call her, then says, not necessarily about the car. Then he bends down and grazes her cheek with his soft lips and wishes her a happy New Year. He smells of oil and old memories of running wild.

She power walks up the road to The Briars, trying to get some control over her raging libido. She needs to talk to Siobhan, like now, she was always Mel's voice of reason, even if 99 times out of a hundred Mel didn't follow any of her advice, it turned out later that she was right, though.

As she marches the lane, she thinks about when she first met Jamie. She knew who he was, vaguely, because they went to the same high school, but he was three years older, a lifetime at that age. By the time she started noticing boys, Jamie was done with school. At 16, after her Mum died and she went to live with her dad, she started going out into town with Siobhan on a Saturday night, armed with their fake IDs, to try their luck in the pubs there. That meant catching the one bus an hour that went through the village. Jamie lived in the next village along, Houghton Bridge, and he would climb onto the bus with a couple of mates, swinging noisily up the stairs to take up residence at the back of the bus. They were a rowdy bunch, so they always drew her attention. Jamie stood out to her with his long hair and scruffy leather jacket. She liked to sit in the front seat over the driver, and from above, she could see his bus stop coming up.

After a few weeks, she knew that she was secretly looking out for him, gutted if he wasn't there. She was still going out with Chris, so she kept all these feelings to herself. Chris was not interested in going out drinking with them; in fact, he tried everything to stop her from going, but she just ignored him. He was worried about her; at that point, she was regularly drinking until she blacked out. Of course, Mel didn't listen to a word of his lectures; in fact, they started to have the opposite effect. She would drink more just to rebel against him. She didn't want anyone mothering her if it wasn't her mum.

Jamie paid zero attention to her anyway until one snowy winter night. She would always catch the last bus home at 11 pm. Back then, taxis were a luxury they couldn't afford, and their parents would only let them go out if they stuck to this rule, thinking they were only at the cinema or the Super Bowl. Jamie and his mates would hang out at bars that they were far too scared to go into, and they would never catch the last bus home, but she would look out for him anyway. That night, it started to snow heavily, and they weaved through the sudden blizzard to make it to the bus stop on time in Chapel Hill, only to find a larger queue than normal. No one was taking the chance of getting stuck in town as the snow came barreling down. The bus was late, and the queue began to dissolve into groups. Barely dressed girls gathered for warmth under the bus shelter, while the boys sat up on the wall in the snow, smoking cigarettes. She huddled with Siobhan and some other friends, but she couldn't keep her eyes off Jamie, who had turned up with his boys, drunk and mouthy, swigging from a bottle of Newcastle Brown ale.

She wasn't quite sure, but she felt like he was watching her too. She was talking to Siobhan when a snowball hit her on the back of her neck, spinning round to see him look away, scratching his head as if he didn't see a thing, so she scooped up some snow and threw one back at him which he ducked, aiming his wicked grin right at her. It started a huge snowball fight, and pandemonium broke out around them. She looked up to see Jamie right in front of her. Before she could protest, he crushed a snowball into her face, laughing. Then, amidst the rowdy chaos, he proceeded to gently wipe the vestiges of snow from her face, tracing her features with frozen fingertips. He looked right into her eyes, his lip curling with suggestion, and Mel, well, she fell totally under his spell.

As she gets up to Siobhan's posh house, she thinks that perhaps she should have rung her first, hesitating on the step, but as she dithers, the front door flings wide open and a sophisticated version of her old partner in crime lunges in for a huge hug, sweeping her inside. Mel finds herself inside a very stylish home, which suggests that Siobhan is doing well for herself. The two little girls she'd seen on Jackie's photos bob behind her, "Girls, this is my oldest friend in the world, Melanie. I've known her since I was your age."The girls look at her wide-eyed, probably wondering where the hell Mel has been their whole lives, "Go play in the playroom, you two, Auntie Mel and I have a lot of catching up to do, we'll be in the kitchen." She follows Siobhan through into an enormous, airy kitchen, sinking gratefully down on the squashy green velvet sofa, looking round appreciatively at all Siobhan's tasteful touches, whilst trying not to think about her current homeless situation,

"Brew? Or what time is it? I mean, it's past 12, so could we open a bottle of fizz? It is New Year's eve, and this is a special occasion! It's so good to see you, Mel."

Sod it, thinks Mel, it's been quite a day already, and she's walking home now anyway. She gives a firm yes, ignoring the voice in her head reciting her to-do list; there are still a few hours until Andrew arrives. After seeing Jamie again, she desperately needs something to steady her nerves,

"I'm so sorry about Kath. Mrs. Oldswick said she left you the house, though. Are you finally coming home, Mels?"

"God no!" Mel splutters, "No offence, Sib, but no, you remember the state of it? Well, add twenty years of mess and crumbling plaster onto that. I just need to clean it out, look for some paperwork for Ken Braithwaite, and find homes for all the animals. It'll probably go to auction. Connor and I have been left half the value between us, less the fees, of course."

"Just a few things to do then? Jesus, Mel, let me know if I can help, it's been years since I've been inside, but we go up to the farmshop quite often, so I know what you mean...I take it you've seen Chris. How did that go?"

Mel sighs, "As well as you can imagine..."

"Still sulking?! I did hear there was some dispute about you in the pub, from Mr.Nelson obviously,"

Mel groans, "I just want to get the house sorted and out of here with no drama, no offence, Sib."

"By all accounts, you've already upset the apple cart, Mel. I don't think it's gonna be that easy."

Mel takes a large swig from her glass; the bubbles go up her nose. She is beginning to think the same.

"How's Aaron? And Connor? I can't believe you've got an 18-year-old son, Mel, that's crazy!"

"What's crazier is that he's now living in Ibiza with Aaron and his new wife," Mel shakes her head.

"I know. Jackie rang me and told me you went there for lunch. She couldn't get over how civil the two of you were. I think she may have even said *flirty!*"

"Not flirty, no, honest Sib, it's taken its time but I'm officially over Aaron, besides, he's having a baby and his wife, Maya, is lovely."

"Was it weird to be back in Ibiza? Dave and I took the girls a few years ago, but we didn't exactly go clubbing. We walked down the strip, but I just felt old when I saw all the kids in the streets. Where did the time go, Mel? I feel like I blinked and we're nearly 40," she tops up Mel's glass,

"Being back here makes me feel like I'm still eighteen again, though, Sib, and not in a good way… Chris still hates me, and when I saw Jamie,"

"What? Wait?! You've seen Jamie as well? When? How did that go?" Siobhan interrupts,

"Someone could have warned me he was back in town! Why is he back in town?"

"He's got a kid with Lindsey Mellor, Jake, he's in Bella's year, I take it he didn't mention that fact?"

Mel feels like her brain is about to burst with all the things she needs to get her head around,

"They're not together, I don't think they even lasted until Jake was born…She always fancied Jamie, remember? She was *furious* when you started seeing him. She tried to snog Chris to get back at you, but Chris wasn't having any of it…Anyway, to his credit, he's a pretty good Dad, I think, I see him at school pick up on a Friday, and he comes to all the parents' evenings and stuff, even though Lindsey lives with another bloke and has another kid with him. Jake's pretty cute, got Jamie's looks. I think our Bella has a bit of a crush on him. Anyway, tell me *everything!*"

It's funny with true friends; it doesn't matter how long ago you last saw them, when you start talking, it's always as if it were just yesterday. Mel could've talked for hours, filling Siobhan in and hearing the news from her life and all the village gossip, but vaguely mindful of Andrew's imminent arrival, she finishes the contents of her glass and says she'd better get going to have any chance of getting the house clean before he arrives.

They arrange to meet up again soon, and Mel staggers off down the drive. Too late, she thinks, yet again that she's been drinking on an empty stomach and is way more drunk than she should be at 1.30 pm. If she ducks into Nelson's, she can get something to mop up the alcohol (and maybe some more for good measure). Then she'll ring Andrew and ask if he would mind picking up some bits on his way.

Mr. Nelson looks up as she tries to sidle in unobtrusively. "I hear Lindsey Mellor isn't happy that you've been seeing Jamie Hirst again," he offers as she goes to pay. The jungle drums must've been working flat out if her meeting with Jamie has reached Lindsey's ears already. She decides that Mr. Nelson is just making things up to bait her. "I don't hold with rumours,"

he adds, "But it's going round that you pulled that bit off your car exhaust on purpose."

Mel does not dignify him with a response, gathering her bottles of wine, she clanks out the door. Mr. Nelson mutters something about her drinking habits also not changing, over the clanging doorbell. Hoping she doesn't sound too drunk, again, she fishes her phone out of her bag to call Andrew to find it's dead. Bugger. She decides on the spur of the moment, to save time, that she'll take what they used to call the track back, up through the wood and over the fields. With zero dignity, she slings her leg ungracefully over the dry stone wall by the pub, heading unsteadily up through the trees.

In the past, they always used this shortcut. It shaved a good half off the road's distance. However, she was also agile enough to duck between barbed wire and scramble over dry stone walls back then.Halfway through the woods, she is forced to acknowledge that, just like old times, her drinking leads her to make rash decisions.This is most definitely one of them.

The path they'd trodden down over the years is no longer visible; the way now thick with brambles. She gets snagged every few steps and isn't sure if she is heading in the right direction, as she keeps having to double back when it proves impassable. She ploughs on, the woods aren't that big, she'll reach the perimeter sooner or later, but time is ticking by, and it starts to get cold as the afternoon draws in. She's only wearing a thin jacket as she'd set out in the car. Pulling her jumper down over her knuckles, she tries to pick up her pace, but the terrain is impossible, stumbling over branches and pushing her way through the undergrowth with no real clue if she's actually getting anywhere. The possibility of Andrew arriving and finding her AWOL is mortifying, though, so she ploughs on. After what feels like hours, Mel admits she is lost, possibly in more ways than one.

She briefly considers lying down on some soft moss, covering herself in leaves, and giving up like the babes in the wood, but she acknowledges that she is perhaps being a tad dramatic. Instead, she unscrews the red wine and takes a large swig from the bottle.The wine gives her a warm kick, giving her the push to carry on. She forces her way through more banks of brambles, which claw her hair and scratch her skin. At last, with huge relief, she spots the dry stone wall that marks the perimeter, scrambling over the mossy stones with joy but zero finesse.

THE TRACK BACK

From there, it's just a short walk up through Oldswick's frozen fields until she comes around to the back of Kath's house. As she gets closer, however, she can see that all the lights are on. As she gets closer still, she notices Andrew's Audi is pulled up next to the truck, bollocks.

Breathless, she bursts through the front door, which sets the dogs off barking, to find Andrew, Chris and Marlowe all sitting at the kitchen table. All three look at her for a minute in stunned silence before Andrew speaks, "Where on earth have you been, Melanie? I arrived as we agreed, but obviously, you weren't here and your phone was off...Then I saw these guys at the cabin across the field. Chris here was good enough to call around, " His lips are thinly pursed. Dressed in his smart overcoat, he looks ridiculously out of place, but not quite as much as the staggeringly immaculate Marlowe, who appears to be wearing an all-cream cashmere ensemble. Mel is still in the goat poo jeans,

"Ummm, I took the track back, but err, our path is not a path anymore though, Chris, so..." Mel flounders, this is her worst nightmare come true, Chris, Andrew and Marlowe are staring at her like a judging panel. It's very clear that she's not going to advance to the next round.

Chris speaks harshly, "Mr. Nelson said you left the shop ages ago and that you seemed quite drunk to start with... Then you bought more wine and staggered off. He was concerned about your mental state. He suggested that you might have gone off somewhere with Jamie Hirst," he spits out Jamie's name, his flint eyes flashing,

"I'm fine, everything's fine! I wasn't with Jamie, I wasn't, honestly, I just got a bit lost, that's all! "She insists, hovering in the doorway, unable to look anyone in the eye, least of all Chris,

159

"Excuse me a minute."

It feels horribly like deja vu. There had been a fair few similar conversations in this kitchen before, though those times she was, of course, actually out with Jamie.

Locking herself into the downstairs toilet, she tries to get a handle on the awkward situation taking place in the kitchen. As she catches herself in the mottled mirror, she understands why everyone's jaw had dropped. Her hair is full of leaves and twigs. There are at least a couple of bleeding scratches on her cheek, and around her mouth, there is a red wine stain that makes her look slightly like a crazed vampire. Plonking herself heavily on the toilet, she rubs at her face with an old towel, quickly redoing her hair and practically eating the dried-up sliver of soap to remove the wine stain. She couldn't take too long lest Chris come to check if she's climbed out of the window, something she'd done on several occasions, in a bid to escape varying interventions.

Taking some deep breaths, she re-enters the kitchen, plastering on her best smile. Andrew and Marlowe are chatting, Chris thankfully is nowhere to be seen, "Christopher has gone to put your animals to bed for you, Melanie!"trills Marlowe. God, she is so perfect looking. Mel feels like a troll in comparison, looking down to realise her jeans are now also covered in green streaks from scrambling the dry stone walls.

"Marlowe was just saying that she might be interested in buying the house, "says Andrew, smiling at Marlowe brightly,

" That would make the sale nice and straightforward."

Over my dead body, Mel thinks, "Well, I haven't decided if I'm going to sell it yet, so…"

"Really?" says Andrew, "Look at the state of the place! I don't want to put you off, Marlowe, but it's going to need a lot of money spending on it."

"I know it's an absolute dump right now, " She shudders, pulling her cream pashmina tightly around her.

" But Christopher is so talented, we could totally modernise it. It's so dark and poky in here. We could open it right up, put in a glass box extension, some big windows, imagine a white marble open plan kitchen" Andrew nods along with her, seemingly besotted,

Marble kitchen my arse thinks Mel, wanting to throw both of them out the door,

"The kittens are adorable!!" Marlowe continues, "Chris said you're rehoming them? I might take one," She plucks Kim from the floor. Kim K starts hissing indignantly, then gets her claws caught in Marlowe's wrap.

Mel tries not to smirk, "I'm keeping them, actually, *all of them* and the dogs, so yeah, nobody needs rehoming, thanks."

"I'm allergic to cats," pipes up Andrew, "I thought they'd be farm cats, you know, living outside."

You'll be living outside in a minute, thinks Mel, if you don't stop simpering over Marlowe,

"We found him an allergy tablet. He couldn't stop sneezing!" Marlowe pats Andrew on the arm, "It's very hairy in here…" she says accusingly, looking round with a sniff,

"You didn't mention those log cabins that I told you about are right there," Andrew gestures out the window,

"Didn't I? I mean, you said they were booked up anyway."

"We've got two bedrooms in ours, if it's too much for you here, Drew. I'm sure Chris wouldn't mind."

Coming through the door with a heavy sack of dog food, "Mind what?" he asks, looking anywhere but in Mel's direction,

"If Andrew and Melanie stay with us at the cabin, we could have a party, it is NYE!!"

Chris throws down the bag, looking like he'd rather slit his own wrists, Mel recognises this because she feels exactly the same,

"Gosh, thanks, that's such a generous offer. We couldn't possibly intrude!" Mel interrupts, forcing a smile that she hopes conveys sincerity onto her face,

"It could be fun!!" Marlowe isn't deterred,

"I've got plans for later!" says Chris, glaring at Mel as if she is the one who had the idea.

"So have I," Mel doubles down,

"If you mean going to that pub again, I'd rather hang out at the cabin, thanks." Marlowe pouts, "Andrew and Melanie are supposed to be in Paris tonight, you know Chris... Mel *cancelled* it to come *here*. I told Andrew that you would've looked after the animals for a few more days. Mel should have just asked you,"

"Yes, she should've," agrees Chris primly, squeezing Marlowe's shoulder while she kisses his hand. Mel looks around her for something hard and heavy to belt both of them with, while Andrew looks at Mel like he wants to do the same.

Happy NYE, Y'all.

"I've put all the animals in. I'm a bit worried about Eddie. Have you noticed if she's been eating?"

"I don't know which ones which," Mel admits.

Chris shakes his head. "She's the darker one. They're both old for donkeys, so they need constant attention. Clearly you're too busy... I'll give Dixon a call. He might just think it's kinder to put her to sleep."

"What? No, no, she might just have a cold or something?" Mel suddenly can't swallow properly,

"It's just a fact of life, Mel. What are you going to do with them anyway? You can hardly put them in your back garden in Manchester. "

Even Andrew looks a little taken aback by Chris's vitriol.

"I'll come by tomorrow and check on her. Tom Dixon can make the call if you can't face it."

Mel nods, not trusting herself to speak without crying. Thankfully, Chris sweeps Marlowe away, muttering he has something to do before she can start inviting them to come over again. It's too quiet once they leave. Mel shuffles around the kitchen trying to minimise the cat situation. Andrew gives her what feels like a very stiff hug. "I'm sorry, Andrew," she says, aware of how woefully unprepared she is for his arrival.

"Honestly, Melanie, I feel like that's all you ever say to me these days," he says, not looking very happy.

"I know and... I'm, sorry," she trails off, "You found it ok then?"

"You could have warned me about the state of the place. I'm worried about my car."

Mel thought it best not to share her car news. "Sorry..." God, this is awkward. After a tense silence, Andrew asks, "Are you okay, Melanie? You don't seem like yourself. "

Mel doesn't know how to answer that question. Ever since she arrived back, she feels like a ball of wool rapidly unravelling,

"I'm *fine. I just haven't slept too well;* that's all."

Not to mention feeling like she's in some kind of temporal time slip, like a Dr. Who episode where all her bad behaviour comes back to haunt her at once. She reaches for the wine. Andrew seems unconvinced, but for argument's sake, he lets it go,

"So, how do they celebrate New Year's Eve in Greenleigh then? I mean, we should've been at the Eiffel Tower, but you know..." She hopes he won't bring up Paris all night. Reeling from Chris backstabbing her to Marlowe, Mel hopes they have a terrible 'NYE', wondering what Chris' plans are, before remembering that she never actually made it to the shops. There is nothing much to offer Andrew, apart from the crisps she bought yesterday, bugger. She doesn't have a clue how they are going to celebrate because, really, she only invited him to prove to Chris that she isn't the total loser he thinks she is.

So far, that's working out well...

She remembers what they used to do on New Year's Eve; she and Chris would go up to the highest point in the valley to watch the fireworks go off in the distance for miles. It had always been magical, "Well, I've planned something romantic for us. It does involve a walk, though?" She says brightly as if all along she had a plan,

"Is it far? It's pretty cold out there. I didn't bring any walking gear. Isn't there something going on at the pub we could go to? Chris mentioned,"

"Oh no, no, NOPE! It will be rammed and there's a rock band on so it'll be noisy,"

"Will *Jamie Hirst* be there?" He'd picked up on that part of the story then. She's going to have words with Mr. Nelson, but then again, if she does, that will also be around the village in no time. Suddenly, the anonymity of Manchester seems like heaven,

"I don't know, and it doesn't matter, honestly, Andrew, he's just an old *friend,* and besides, I've got a plan! I just need to err, get some stuff together. How about I put the TV on in the other room? You can put your feet up and relax while I just sort out a few things."

Andrew follows her into the lounge, which, as she hasn't got around to cleaning it yet, is a fairly depressing place to sit. Andrew hovers in the doorway,

"I can't believe someone lived like this," he sniffles into a hanky, a tad dramatically,

"Don't be so judgmental!" she snaps, even though she initially thought the same.

"Kath was busy, Andrew. Not everyone wants to live in a sterile penthouse."

Andrew shook his head. "Wow, there I was planning on asking you if you wanted to move into my sterile penthouse. I guess that's a no?" He looks at her, hurt, while cleaning the remote control with a wet wipe. Mel had not seen that coming, after all, they had not been together that long. She reels around from the frantic tidying she is doing,

"Really?"

"Yes, really, I know you're having a hard time finding a decent place you can afford, you can't stay in Janet's spare bedroom forever and the flat seems so empty with just me in it."

Not 'You had me at hello, you complete me or even you're my lobster.' The underlying understanding is that Andrew does not like being alone. It is, however, an amazing apartment. Mel feels that she could make a lot of compromises if she knew she could have a spa jet bath at the end of every day,

"Wow, Andrew... I don't know what to say."

"You aren't serious about keeping this place, are you? It has money pit written all over it, Melanie. You wouldn't want to live out here in the back of beyond, would you? I swear it's like stepping back in time, no phone signal?! You could keep it as a holiday let, I suppose, that's not a bad idea. Marlowe is onto something. I mean, I saw what they're charging next door, they're booked up for weeks." His thoughts tick over, "Once you get rid of the animals, there'd be enough room for some glamping tents or those pods, we could go through the figures. My broker is always telling me to diversify. What do you think?"

What Mel thinks is, "Back off, mate. The house is perfect as it is, save a bit of cleaning." (Okay, a lot of cleaning.) Desperate to shut him up on the subject, Mel kisses him, which seems to do the trick. Then, leaving him with a bottle of wine and the task of blowing up the bed he brought, she extricates herself to the kitchen, hoping to find a miracle in the cupboards.

She didn't think she'd ever felt so confused in her whole life about exactly what to do with her whole life.

Picking up the kittens, she cuddles them tightly, seeking comfort. They certainly wouldn't be welcome in the penthouse, despite their namesakes. Somehow she manages to cobble together some sandwiches, (Thank god for tins, there's some tuna, nearly at its best before, she gives it a good sniff first and Mel makes herself a jam one, scraping away the mould off the top of the jar.) There are crisps and a packet of jam tarts that are only a bit out of date. It isn't artisan or award-winning, but it will have to do. Andrew has brought several bottles of champagne. If she plies him with enough alcohol, hopefully, he won't notice the basic quality of her offerings.

Digging around in the utility room, she finds a torch, thinking too late of the picnic blankets in the back of her car now down at the Garage. She scouts around for something not covered in cat hair and bundles everything into a tattered rucksack, which is not ideal, but on the fly, it's not bad. She pops open the first bottle of champagne. The only way to get through this potential car crash is to keep drinking.

It isn't a long walk, a mile or so, all uphill, thankfully up a cart track, no more bramble scrambling. Having plied Andrew all evening with a lot of champagne, he has become quite amenable, although he hasn't let go of the topic of her moving in with him or the potential of the house, neither of which she is sober enough to consider seriously right now. Once they are high enough up the hill to get a phone signal, she rings Janet and tries Connor, imagining he'll be working. She leaves him a message wishing him a happy New Year, asking him to pass it on to Aaron and Maya. Siobhan sends her a message which makes her laugh. She thinks that if nothing else comes out of being back home, she is so happy that they are reconnected. Funny, she thought of Greenleigh as home, though she ruminated. Josh has sent her a chain of messages demanding the details of her meeting with Jamie and asking her to come down to the pub. She sends him a middle finger emoji with some kisses.

As they climb higher, the landscape opens out below them. It's a clear night, so the glowing street lights thread for miles across the distant valleys, flickering like a thousand tiny bonfires, a sight that has always made her catch her breath. Above, the stars seem to twinkle back in reflection. As she stops to admire the view, Andrew, who doesn't share her appreciation, wanders off to empty his bladder behind a tree. She shouts at him that she'll keep going up.

She rounds the corner and instead of the dark bench on the hillside she was anticipating, she finds a breathtaking fairy lit grotto of elegant candles and twinkling lights strung from the trees, under which a beautiful array of artful blankets and cushions are piled up, next to a picnic basket with champagne in a bucket. She looks around wildly like she is being pranked, but there is nobody in sight. Spinning around at footsteps, expecting the picnic's owner, but it's just Andrew. She's perhaps plied him with too much Champagne to soften the blow of his limp Tuna sandwich, as he starts reeling dramatically around in drunken delight while he takes in the romantic scene,

"Wow, Mel, this is 'mazing!" He slurs whilst trampling regardless through the artful scene, "You're amazing! I thought you didn't care when you were out doing god knows what earlier but this is really what you were doing this afternoon, isn't it? It all makes sense now!" he declares, before throwing himself down on the pile of designer cushions, grabbing her hand on the way to pull her down on top of him. Before she can tell him the truth, a bit befuddled by her champagne brain, he starts kissing her hungrily.She lets him as she desperately tries to devise a way to get out of the situation without looking like a terrible person. As she racks her brains, she realises that Andrew is trying to drunkenly wriggle out of his clothes,ducking out of his clutches, she gets to her feet, unsteadily. They need to get out of there pronto before the real recipient turns up.

"C'mon Melanie, this issssh perfect, soooo romantic, who needs Paris, eh?" he slurs, trying to get his jeans over his boots,

"I know it's cold, but I want to make love to you under the stars!!"he booms from under his jumper, which appears to be stuck on his head, oh Jesus, his boxer shorts are halfway down his legs,

"Look, Andrew, I'm sorry but truthfully..." She takes a deep breath," I didn't do this for you, you've got to get up, now, this is someone else's picnic."

"Whaaaat?" He's wrestling about, trying to get out of his coat and doesn't hear a word she says,

"You need to put your clothes on, we have to go..." she begs, frantically,

Somewhere in the valley below, the first fireworks began to crackle into life. It must be almost midnight,

"Andrew, seriously, we have to go!" She gets down on her knees and starts to pull up his boxer shorts, but he just keeps trying to get her clothes off and won't listen to her pleas, when the sound of voices behind her announces the arrival of the picnic's true owners.

Silence falls, Mel tries to do something quick to hide Andrew's brewers droop. In desperation, she grabs one of the beautiful velvet cushions and plonks it on his crotch, then turns around to face the music,

"What on earth are you doing!? "roars Chris, staring at them in utter disbelief,

"What do you mean? "Marlowe says, she is wearing a blind fold, Chris' arm draped round her to guide her forward,

"Who' isss that? "Andrew is still rolling around on the floor, his head entangled in his jumper.

The fireworks kick up a notch. Distant cheering can be heard from all over the valley,

"...Happy New Year?" Mel offers weakly,

"Oh Melanie, it's you, are you part of my surprise?" Marlowe squeals, "Chris won't tell me anything!"

"Not exactly…" She can't look Chris in the eye, "I can explain…" she mouths to him, he looks at her like he might actually kill her,

"You don't have to," he snaps, "After all, Mel, I'm quite used to finding you having sex in random places."

Mel can say nothing back to that. Andrew finally extracts himself from his jumper and sits up, "Sorry mate, this hill's taken! Look what Mel did for me, you know, when she said she was out getting lost?! Isn't she the best?" The cushion slides off his lap, he doesn't appear to notice, Mel cringes, wishing desperately for the apocalypse to happen like, now,

"Oh, Mel did this, did she?" The venom in Chris's voice is palpable.

"Can I take this off now?"Marlowe asks,

"No!" Chris and Mel shout in unison,

"Chris, I'm so sorry, it's just a big, err, misunderstanding. We're going," Mel grabs Andrew by the hand to get him on his feet, hissing at him to pull his pants up,

"Oooerrr!"says Marlowe," I wasn't expecting a sex party! I thought Chris might be popping the question, aren't you country folk full of surprises?" she giggles.

The last of the fireworks explodes into the sky, then a deafening silence falls. The smell of spent sparklers and smoke drifts across the valley. Oh God, of course it's a proposal Mel thinks with a sinking heart, this is exactly the sort of thing Chris would do, he was always amazing at romantic gestures and here on this hill, under the stars, with all the fireworks, at the beginning of a New Year, the beginning of their new life together. It was perfect and she had just completely ruined it.

Hustling Andrew to get dressed, she starts straightening up the blankets and rearranging the pillows, "Leave them!" Chris barks. Grabbing a very confused Andrew by the arm, she drags him back down the track. To stop his insistent questioning as to why they are leaving, she force feeds him the jam tarts while she cracks open the champagne and swigs it from the bottle like it's pop, because if ever she needs to drink to forget something, it is right now. The look on Chris's face, what must he have thought? That she was about to have sex on his perfect proposal picnic rug? Or worse, even, that they'd already done it and she was casually putting Andrew's shorts back on? If she'd thought about it in the moment, with a clear head, she should have known that only Chris would think to do something so romantic as that. She wonders if he will go ahead with the proposal anyway, tipping up the bottle, she drains the champagne.

CHAPTER EIGHT

Mel's slow rise into consciousness is aided by a steady licking on the side of her face, "Gerroff, Andrew," She mumbles, trying to find him with her groping hand. She does not yet possess the power to open her eyes, which seem to have retreated into her skull, along with any memory of where she is or how she got there. The ground beneath her is hard and cold. She establishes, eventually, that the tongue belongs to Milly, who then starts to yap, a noise that splits her head open like a jackhammer. She still can't find the strength to get up, "Shhhh," she croaks, her throat constricting,

Slowly, she opens one eye, trying to work out where she is, which turns out to be on the lounge floor, half off the air bed, which has gone flat anyway, or did they ever even blow it up? She can't remember. Rolling over, she expects to find Andrew next to her, but he's nowhere to be seen, at least from as far as she can raise her head, which is not very far. There's just a wall of cats and dogs waiting to be let out and fed. She pats around the floor looking for her phone. All she finds is a half-full wine bottle, which she knocks over, the tide of it seeping towards her head, which appears to be stuck to the floor. The smell of Sauvignon Blanc wafts up her nostrils, making her gag.

With huge effort, she sits up, mobilising the menagerie, who surge hungrily towards her. Is this really how pet owners get eaten? They were just hungover and didn't get the Whiskas out in time? Somehow, she makes it to the back door, letting the dogs out as her pupils cruelly retract in the bright morning light. Hastily, she retreats to slop some food into bowls. Once every animal inside is finally engaged in eating, she shakily pours herself a glass of water, flopping into the armchair to survey the scene and gather her wits. (Although she suspects they are still in Manchester somewhere from the way she's been behaving since she arrived.) She needs to summon the strength to go outside and deal with the rest of the menagerie.

Where on earth is Andrew? She tries to piece together her patchy memories from last night, slowly it all starts to come back to her; Chris's furious face, Andrew's lilting penis and Marlowe's ruined proposal replay in a horrifying show reel. As the agonising shame washes over her, she curls back into the chair with mortification. There is no doubt about it now; she is officially going straight to hell.

But first coffee…

After filling the kettle, she goes to find Andrew but he's nowhere down here, with a groan she crawls up the stairs thinking he must have gone in search of a proper bed but there's no sign of him up there either, just a sobering reminder of how much stuff she still has to do. With the hideous shame game playing repeatedly in her head. She forces herself to pull on some of Kath's old wellies, staggering out into the yard. Andrew's car is still there, thank god, because he could barely walk back down the hill, let alone drive; he is not asleep in it, however, as she was presuming.

After letting the chickens and ducks out, she begs Arlo to help with the rest, as usual, he completely ignores her. She is forced to fall back on the crazy dance, mid arm wave she hears Josh laughing, "Come and help me you arsehole!" she begs, desperately needing to sit down,"Got a sore head, have we?" He shouts in her ear,

"Unless you've come to be of assistance you can piss off Josh," She rests against the truck bed,

"And a happy new year to you too, Melsbells…" he corrals the last sheep into the field, "Chris sent me to check on Eddie…"

He takes a fresh hay bale over to the donkey shed. Mel trails after him. Please let Eddie be OK, she prays, the last thing she can cope with right now is a dying donkey. Thankfully, she seems all right. Josh looks her over while she munches her breakfast,

"How are you so bright and breezy?" She feels like she might die at any minute,

"We've been up Broadholme for the annual New Year's Day swim, remember? You should have come! It sobered you up in a second! We had to crack the ice this morning, though. It was chuffing freezing, but I did my lap. Obviously your name came up 'cos, errrr, we were planning a congratulations 'do today… Honestly, Mel, I thought nothing could top Pool Table 'Gate, but you've given Greenleigh next-level gossip for another twenty years! Chris caught you having sex on his proposal picnic blanket? I mean, everyone was pretty shocked, but then no one was surprised, given…" Josh nearly keels over, he's laughing so much.

A lightning strike, an earthquake, anything, please just swallow me up right now, she begs. The facts are a thousand times more excruciating coming from someone else's mouth, "We did not have sex!" Did they?

"Not what Chris saw,"

"Chris did not see us having sex." Oh god, oh god, not this, not again,

"He saw Andrew's weener," Josh chortles, thoroughly enjoying this new turn of events,

"It is not a weener! He was just very drunk, you haven't seen him anywhere, have you? Andrew?"

"Yeah, he's at Marlowe's cabin, in the spare bedroom."

Mel, who thought this situation couldn't possibly get any worse, gasps as the horror plummets another ten levels, "What is he doing there?" She croaks in disbelief,

"Turned up at 4 am apparently, banging on the door saying he couldn't sleep with all those cats around him. Chris was forced to let him in to stop him from disturbing the other guests. "

I just need to die, Mel thinks, sick rushing up her throat,

"I have to say, Mels, I don't think he's the one for you. I met him yesterday when you went AWOL. That was just like old times, eh? Hilarious! He's a skanky manc Mel, you need a good Yorkshireman! Thinking about it, he'd be perfect for Marlowe. We could kill two birds with one stone,"

"Josh! You can't say that, she's your future sister in law!"

"Not yet, she's not. Thanks to you, the proposal got delayed. Did you think he would go ahead after Andrew jizz/"

"Josh! We didn't, I swear!" Mel feels faint.

" Well, Chris is soooo livid!! I owe you one, Mel!" He gives her a high five,

 "Though if you ask me, the only reason he suddenly decided to propose is "cos you're back. "

She just about makes it to a bush before she spews up her guts. Josh pats her back, still laughing. She feels marginally better for throwing up, not mentally, obviously, because she isn't quite sure how she's ever going to get over last night.

Josh makes her a brew while she starts to clean up the mess from last night. It looks like they had quite the party, as she puts five empty bottles in the recycling. No wonder she feels like dying. She knows she should go and get Andrew, but the thought of seeing Chris is terrifying. She begs Josh to go, but he refuses unless she spills the gossip on Jamie: "Honestly, there's nothing to say, Josh. I don't know what you were expecting?"

"Hot sex on the forecourt?"

"Too rough, it's that pebble-dash concrete…"

"Back seat of your car?"

"Not that agile these days!"

"That's not what Chris said about last night."

Mel knows the hard way that it doesn't matter how many times she denies it; once Greenleigh decides about a version of events, the story sticks like glue.

"On a scale of 1 to 10, exactly how mad is Chris?" Mel grimaces, Josh sucks in his teeth, "…. About a 1000?"

"Josh, please, *please,* will you go get Andrew? I'll pay you anything."

Josh tells her to woman up and goes to the pub for a post-swim pint. He begs her to come down later, but Mel will never show her face in Greenleigh again after last night.

Andrew returns, thankfully, after apparently taking a hot bath in the vintage tub, happily raving to her about the incredible view. He looks well-rested. He has a coffee and a buttery-looking croissant in his hand. Mel's thoroughly empty stomach starts to growl. Marlowe could have sent her one. Andrew doesn't even offer to share, too busy talking about how wonderful Marlowe is. Luckily, it transpires Chris went out to swim and had not come back yet (probably clearing up the picnic, Mel thinks shamefully), but thank God, she can only imagine how awkward that scene might have been, coming back to find Andrew soaking away, oblivious, in their bathtub.

Andrew claims to have no memory of going over to the cabin, pointing out unperturbed that Marlowe had invited him to stay there earlier in the day, though, so it wasn't a problem. His memory, as it transpires, gets fuzzy beyond getting to the "Amazing romantic picnic that you did for me, to make up for Paris." Mel opens her mouth to tell him the truth, then closes it, then opens it again, "The thing is, Andrew…" Then she thinks about the ramifications of telling the truth. She is far too hungover to deal with that right now; she will, she must, but at another, better time. I mean, why burst his bubble when she's back in his good books? She will just have to keep him far apart from Chris forever.

She excuses herself outside to ring Connor. With the time difference, he should have surfaced by now, but his phone goes to voicemail. She checks her messages. Jamie sent her a picnic basket emoji with an aubergine, and Siobhan a lot of laughing faces. News spreads as fast as ever, she groans, picturing the gaggle of gossiping swimmers before they all ran into the freezing reservoir, a tradition long held by the whole village.

The sooner she gets out of here, the better. All she's done, at every turn, is behave like a complete idiot since she got back. It's almost like she's just carrying on from where she left off, all those years ago. Drinking far too much and getting into all sorts of trouble. Chris is never *ever* going to speak to her again, all over again. She legitimately worries that if she spends any more time around Jamie, just like old times, she'll find herself with her knickers around her ankles in a field somewhere.

Staring out across the beautiful valley, somehow she rallies herself. It's a New Year! No more old Mel! Tomorrow she will hire a skip, ring the vet, find homes for the animals, organise the funeral with the Oldswicks (via email?) and focus on getting out of here and on with the next stage of her life. Andrew is a nice man, with a great family, that she would be very happy to be part of, not to mention the option of living in his luxury apartment; she doesn't want to mess that up, even if she has a few nagging doubts that they are not compatible.

 She doesn't want to have to kick Andrew out, but she doesn't have the energy to entertain him. If he stays any longer, she'll have to offer him more food. There is no more food. She can't risk him offering to go into the village for supplies. She doesn't need him to find out from Mr. Nelson, what the whole village thinks they were doing it on Chris' proposal picnic blanket, the picnic that he still thinks was especially for him.

Thankfully, another sneezing fit sends him on his way. He has plans with his family later. Hustling him to his car, he says he will be back for the funeral, she insists he doesn't have to, reminding him it's just a small gathering, "I want to come and support you!" he says chivalrously,

"Thank you, that's sweet, honestly, you don't have to. I'll be fine, I'll be home straight after anyway," She counters (and they will never, ever have to come back here again). She kisses him chastely on his cheek because she can't honestly remember if she's brushed her teeth today. She waves him goodbye, finally breathing out. As he is about to drive away, out of the car window, he remarks,

"I think you need to get back to the city, Melanie, out here, you've gone a bit *feral*,"

Maybe I always was, thinks Mel, looking out at the moors. It just takes the wild places to remind you.

Putting the kettle on for the umpteenth time, she takes stock of everything that she's done in the last few days. None of it's pretty, well, Jamie is quite pretty, she thinks, remembering when they were young. She may still be drunk. She reaches for the squashed jam tarts; she needs to get a grip. Why doesn't she ever know what's good for her?

She busies herself with the animals for the rest of the day because at least they don't judge. She also feels guilty that she's not given them her full attention. Hats off to Kath, she thinks. Sweeping out all the varying beds and trundling fresh straw back and forth is bloody hard work, but she is actually enjoying herself in the fresh air and the peace and quiet.

As she mucks out the donkeys, she catches sight of Chris and Marlowe coming out of the cabin. She ducks into the doorway, desperate not to be spotted. Of course, she absolutely wants to see what they are doing. Nobody can deny that Marlowe is stunningly beautiful, but she seems out of place here. She wears an awful lot of white for someone going out with a farmer. Does Chris think their two worlds could combine?

Would she be a farmer's wife, or would he leave the farm and live in London? Chris doesn't even like going into Huddersfield. She must get Josh to spill some more beans. Is he going to propose again, she wonders? She needs to be miles away this time, not because what Chris does with his life is any of her business, she tells herself.

Down in the donkey field, she isn't that far from the cabins, so she can see that they are having a heated discussion as Marlowe puts her Louis Vuitton bags into her car, which is also white, or was white until she arrived in Yorkshire. Chris keeps trying to get her to listen, but she slams the car boot and climbs inside. Mel watches Chris bend to the car door, imploring her as Marlowe throws the car into reverse, leaving him bent over nothing as she shoots off. Chris watches her go, looking utterly dejected.

Unfortunately Skippy and Arlo, who were a minute ago contentedly sniffing around her feet, choose this moment to spot Chris, running towards him, barking excitedly. Flattening herself as best she can behind the door, she can see Chris scanning to see if the dogs are out alone, the last thing she wants is for him to come over and bring them back. Reluctantly, she inches out of her hiding place, "Arlo! Skippy! "She shouts, looking around in every direction but at Chris, whilst wheeling the barrow back to the yard as nonchalantly as she can muster.

In penance for her bad behaviour, she exudes what little strength she has left, scouring the wonky kitchen floor on her knees with the radio on to drown out all the guilt and shame. Later, when every last animal is fed again and put back away for the night, she blows up the inflatable mattress that, thankfully, Andrew left for her. Tomorrow night, she will sleep upstairs, she tells herself, but for now, she stokes up the fire, piles up the blankets and plants, and, exhausted, falls face-first onto the airbed.

She wakes up in the morning to find her bed flattened by the weight of herself, Milly, Skippy, and varying cats curled up next to her—it is literally a two-dog night.

With a renewed energy (she isn't hungover for once), Mel is up with the larks, or rather, an incontinent dog and some hungry cats meowing loudly for food. How on earth had Kath done this every day, she wondered? It's relentless, feeding everyone, washing bowls, clearing up after Milly who would just wee on the floor if you didn't get her out the door quick enough, then there's the farm animals to deal with, all of whom seemed to spend their lives eating, then crapping, in a constant round. She's already shoveled what feels like a lifetime of poo onto the manure pile. She adds buying animal feed to her to-do list and wonders where to go. She'll Google it (she certainly isn't asking Chris), then she remembers that her car is still at the garage.

Locating the keys to the truck, Mel turns it over a few times, but it isn't having any of it. Her stomach growls all the while, not satiated by a pitiful breakfast of tea and the last stale jam tart, she must get to the shops today. After much internal debate, she knows there is nothing for it but to ring Jamie.

Sat on the flatbed of the truck, her feet dangling down, she stares out at the view ahead of her; the patchwork fields of green, divided by the warm grey of old stone walls, the dusky moors rising beyond, spanning the endless horizon and the vast expanse of sky that you never see in the city. Growing up, she took it all for granted, running through the fields to get to school, surrounded by nature and animals, playing out in the woods until it got dark, trekking miles over the moor to swim in the reservoir on hot summer days; they were so free as kids. It was very different from Connor's childhood, which was all about pavements, playgrounds, and soft play centres.

Everything you needed in life was here in this valley, and yet she couldn't wait to leave at 18, making the ironic assumption that the grass was greener elsewhere and not caring at all about what she left behind.

As her phone kicks into life, the messages pile up. Aaron has sent her a sweet message asking if she wants him to bring Connor over for the funeral. Although she is very grateful that they are willing to support her, she isn't sure if she can handle Jamie, Chris, Aaron and possibly Andrew in one room. It feels a bit like one of those quantum physics equations where if all the elements ever met, boom! She will be sucked into a black hole forever, though perhaps no bad thing at this current juncture.

There is also the very real possibility that Connor might overhear any one of the varying rumours about her. No child ever wants to hear that about their parent, so she can at least spare him that shame. Kath would have understood. According to Josh, the whole village will be coming anyway.

Jamie picks the phone up with a snort, "I've got some more places for you, the war memorial...In a bunker at the golf course?

"Been there, done that", Mel starts to flush all ready, bloody Jamie,

"Oh, I *remember* Mac, I was just testing you, you wanted to know what sex on a beach would be like."

"It wasn't *on* the war memorial, we weren't that disrespectful," Mel counters.

"Up against the wall next to it, as I recall."

She remembers it well, blushing. Jamie had led her so wildly astray, and she had been a very willing follower; no matter what Chris thought, she had known her mind. It was just at that point, her mind was hell bent on blocking out all the pain of losing her Mum by drowning her sorrows in the arms of a boy who didn't know anything about that part of her life. These days she's wise enough to understand that she did many stupid things to mask her trauma, but back then, she just did whatever made her forget.

"I didn't ring to discuss all the places where we…"

"Shame. I'm still waiting on delivery of your exhaust, I'm afraid."

"How long will it be? 'Cos I've got to go get animal feed today, it's pretty urgent,"

Jamie laughs, " Got a hungry Pussy?"

"Grow up, Jamie!"

"You walked straight into that one… I thought your boyfriend was going to help you with the truck? Oh no, you were too busy ruining Chris' life, again." He can't stop laughing, revelling in Chris' misfortune,

"I didn't know it was Chris' picnic, honestly!!"

"Does that make it better or worse, Mac? You decide!"

"We weren't having sex either, despite the rumours."

"Come on, Mel, this is me you're talking to, I know how much you like it al fresco."

"Can we just focus on the Ford Focus, please, Jamie?"

"Did you try starting the truck? You'd be better off in that anyway, if you're buying sacks of feed, you can just chuck 'em on the back."

"Battery's flat, I reckon."

" You want me to come? And help, I mean? Get the kettle on, Mac, I'll be there in 20."

Exhaling, every day is a different flavour of hell. Mel lies down on the truck's flatbed, looking up at the sky above her, thinking about how much fun they used to have. She knows it will take all her strength to stay away from Jamie Hirst; she also knows exactly what he would say:Resistance is futile. She doesn't even give Andrew a guilty thought, which pretty much tells her everything she's trying to ignore about their relationship.

Watching the clouds drift by, she thinks about how ironic it is that she's ended up back here, back in all the same boats, despite all her best intentions never to lay a foot in Greenleigh again. They say the past always catches up with you, though, and Mel has been running for twenty years.

She hears the familiar sound of Jamie's motorbike and gets up. If he gets there and finds her lying flat in the back of the truck, she'll never hear the end of it. Is he still doing that hair toss when he takes off his helmet? She watches, yep, there it is. Jamie's hair is probably one of the first things that attracted her to him; it was so glossy. She would comb his bathroom for evidence that he was using posh women's products. Her hair was certainly never that bloody shiny, and she used all the posh women's products.

 Too late, she remembers that it's now been some days since she has washed her hair, or herself, for that matter. She zips up her coat swiftly to keep any odours in. Maybe she can nip up for a shower while he fixes the car? She needs to go out into public today, and she does have a modicum of self-respect left, though to be fair, it's pretty much hanging on by a thread. He unzips his leathers (sigh) and gets the new battery out from his bike box. The dogs both run to greet him like old friends. He fusses them soppily. I mean, they say dogs are a good judge of character, she thinks, remembering how Milly nipped at Andrew on several occasions.

She's never driven a truck, you're so high up. She likes how *country* it feels. While Jamie works his magic, she looks up animal feed stores and finds one on the outskirts of town. She scribbles a list: goats, sheep, cats, dogs, donkeys, ducks, me. Jamie shouts to start the engine, and the truck sputters back into life. He comes round to her window, "Suits you,"

"I like it! I couldn't take it back to Manchester though, I'd never be able to park it anywhere,"

"You're still hell bent on going back then? I thought your son was living with his Dad now? Just come home, Mel, I'll give you a warm welcome," he grins wolfishly,

"I have a job, friends and a *boyfriend* there,"

"I hear he's not your type at all."

"Have you been talking to Josh? "

"He's a good lad, not like his brother. We're on the darts team, and he fills me in on *everything*."

"Don't believe everything Josh says; he just loves a good story."

"Let's be honest, you have form, though, Mel... Will you be okay driving a truck? I think it's got a reversing sensor so you don't back into anything, and it's a diesel so don't go chucking unleaded in it."

"Noted, thank you, umm, are you in a rush to get back? It's just, well, I *really* need a shower,"

"You want me to wash your back? *Watch* your back, I mean?" His lip curls suggestively,

Mel suddenly feels ridiculous. It's broad daylight. What is she scared of? Kath's ghost?

"Mac, seriously, you go shower. I'll put the kettle on and wait in the kitchen. If you get the heebie-jeebies, just shout. I promise to behave."

They go inside, and she rifles around to get clean clothes. "It's been a long time since I've been in here," Jamie leans on the sink, remembering,

"My Dad was never exactly welcoming towards you, was he?"

"He was Team Oldswick all the way…Can't say I blame him, Mac. I was a little idiot back then, but you know, I'm a dad now, I've grown up, finally."

Mel swallows. What she does not need right now is for Jamie to become her dream partner, twenty years too late. Gathering her things, she goes up the creaky stairs, ignoring all the creepy closed doors. Shivering, she starts to undress, trying to ignore the grimy tiles and all the cobwebs. God, there's still so much to do. The 10 days she's earmarked are looking less and less likely at the rate she's dragging her heels. Resting her chin in her hand, she considers her last thought: is she dragging her heels and if so, why?

The shower eventually runs hot. She washes her hair, luxuriating in the feeling. Andrew's jet shower should have made it seem like a bargain basement experience, but she's just thrilled to be washing the shame of the past few days away. She didn't take any clean underwear up with her, though, weighing up wearing yesterday's pants against Jamie seeing her in a relatively small towel. Deciding he's seen it all before anyway, she nips down. Too late, she goes into the kitchen, hears voices, and sees Chris standing there.

All ready, obviously, *very* unhappy with her, add that to him finding Jamie sprawled out casually in the kitchen like he's well at home, Chris takes one look at her in the tiny towel and his face goes so red, she's scared he is about to burst a blood vessel,

"Unbelievable!" He mutters, shaking his head, " I just came to check on Eddie. I'll leave you two to it," he stomps back out of the door, banging it shut behind him before Mel can say anything, the dogs go with him, the traitors.

"Jamie, why didn't you say something?!"

Jamie shrugs, "I was distracted by your towel slipping down"

Mel looks down, her towel is fine, "Now he thinks I'm a total ho!"

"Oh, *now* he thinks you're a ho?" Jamie snorts, his eyes travelling over her,

She snatches up her things and shoots back upstairs. Maybe she'll have to make peace with never redeeming herself to Chris. She opens the bathroom window to let out the condensation and sees him checking the donkeys as the dogs trot after him. Before she leaves, she must at least try; she's owed it to him for a very long time.

CHAPTER NINE

After her Mum's cancer was diagnosed as terminal, she and Chris became inseparable. Mel was well aware that his mum would have told him to be kind to her, and at first, she didn't want his sympathy, because that meant it was true. Her mum was going to die, and there was nothing she could do to stop it from happening.

Initially, she was mean to him, teasing him mercilessly, but Chris never rose to it. Although they barely spoke at school, they would get off the bus every Friday night and walk slower and slower up the hill together, as they talked more and more each week. He would always walk her into the yard at Kath's, insisting on carrying her heavy book bag. She started spending more of her Saturdays next door at Holme End, hanging out in the warm kitchen with Sheila, drinking endless cups of tea, playing games with Josh and helping Chris and his Dad out with the cows. They took her in like a stray animal and made her feel like one of the family.

Eventually, when her Mum had to move into a hospice, Mel had to move to Kath's permanently, reluctantly. Slowly, somehow, the sadness she felt was tempered by happiness in her growing relationship with Chris. No matter how miserable she was feeling, he would always seem to know what to say to bring her round. If she wanted jokes, he made plenty; if she needed a hug, he would wrap his strong arms around her and sit with her until she felt better. They would wander the farm talking to the cows (she named the whole herd) they both loved being outside so they would take picnics, (Chris always was great at them, she really should have known), roaming the hills and valleys, swimming in the reservoir on hot days, tramping through the silent, frozen woods in winter. It was a symbiosis; he loved to care for things, and she needed to be cared for in return.

One day, when they were sitting on the old standing stones, high up on the moor, he told her earnestly that he knew they were young, but he loved her and he wanted to love her forever. Mel had crawled into his lap in tears. They made rings for each other out of grass. She would never leave him, she promised, and she would never stop loving him. She could see herself happily spending her life with him at Holme Farm; it had everything she'd ever need for a good life.

What a mess she made of that.

She didn't like living at Kath's house; it was messy, always freezing, and everyone walked on eggshells around her. The only saving grace were the animals, and that she could jump the fence and run up the track to see Chris in five minutes. The door was always open at Holme End. Mrs. Oldswick would make her eat, even though she could barely swallow.

It was Mrs. Oldswick who baked her a cake for her 16th birthday. When she blew out the candles, she made a wish for a miracle that her Mum would somehow pull through. The life that was leaving her Mum started to leave her too; she was thin and pale from days spent sitting in the hospice, holding her Mum's hand. Her Dad, the Oldswicks, and her teachers tried to get her to leave, to sleep, to eat, but toward the end, she wouldn't go home in case her Mum slipped away without the chance to say goodbye. Chris would sit with her as often as he could, sometimes all night, holding her hand tightly while she held onto her Mum tightly. When her Mum finally slipped away one cold, grey afternoon, Chris was with her. He scooped her up into his strong arms and held her until there wasn't a tear left for her to cry.

THE TRACK BACK

The first time she got drunk was at her Mum's funeral. In the back room of the pub, no one was paying attention to the kids; her mum's distant family, whom she never knew or saw again, held the fort next to the sandwiches. Mel's Mum was not close to her parents for reasons she was never told but had always wondered about, so Mel never knew her Nana or Grandad like other people. She had thought over the years about reaching out, but then remembered that they knew Mel's Mum was dying and never came to see her or enquire about Mel's well-being.

Her Dad was from County Cork, Ireland; his huge family are all still there that she knows, in the same village. They'd visited a few times when she was small; she remembers being crowded by cousins she'd never heard of, with names that seemed mystical. A big group of them had come over to his funeral, but Mel never kept in touch with them either; they had tried. She resolves to reach out.Watching her dad take all the commiserations at her funeral, despite their separation, made her so angry she could barely be civil. She had it in her head then that it was him leaving that had caused her Mum to get sick.

Later in the day, after people were tipsy, she picked up people's drinks for herself and talked sympathetic strangers into buying her cider and black, then, when she was drunk, she decided to take up smoking. Chris had held her hair back while she retched pink sick into a flower pot in the beer garden.Chris was steadfastly supportive the whole time, anything she said, anything she did, no matter how stupid (and she had been pretty stupid at times), he had stood by her side, a rock in the sea of her tsunami of grief. Unfortunately, she quickly found drinking to be the quickest cure for her unhappiness. If Chris were with her, he would slow her down and keep her steady, but she had other friends who were always happy to accompany her when he was too busy on the farm. Siobhan, who was a wild flirt, would go where the boys went, and the boys would go where the beer was, so she was always a reliable drinking partner.

Often when she was drunk, she would ring Chris to come and get her, or she would stumble up the shortcut to the farm to find him. He would let her cry or be sick or rant, and then he'd take her home and get her into bed, with a bucket next to her, often sleeping on the floor next to her, just to make sure she didn't choke on her vomit in the night. Her Dad and Kath had lost all control over her at that point, so they acquiesced to Chris, who was the only one she would listen to, but as the weeks went by, even that was becoming precarious. The more Chris tried to stop her, the more she began to rebel against him.

When she started college in town that September, Mel began drinking there instead, well away from prying eyes who would report her behaviour to her dad or Chris, who himself had got a place away at an Agricultural college but chose to defer as he didn't want to leave her.

She and Siobhan got fake ID's and hung out in dive bars that didn't check them closely. That night, after the snowball fight, she'd climbed onto the bus, trembling with cold and from excitement at the interaction with Jamie. He'd stood right behind her as they jostled to get on the bus. Every inch of her skin felt his presence. He slipped past Siobhan and sat down next to her on the front seat, resting his long legs in those skinny jeans up on the window ledge.Siobhan raised an eyebrow, sitting as close by as she could. They were both wet and breathless from the fight, skin tingling with the cold. She was shivering, so he took her blue hands and rubbed them in his. From across the bus, she caught Siobhan's warning look and ignored it. They barely spoke; they just sat looking up at themselves in the overhead mirror and smiling at each other in their reflection. Eventually, his mates started yelling at him insistently from the back of the bus, as they got more rowdy, he stood up reluctantly and with an apologetic shrug sauntered off to join them. Siobhan plonked herself down in his empty seat with a frown, gripping Mel's arm to stop her turning around as he got off the bus, but she wanted to. She looked out of the window as it pulled away. Jamie stood in the snow, staring up. He bowed to her as the bus pulled away.

A few weeks of bad weather followed, with heavy snow trapping her frustratingly at home. She hung out with Chris, but she thought about Jamie all the time; he was like an instant cure for her grief. She turned 17, the drunken celebrations got way out of hand, someone called an ambulance and she had her stomach pumped. Her dad fetched her from the hospital and grounded her for the foreseeable future. She was allowed to see Chris, but only at home. Relative calm fell for the next few months, everyone thought she was "Getting better" as if grief was a thing that you recovered from like the flu.

Chris, ever thoughtful, made plans for their anniversary, a date she kept no tabs on because they got together, officially, in the months that her Mum was in the hospice, and those months were all a blur to her. He told her nothing but to come to the farm at 8 pm sharp. Mel was excited because she thought Chris was finally going to give in to her desire to lose her virginity. When she was drunk, she kept trying to seduce him, but he always said that she'd had too much to drink and it wasn't right to take advantage; he wanted it to be special.

When her dad asked her what time she was going over there, she didn't think twice about lying, thinking a few drinks in the pub first would amplify the evening ahead, Chris would only be providing soft drinks, he was always on her case about quitting alcohol or going to see a grief counsellor these days and she was getting sick of it. The barman at the horse was never fussy about ID for the locals, so, dressed in her most seductive outfit, hoping it was her lucky night (with a jumper on top for her dad's benefit), she legged it down the track through the woods down to the pub. She sat at the bar chatting to the regulars as she quickly downed a couple of happy hour double vodkas and Coke. (Didn't make your breath smell so Chris would never know.)

With an eye on the clock, debating one for the road, the door to the pool room opened and out strolled Jamie Hirst, and just like that, all concept of time and any other plans simply disappeared. He bought her a drink, she followed him into the dark pool room at the back of the pub, his mates melted away as they played a game of pool, she took off her jumper, her dress was barely there, meant to seduce Chris. She leaned low over the pool table, and they flirted mildly, then wildly. She was now running ridiculously late, but she didn't even think about it. Alcohol had numbed all her common sense; she just wanted to be with Jamie. She asked him to help her take a pool shot; she didn't need him to, she just wanted him to get close. He leaned in behind her, his hair brushing her shoulder. He always smelled faintly of motor oil, which was somehow intoxicating. His arms went round her, and he leaned into her from behind, and something inside of her blew a fuse; she twisted around and kissed him.

Years later, it seemed apparent to reflect that the quickest way out of pain was by pursuing pleasure, and Jamie was even better than alcohol for sweeping all her misery aside. He didn't know anything about her Mum, and he didn't look at her with the pity she saw in Chris' eyes. He was reckless, lived in the moment with no thought for consequences, and that was exactly how she needed to feel right then.

Her tiny dress rode up to her waist. Jamie was on top of her, and they were kissing madly against the pool table. Jamie was running his hands all over her, pushing into her as she arched into him. Vodka always made her a brazen drunk, but it was nothing more than that; no clothes were removed, she wouldn't have, not then and not in there.

It was just unfortunate that Chris had come to find her, worried about her no show, enraged when the bartender confirmed that she was indeed in the pub, "She's outback...wi' Jamie Hirst!" The sucking in of air amongst the locals palpable as Jamie's mates sat sniggering. Chris had the worst-case scenario in his head before he even pushed open the pool room door. In the dim light it maybe did look like they were going for it on the pool table, Chris certainly didn't stop to check, backing out of the room at top speed and stumbling back into the bar, " 'You find her?"asked the barman, "Yeah, having sex with Jamie Hirst on the pool table!" he'd announced, stunned, to the whole pub.

And that, my friend, is how legends are born.

Chris stormed out the door. The regulars looked to the bartender, who was more worried about the potential damage to the pool table, and followed him down the corridor to find out if it was true. Over the years, many claimed to have been there and that it actually happened, but by the time anyone stuck their head round the door, Mel was hiding in the toilet in shame because she'd seen Chris backing out of the room, and she knew exactly what she'd done.

She left without seeing Jamie again, crashing through the woods with tears in her eyes, but at the farm, Mrs. Oldswick told her it was best she went home. As she drunkenly stumbled across the yard, she noticed that one of the outbuildings was all cleaned up and fairy lights hung around the ceiling. There was a table set for dinner, vases of wildflowers and candles. She felt sick with guilt and wretched with betrayal, yet also secretly exhilarated by her experience with Jamie, half wondering when she might see him again. She rang Chris for days, but he wouldn't answer, turning his phone off and ignoring all her apologies.

When she found out that the whole village believed what he'd said about her, Jamie and the pool table, she sent him long letters telling him the truth, but he never responded. Mrs. Oldswick was firm and told her to give him some space after what he'd been through. Mel was too ashamed to face her again once she knew what everyone thought they knew. One day, Josh shouted, "Chris hates you, he never wants to speak to you again! Go away!" from his bedroom window. Mel gave up going round after that. If Chris wouldn't believe her, well, it was his stupid fault, she consoled herself, but deep down, she was so ashamed that she'd treated him terribly. She added it to the pile of feelings that she would drink away.

Now that the whole village had condemned her anyway, when she got the chance, one Saturday night (her dad and Kath were away at one of their Goat shows). She got on the bus to town to find Jamie. If everyone thought that they were having an affair anyway, then she was going to make it so. When she saw him waiting at the bus stop, she could hardly breathe. She'd sat by the stairs so he couldn't miss her when he came onto the top deck. He swung up the stairs, stopping dead when he saw her, before sliding into the seat next to her and not saying a word, they started kissing.

And so it began, the ballad of Jamie Hirst.

CHAPTER TEN

At the feed store, the man behind the counter says he's been a friend of Kath's for years, they'd been colleagues once, he tells her, as he expresses his commiserations. Somehow, he knows who she is, telling her that Kath would talk about her and her son over in Manchester. Mel drives back to Greenleigh, plagued by terrible guilt; she should have done more. The years had gone by so fast. The early ones with Connor were such an exhausting blur of stress and Aaron's mess. They were just a pair of clueless kids raising a kid. They'd struggled along financially for years. It was hard juggling the bills and trying to give Connor nice things and good memories, but somehow they managed, or she did, for the most part.

She didn't have a car back then, so Greenleigh was practically a foreign country to get to, especially with a restless toddler in tow. She had never invited her father or Kath to visit her, though not that they, like Chris, had ever liked going into cities. He hadn't supported her decision to have the baby, telling her she was throwing her life away. He had no time for Aaron, who was still unreliable. It had become easier not to see her Dad than to have him judge their life all the time, so Mel kept in touch only when necessary. She had grown to understand his stance a little better now, especially since Connor was that age, she wouldn't want him to go down that same road. They were far too young and immature, and looking back, it was a miracle, to be honest, that they had made it through those early years, something she never really gives herself credit for.

After she unloads all the sacks from the truck, she sits down with a cup of tea, mindlessly stirring in the sugar as she looks at her still endless list of things to do. The funeral is now mainly organised, thankfully. There will be a service at the village church, and then Mrs. Oldswick is hosting the wake in the barn. She'd told Connor and Aaron not to come, insisting she'd be fine on her own. It will be much easier that way. Aaron suggested donating to an animal charity and made a substantial contribution on their behalf. Janet offered also, but as it was term time, Mel told her not to worry either. Honestly, the fewer people who know the truth about her past, the better. She listens to their concerned messages, guiltily feeling that she doesn't deserve their sympathy.

From her office in the back of the truck, she orders a skip and reaches out to an estate agent. She's found an animal charity that would come and take anything donation-worthy, but there was so much junk to sort through first. Then, dreading it, she rings the vet, who tells her he's coming by later anyway because Chris has already asked him to (of course he has). She messages Siobhan about bringing the girls to see the kittens, then replies to Andrew, who is still insisting that he will come to the funeral. Not ideal, considering all the lies she told from New Year's. Might she have to break up with him just to stop him coming, or should she, realistically, break up with him because she's struggling with thoughts about their compatibility?

She also needs to try to find the paperwork that Ken keeps asking her for, so armed with bin bags and boxes, she sets aside the afternoon to do a thorough search. Starting with the overstuffed sideboard in the lounge, she pulls out the drawers, trying to be methodical. Some things are easy to throw away, such as old receipts and invoices, out-of-date catalogues, and a hundred copies of the Farming Times. The kittens, fascinated by the piles of paper, jump in and out of the bin bags with glee. Mel is glad of their company as a maudlin mood settles over her. *After we die, are our lives just condemned to a dustbin?*

Tucked amongst the rubbish, however, she finds a lot of old photos, mostly of animals; they kept Show Goats for years, so she's startled when one of herself falls out. She is probably twelve, not long after her Dad moved in with Kath. She is holding a lamb up to the camera. Smiling, a memory flashes up. Did she used to like coming here before her Mum got sick? Would she have liked Kath more, perhaps, if her Mum had lived and Kath wasn't promoted to her replacement? Not that Kath had ever acted in that way; she believed in free-range kids as well as animals. Mel had loved being out on the small holding back then. She had wanted to work with animals and live on a farm herself, happily daydreaming about her future, in which she would marry Chris and live at Holme End. How much joy in everything she had lost in that one defining moment?

Chris had begged her to get some professional help, to deal with things less self-destructively, but she didn't want to hear it. Counselling meant talking about it, and Mel just desperately wanted to forget, no matter how she did it.

How different would things have been if she'd listened to him for once?

A bin bag full later, she'd still found nothing that Ken needed, but she did have a lot of old photos that she decided to take to the funeral so that people could share the memories. There are several old ones from the village show.She picks out a young-looking Mrs. Oldswick, manning the tombola, and Mr. Nelson from the shop, almost unrecognisable with big hair, in the crowd.

With the lounge combed, she'll have to start looking elsewhere. Kitchen drawers reveal old takeaway menus, recipes from old newspapers, keys to mysterious locks, one buried at th e bottom is at least labelled- 'Studio'. The studio is a small stone building behind the barn. It was locked when she tried the handle, and with everything else she'd had to do, she'd sort of forgotten it was even there.

Needing a break from emptying drawers, she takes the dogs outside to check on the other animals. The sky is restless, grey clouds skip by and out over the distant moors, and rain gathers. Arlo and Skippy run out and she carries Milly, putting her down in the yard. The wind whips up the dust on the driveway, and the tall trees in the woods sway back and forth. It feels like there's a storm brewing. She has the studio key in her pocket and decides to take a quick inventory. At this rate, she's beginning to wonder if one skip will do the job. The big iron key takes some turning, but with a few shoves and a large puff of dust, the old wooden door finally opens.

In the bleak winter light, dust motes dance in front of the high windows. It feels like no one has opened the door for a long time, so she props the door open to air out the stale smell. Skippy sniffs about enthusiastically under the long benches. Mel prays he doesn't flush out rats; the stuffing in a chair in the corner is being eaten by something, spilling out like guts.

Shrugging up her jacket, she watches her breath cloud around her. The chill in here is palpable. On the bench are old paint bottles, dried-up palettes, assorted jars with rusty paint brushes, and a wire drying rack. On the table is a stack of canvas, some of which are empty and some of which used. Everything smells faintly of turps.

On one easel, a painting of the moors, mottled by mildew, its colours faded, but you could still appreciate the image, she stares at it for a while before noticing that the signature in the corner belongs to her dad. She looks at the other easel, it's unfinished, but from the style, she presumes it's one of her dad's too. She rifles through the paintings on the side. They are dusty and a bit mouldy in places, but salvageable, primarily landscapes, all her dad's work. Looking at them with fresh eyes, she appreciates his talent, something she never even knew about. Guilt starts gnawing at her stomach again.

She had never once asked him about his painting, thinking it was more Kath's thing. Looking around, she notices none of Kath's work in here. In a moment of clarity, she knows that Kath shut the door to the studio after he died and never came back in. Her heart squeezes. "I'm sorry, Dad, I'm sorry, Kath," she murmurs. I really should have been there for you."

As she stacks up his paintings to take inside, she turns one over and is completely floored by seeing her mum's face staring back at her. It's drawn from a photo that she'd long forgotten, the memory rising in her mind. It used to be in a frame in her mum's bedroom. Her Mum was young with long wavy hair spilling everywhere, just like hers. She's laughing up at the camera. When you're a kid, you can never quite reconcile old photos; she knew it was her Mum, but she could never quite imagine her mum as a person existing before she did.

When Connor had turned 16, she'd gone through a rough few months, haunted by the thought of dying herself and having to say goodbye to him. She put herself in her mum's shoes, thinking of those scenes in the Hospice that she never usually allowed herself to recall. Her Mum was given regular morphine, so she was asleep mainly, at the end. Chris would tell her over and over that she didn't know what was happening, but Mel knew she did from how tightly she would squeeze her hand when it was time for Mel to go, in case this was the last time.

Her mum was younger than she is now when she died; she had also had Mel when she was young. Paranoid that it was genetic, she'd had all the tests. She never told Connor about it, but she'd had nightmares for weeks waiting for results.

The painting is a brilliant likeness, the glint in her eye makes her look so alive that before Mel can compose herself, her chilled cheeks flood with hot tears. It's always been so hard to think of her mum without her memories clouded by the frail paper of her fingers, the white coffin covered in her favourite pink roses and the cold marble headstone with its birth and end dates. The painting drifts to the floor as Mel bends in two, the sudden pain of recall causing her to double over; memories she'd kept at bay flood back in an overwhelming rush. She doesn't hear a car pull into the yard or hear the voices outside; she just looks up to see a shadow in the doorway, Chris.

For a split second, she is sixteen and all she wants is for him to pull her into a hug, stroke her hair and tell her she can cry all day if she needs to, and he'll stay right there. He looks down at the painting, then steps hesitantly towards her, and Mel could've sworn that he was feeling the very same impulse, but his self-preservation kicks in, stopping him from acting on it. She knows all too well that she doesn't deserve any of his compassion. He hovers in the doorway as Mel straightens up, wipes her eyes and stuffs her mum's picture back into the pile.

"... That's your Mum, isn't it? Are you alright, Mel?" he asks, eventually.

She pauses, "I don't want to talk about it," her age-old stock response.

"If you'd talked about it to someone, Mel, you probably wouldn't still be in a mess about it twenty years later," he says in that gruff, very Yorkshire way,

"Twenty years later, you still think you know what's best for me!" Mel bites back, unable to help herself. (She hears Mrs. Oldswick's words as soon as she says it,' Hurt people, *hurt* people'.)

Chris just shakes his head and turns away, "The Vet's here."

She takes the paintings into the house, washes her face and tries to get herself together. The vet, Matt Dixon, is precisely as a country vet should be, wearing a tweed jacket and cracking terrible animal-related jokes to relieve the palpable tension. The wind has picked up, and it starts to patter with rain. Mel hovers as far as she can from Chris, who stands as far from her as possible, making the tension obvious.

The vet examines the donkeys, thankfully only pronouncing them geriatric. She suggests she boost their diet with varying supplements and perhaps stabling them at night rather than leaving them in the half-open box. There are some stables in the yard, but they are also full of crap.

"So you need homes for all the livestock, Chris tells me? I mean, honestly, at this stage, you'd be kinder to put these two to sleep than rehome them, even the stress of going in a horsebox would probably be too much," he says matter-of-factly.

Mel tries, but she can't stop the tears from welling back up. Blinking furiously, she tries to speak, but before she can, Chris steps in. "We'll take them up to the farm. We only use the top field for weddings in the summer, and they can share a stable in the yard, live out their days there."

Mel's heart swells, "Thank you, I'm so grateful, I can pay you for all their food and vet bills and"

"I'm not doing it for you, Mel, I'm doing it for Kath," Chris says, any hint of earlier compassion gone,

The vet blusters on to counter the unpleasant atmosphere in

the air, "I do know someone who'll probably take the chickens and ducks, they're all very healthy animals. Kath was a stickler. I'm sure Pat Harper'll have the goats. That just leaves what? The sheep? Bob Peel will take them; he was very fond of Kath, we all were. What does that leave? A few hundred cats and this lot," he ruffles Skippy's head whilst checking him over as a habit,

"I'll take the dogs too," Chris says, Arlo and Skippy devotedly at his feet, he scratches their heads,

"The dogs are coming with me!" Mel snaps, smarting from his earlier comment,

"Don't be ridiculous!" sneers Chris

"Why is that ridiculous?"

Tom Dixon starts studiously examining his muddy boots,

"You can't take working farm dogs to live in a city!" Chris says in a tone that suggests she is being stupid,

"They do have parks in cities, you know,"

"Parks!" scoffs Chris, "My point exactly!"

The vet sidles off to inspect the chickens, in case he missed something the first time, "I'll make those calls and be in touch."

"I'm going to buy somewhere with a big garden,"

"A *garden*?!"

Mel sees red, "I think you'll find that they are **my** dogs now, so if I want to take them to live with me, I can!"

Chris flushes, "Well, isn't that just standard Melanie McCarthy?! Only thinking about doing what makes Mel happy, never considering how the dogs might feel, so long as you get what you want, nobody else matters."

He stalks away up the field, sending the dejected-looking dogs back to Mel with a harsh command. Mel watches him storm away, turning to the donkeys and scratching Patsy's soft nose with a large sigh, "He hates me, doesn't he? I know he's got good reason, *reasons,* but I wish I could change his mind. Do you have any ideas?" Patsy chews her hay thoughtfully but has no suggestions.

Mel pours herself a glass of wine, pushes it away, and sips a bit. What Chris said stung her so much because she knew he was right. The dogs should stay here, and yes, twenty years later, it appears that she is still a heartless, clueless cow.

Stuck wallowing in the impact crater of the day, she'd forgotten all about her appointment with Siobhan, who wanders in with the girls, takes one look at Mel's puffy eyes and her large glass of wine, looks pointedly at the clock and sends the girls off to play with the kittens. She puts the kettle on for herself, "Tell me everything!"

"Honestly, Sib, I don't even know where to start...I've 5 days before I go back to work to find homes for all the animals, clear the whole house, host the funeral, and find Ken's paperwork... Meanwhile Chris hates my guts more than ever because, yet again, he thinks I'm some crazed nymphomaniac who, this time, shagged her drunk boyfriend on his picnic blanket and ruined yet another perfect moment for him. On top of which, yesterday, he found me half-dressed with Jamie Hirst in the house...Also, my son has abandoned me to live with his "cool" dad in another country. I was a shitty step daughter and daughter and actually, I think I resent my mum because she died on me and oh yeah, I'm about 5 minutes from cheating on yet another boyfriend with the leader of the bloody pack... Apart from all that, I'm just peachy!"

Siobhan leaves with the kittens. Mel cries for about the 5th time that day after they leave. She tries to do a headcount of the other cats, thinking she could maybe at least give some of them a home, depending on Janet's goodwill. To keep her mind busy, she returns to her earlier task of emptying drawers and throwing out rubbish, finding herself forming a clearer picture of Kath as she clears out each nook and cranny. She reads all of her recipes and all the scraps she saved from newspapers, looking at her sewing projects and finding a secret booze cupboard with all sorts of random liqueurs which she puts in a box for the wake. (Somebody in Greenleigh will drink it if it's free.) She also finds a lot of things that belonged to her dad, his wallet is in a drawer with his glasses, as if he too had just popped out of the shops. Of course, it must've broken Kath's heart to lose him too soon.

At his funeral, Mel had felt like a total imposter; she nearly didn't go, but Aaron told her she would regret it. He was clean by then and all about amends. Still, she felt guilty taking people's commiserations when they all knew she'd barely been back to Greenleigh in ten years. Feeling exactly like the terrible daughter she knew Greenleigh thought she was, she had slipped away from the wake, using Connor as her excuse to leave. She could never look Kath in the eye all day. This time around, she's determined to do Kath (and her Dad) proud.

Finally deciding she'll never get it all done by herself, she bribes Josh to help her finish clearing the house. She still needs to find those documents for Ken, so every room needs to be thoroughly combed. There's so much legwork that she sleeps like a log on her air bed every night, surrounded by the animals.

The skip turns up, and she soon decides she needs another one. The chicken man arrives in his van, pops them all into crates, and leaves without fuss. Mel waves them goodbye until he goes out of sight, as if the chickens and ducks can see her. Chris and his dad come by, walking the donkeys slowly up the fields to their new home. He didn't ask, she just catches sight of them out of her old bedroom window, but she is incredibly grateful and is determined to give them some money from the house sale to pay for their care.

It does make for a lot fewer animals for her to round up at bedtime. Her cat count is at 5, possibly 6. She has a plan to guilt all Kath's friends into adopting one in her memory. There is still so much to get done, though, but the joy of not having any phone signal is that she can ignore Andrew and Jamie and everything else that gives her a headache until she chooses.

After weighing the pros and cons, she finally decides that Andrew should attend the funeral; he's the ultimate security barrier between her and Jamie. For once, she wants to leave town without his tail between her legs. All she has to do is keep Andrew away from Chris, which should be doable. Proud of herself, she manages to pick up her car from Jamie with minimal flirting, well, as minimal as any interaction with Jamie can be. It feels dull to drive after the thrill of bouncing along in Kath's truck and being able to see over all the dry stone walls.

She starts making a pile of things that she is going to take back to Manchester, and it's getting bigger all the time, especially as she clears her old room out. She surprises herself by how suddenly attached she is to things from a past that she has spent the last twenty years consciously not thinking about.

It's Josh who mentions the attic, just when it felt like they were also making progress. Mel does not want to get rid of more stuff. She wants to pretend they've never noticed the loft hatch, but Ken is pushing her, and if they can't find specific papers, it will take much longer to get everything tied up. With a sigh, she sends Josh off to find some step ladders.

Josh is very quiet for Josh, she half wonders if he is mad with her on Chris' behalf but when she asks him what the matter is, he tells her that Lacey dumped him for Darren Clegg and that he's gutted, "I guess us Oldswick's are just unlucky in love," he says with a shrug, climbing up the loft ladder,

"What about Chris and Marlowe? They seem happy. "She asks, climbing up behind him,

"Where've you been, Bells? Didn't you hear about the proposal row?"

"I haven't been to Nelson's for a few days," Mel retorts as Josh pulls her up in the attic, dust swirling with every step along the boards. To her dismay,there are more piles of boxes lined up under the eaves.

"Well, after you ruined his proposal by having sex on his picnic blanket…" Mel starts to deny it, again, but knowing it's futile, she lets him continue, pulling the yellowing tape off the boxes to explore their contents.

"Chris decided to postpone the event and not say anything to her so he could plan another surprise but then Marlowe went to the shop and Mr. Nelson told her he was sorry to hear about you ruining the proposal, so then Marlowe told Chris what she'd heard and said that she was glad that you'd ruined it because if they were going to get engaged, they needed to plan it properly, make it special and she would make sure someone was there taking photos for her social media. Chris was hurt. I mean, I put up all those bloody fairy lights after he decided to do it, at the last minute. I thought it was romantic, especially with the fireworks an' all. I wish I'd thought I'd take Lacey up there for a quickie before you got in there, Mels. She might not have buggered off with dickhead Dean! Anyway, I think that's when the penny finally dropped for both of them, that they didn't have a future. We all know he only proposed to her to get back at you, anyway, well, except Chris. He's pretty gutted, but the rest of us are glad to see the back of her."

Mel doesn't want to be happy that Chris is unhappy, but she is also really pleased to see the back of Marlowe.

"What is all this stuff? Honestly, Kath could've been on that hoarders TV show, this stuff looks like it's been here for years." He pulls out some old clothes and trinkets randomly stuffed into a box. It takes a minute to filter, but as Josh pulls out more and more bits, she suddenly recalls a memory of that very trinket sitting on her Mum's mantlepiece. She opens the next box, then the next, to find books from their old house, her Mum's records and a host of other things that stir her memory as she turns them over in her hand. Her Dad must have kept it all, after she accused him over and over of not caring. Had she just conveniently forgotten?

It takes them a very dusty two hours to get everything down. Straight away, her Mum's things go into her 'Keeping it' pile. When they are done for the day, both too knackered to go on, she asks him if he'll wait while she has a shower. Even though they've cleared out a lot of stuff, the bathroom still terrifies her, especially in the dark. When she comes backdown in clean clothes with a towel on her head, he's slumped on the fireside chair, Milly on his knee, looking sorry for himself while he rolls a joint, "It's a shame you can't stay here Mels, I'll miss you and not just for your quality drugs. Can't Andrew help you out to keep the place? He looks rich? C'mon, we could be neighbours again just like old times. I could kick your arse again at Super

Mario!"

Mel collapses in the other chair, exhausted but exhilarated by finding her Mum's things; she thought there was nothing of her left except the one faded photo she'd allowed herself to take to Ibiza. She relaxes for the first time in days,

"Between you and me, Josh, if you'd have asked me a week ago, I would have said never in a million years, but now…" She shrugs," Somehow I'd forgotten how beautiful Greenleigh is and how nice it is to be reminded of my folks and to see old friends, you guys… Being here makes me feel close to them, which I never knew I needed. I always thought I hated it here, hated this house, but maybe I just hated what happened. Now, when I get up in the morning, I look out the window at the view! I love the peace and quiet But you've seen the state of the place, Josh! I can't afford to give Connor his share and do it up; everything needs fixing. I don't earn enough money to get a decent mortgage. I wish there were some way to hold on to it; I don't want a developer to buy it and knock it down, but Manchester is home now. Or is it? What does home even mean?"

Since Connor left, she isn't even sure what a home might look like on her own, which is perhaps why she's dragging her heels over leaving Janet's. Maybe she should consider moving in with Andrew, but would she be using him to fill a void? Deep down, she isn't sure he isn't using her to fill a void, either. She shuts her eyes, confused.

"Home is where your heart is. "Josh is wasted and only capable of cliches. "There's no place like home, No, no, it's wherever you lay your hat. Mel, look, yours is there." He points at her woolly hat dangling off the chair,

"Holme end is your end, home Mel, you've just forgotten where you belong."

CHAPTER ELEVEN

After a few grey days, the day of Kath's funeral dawns brightly. You still need your winter coat on, sometimes until May, but at least it's sunny. Mel rolls off the airbed at 5 am. She wants the day to be perfect, and there is still a lot to do. Yesterday, she finally tackled Kath's bedroom, asking Josh to leave her to do it alone. It felt too personal for just anyone to be emptying the drawers. She found that her Dad's things were all still in the wardrobe and she spent the day in tears, imagining how painful it must be to clear out the belongings of someone you love as if they had never existed. Regret is a tough emotion; you can't change the past, no matter how much you wish. Mel wished it badly. Since she'd found that painting of her Mum and all her Mum's things in the attic, she was thinking about him in a different light. It was breaking her heart that it was too late to tell him how wrong she'd been and how much she regretted her behaviour.

She found all Kath's paintings in boxes in her wardrobe. Mel planned to hang as many as she could at the wake so that people could choose one to take home and remember her by. She kept one for herself, of the house on a snowy winter's day, maybe in that crazy snowstorm that kept them housebound that time, Kath had captured the cosy glow from the windows in contrast to the white hills and grey skies. She desperately hopes that someone will buy the farmhouse and restore it to its former glory. She can't stop builders from bidding on it and knocking it down, but really, it deserves to be resurrected. Now that it's almost clutter-free, you can see how much potential it has to be a happy home again.

She feeds the cats, now down to just three after some

emotional blackmail around the village. Surprisingly, Mr. Nelson took one, renamed it Fluffy, and, by all accounts, is feeding her fresh salmon. As Mel still doesn't know where she'll be living, she had to decide that it would be unfair to consider keeping any of them, despite how attached she's become.

As each one went off to its new home, she felt like running down the road after them, saying she'd changed her mind. She had cried again when the sheep trundled off with Bob yesterday.

After that conversation with Josh about what home means, she's been pondering all sorts of plans, even having a vague fantasy about perhaps moving to Ibiza herself. In her heart, she knows it's unrealistic, but after this week, she craves family, and Connor is all she has. Being away from him still feels like a part of her is missing, but she isn't naive enough to think he feels the same way. Pretty sure, now that he's glimpsed his freedom, that he won't want to live with her again, as it should be. It seems like he's having the best time with Aaron. Going out there would be trying to dovetail her life to his after he's happily flown the nest.

She feels completely clueless about her future. Ironically, now that she has choices, she doesn't know what to do with them.

She loads all the artwork into her car. Jamie's offered to buy the truck, and although she loves driving it, she can't justify keeping it, so she agrees, knowing it will be taken care of. She doesn't accept or decline his offer to christen the back of it.

Mrs. Oldswick is setting things up in the barn, all the tables laid out with beautiful winter floral arrangements and candles. You can see where Chris gets his eye from. They've transformed the barn into a gorgeous venue, rustic but so stylish. A wedding there would be gorgeous, especially on a summer's day when the big doors would be flung open and you could see the views right down the valley to the distant purple moors. Josh has told her all about how they host them; they put up a huge bell tent in the field with hay bales for people to sit on, light a roaring fire pit at night, and bands play on the back of the flatbed trailer with thousands of fairy light strung from poles around the field. Dreamily, she starts to see herself as a blushing bride walking up the meadow in a vintage dress, clasping a wildflower bouquet. Just as she turns to see who her dashing groom is, Mrs. Oldswick shouts to fetch some boxes, bringing Mel back to earth.

Less four weddings, more funeral.

Together, they arrange a table of all the old photos, propping up the paintings along the walls so people can browse. Mel puts labels on them so people can write their names on the ones they want. She puts a tin out for donations for the animal charities Kath supported, and a hand-drawn poster asking for homes for the rest of the cats. She dumps the sticky collection of alcohol on the end of the drinks table, knowing full well even the sickly looking bottle of Midori will be empty by the end of the day.

The goat man is coming to the funeral with his trailer and taking the goats back with him. Mel said goodbye and good luck to each of them all this morning when she let them out, tearily, for the last time. She hopes Kath would approve of all the rehoming.Siobhan sent her pictures of the Kardashian kittens, sleeping in a giant pink fluffy bed surrounded by cat toys.They are finally getting the 5-star lifestyle their names dictate.

She has to be at the church by 11 to receive the funeral flowers, but she wants to arrive early with flowers of her own, well aware that she's been procrastinating about going up there since she got back. She has never seen her Dad's memorial plaque. In a last-minute panic, when she remembers that she didn't bring anything smart to wear and has no time to get into town, she finds, amongst her Mum's things, a black dress with folky flowers embroidered on it. It smells a bit musty, but she tries it on anyway. She never thought that she looked like her Mum because she could never quite remember what she looked like when she wasn't sick, but in the mirror, in her dress, she could see the resemblance. An old memory surfaces, her Mum spinning in this dress, making the skirt fly out. She twirls around in front of the mirror until she gets giddy, trying to hold onto the memory. She unleashes half a bottle of Febreze on it and hangs it out to air, hoping no one will notice its vintage smell.

The Church has stood on the hill at the top end of the village for over 200 years. The smooth flagstones of the path worn in the middle from all the services and ceremonies that Greenleigh has ever witnessed. Her Mum and Dad were married there, and she'd found the photos in a photo album from the attic. They were standing outside the church, her Mum in a lacy wedding dress and her dad in his big-collar suit; they both looked so young. As she walks up the wonky path today, lined with trees on either side, she imagines them coming down it, confetti swirling. Her heart clenches.

She fully expects to find her Mum's grave overgrown after all this time, but stepping round to it, she's surprised to see it well tended. There are even some recently dead flowers in the little vase. Taking them out, she puts fresh ones in, squatting down and placing her hands on the headstone as she used to do, as if by touching it, she is somehow touching her. She shows her the dress and whispers how sorry she is that she hasn't been to visit for such a long time. She blurts out how confused she feels about her future and wishes she could stay in Greenleigh to be closer to her memories. That it sounds crazy, but being here has almost made them all come alive again because everyone here knows them and she can talk about the past, " I didn't know how much I needed that, " she tells her, "I never knew it before, but this is my home. I wish I could stay at Kath's, start over, do right by her and her Dad by keeping it going as it was, be part of the community again." She sighs, surprising herself by how much she means it all. She promises to return soon and bring Connor to see her, "You won't believe the size of him."

So caught up in her emotions, she doesn't notice Chris under the Yew tree where he always used to wait for her. He and Josh are here to help carry the coffin. He listens to her quietly, blinking away his tears as she spills out her secrets.

Aware that the florist will be arriving shortly, Mel traces her fingers along the engraving of her Mum's name, Marie Elizabeth McCarthy, remembering that despite their separation, they never divorced. On Kath's wishes, her Dad was cremated, and a plaque was put up along the side wall of the church. She sees the same bunch of dead flowers sitting in the vase when she finds it. Kath must have taken flowers to both of them when she came here. Remorse courses through her veins. She tells her Dad how sorry she is for everything and how grateful she is that they kept all her mum's things for her to find." I hope you and Kath are back together again," she tells him, trying to stay composed. It's going to be a hard enough day without breaking down yet, but Mel is feeling all the big emotions already.

She waits outside the church door, not ready to greet all the long-familiar faces but knowing somehow that it's a part of her reckoning. Siobhan stands with her until Andrew arrives, immaculate as ever in a sharp black suit. He takes his place next to her, and, of course, he is brilliant at saying the right things to people, as if he were an old, dear friend of Kath's himself.

Out of the corner of her eye she sees Jamie sauntering up

the path, she's never seen him wearing a suit before and well, it's quite a sight, so much so she finds herself stopping mid sentence in conversation with Mrs. Armitage, her old teacher, unable to remember what she was about to say,"I errr, yes, sorry, err," She hears herself stutter. Why does he still have such an effect on her? She doesn't know how he does it, but even the nonchalant angle of his black tie makes her feel a bit flushed. The man could probably wear a bin bag and still look attractive. It was all in that confident swagger and the naughty look that permanently resides in his big brown eyes. She links arms firmly with Andrew to keep herself grounded. Still, Jamie leans in to kiss her on the cheek anyway, warm inviting lips on her wind chilled cheek, they linger there a fraction too long causing Andrew to narrow his eyes, "I'm sorry about Kath, truly Mac, "Jamie murmurs before shaking hands with Andrew vigorously, his eyes flashing at hers as he turns away with a swish of that hair.

Mel steadies herself on the old oak door post with an audible sigh. This is going to be a long day. Behind him, she sees Lindsey Mellor and her new husband. It may have been a funeral, but she's pretty sure that Lindsey Mellor only looks upset because she just clocked Jamie's lengthy kiss. Mel says hello, but Lindsey hurries into the church without stopping. Pat Harper introduces himself, confirming he'll collect the goats after the wake. Mr. Nelson plods up and starts quizzing Andrew so that he can share the lowdown with the whole village later. Mel keeps a tight ear on the conversation, ready to jump in if she hears anything Andrew doesn't need to know. She's already starting to sweat; there are a lot of moving pieces.

She chose a wicker coffin; she thought Kath would appreciate the environmentally friendly aspect. The church is full of seasonal holly and Ivy, so she had the same arrangements for Kath's flowers. It looks beautiful inside with all the white candles lit, and everyone remarks on it throughout the day. She hopes that she has made Kath and her Dad proud. It's hard not to recall herself at her Dad's funeral here, 10 years ago, skulking at the back out of everyone's way, then at her Mum's before that, where everyone was so full of pity for her she felt like she would burst.

If it hadn't been for Chris' steady influence and the Oldswicks' support, she might have turned tail and bolted, as if she wasn't there, it wasn't happening. She looks over to the Oldswicks with a heartfelt gratitude. Sheila gives her a supportive nod. Yet again, they have been so good to her that she feels a terrible pang of guilt for leaving them behind without a second glance all those years ago; they felt like family then, and they do again now.

In true Greenleigh style, the whole village has turned out to send Kath off. Although she's pleased for Kath, Mel isn't immune to the looks and mutters that she overhears as people gather outside the church. After a few loud comments, her face begins to burn: "Never visited." "Where was she when Kath needed her?"

They all fall to a hush, however, as the undertakers and the boys carry the beautiful coffin up the path. Seeing Chris and Josh undertake the task with such dignity is so moving that Mel has to bite her lip to keep the tears at bay; she can't break down yet. The silence is short lived however, once they step inside Caz Mellor remarks to her partner, "And to think poor Chris saw her shagging Jamie Hirst on the pool table," Mel sees the back of Chris's neck flush the same colour as her cheeks.

Mel is relieved when the vicar comes out to gather the last stragglers, and the attention shifts from her. She is burning with rage over Caz's comment. Greenleigh should have a plaque for the village with the longest memory next to the bloody Britain in Bloom award. She squeezes into a pew next to

Andrew, moving up for Josh as they step away from the coffin, but he plonks himself in the row behind next to his parents, leaving Chris to sit next to her, a move she's pretty sure Josh instigated on purpose.

She is aware of the village's burning eyes on the back of her head as Chris hovers awkwardly. She inches up as far as she can without sitting on Andrew's knee. He sits down, but despite his best efforts to press into the pew arm, they are closer than they've been for years. Chris looks straight ahead, shifting his tie. He wears a suit awkwardly, but he seems like a man in it, not the 18-year-old boy she left behind. The boy who had been her best friend, yet she'd let him down in the worst way.

Mel's heart, already way above resting rate, starts to pound in her chest. She feels terrible that she's come back into his life and messed it up all over again. He has every right to hate her, which will be for the best when she leaves. She wonders if he will return with Marlowe, twitching involuntarily as the thought makes her cross. Chris turns his head, holds her gaze for the first time since he got there, and his grey eyes are as warm as they used to be, well, before.

"That's your Mum's dress, isn't it? I remember it. She'd be proud of you, you know Mel." He whispers.

Mel has to look away as a lump forms in her chest; it isn't even true, given the way she's behaved since she got back. God, she thinks, Chris is a good person. Too good to still be the butt of the joke after all these years. It wasn't fair on him then, and it isn't fair on him now. She must find a way to make this situation right somehow. As the vicar reads a psalm, she zones out, wondering how on earth she can make it up to him.

Chris gets up and gives a beautiful speech about Kath's love of animals, which brings even the toughest hearts in Greenleigh to tears. As people reach for their tissues and mop their mascara, Mel stares at him, he's shaved, tamed his hair and despite being more at home in his scruffs with his hands dirty, busy making something, he stands up there talking confidently, not at all afraid to be emotional, she sees him for the first time as a man, instead of the boy she knew.

What an incredible person he's grown up to be, she thinks, going all the way from his beloved Yorkshire to Australia to save the farm he loves for future generations of Oldswick's, supporting his parents, building those beautiful cabins by hand. He had been a sweet boy, whom she didn't appreciate at the time, and now he's grown up to be a good man. Mel reaches for her tissues too.

Now it's her turn to speak, she's chosen a poem she found in one of her dad's books and just about manages to make it through without stumbling, keeping her eyes firmly fixed on the paper. It isn't until she looks up at the whole village with their eyes fixed on her that she knows what she needs to say next. She starts hesitantly, "I know exactly what you're all thinking about me right now…" She begins without much of a plan. There is a collective intake of breath, people sit up straight in their seats, and the Vicar, expecting more meaningful words, looks on anxiously. Mel fixes her eyes on the stone arch over the front door. It's now or never,

"You're all thinking, what right have I got to stand here and talk about Kath and take your commiserations when I was a terrible stepdaughter to her. I never came to visit her after my dad died or before either, and I barely even called, so you have every right to judge me on it, but I've spent the last 10 days up at the farm, living in Kath's shoes, and I've learned a lot of things about Kath. She did love her animals, I mean it takes dedication to get up every day and feed 40 odd mouths and care for them, hats off to you Kath," The Vicar starts shuffling, indicating to her to wrap it up, but she's just getting warmed up,

"And she loved my dad so much, I don't think she threw anything of his away because she didn't want to let him go. I don't think she picked up a paintbrush after he died because she was too heartbroken."

The vicar coughs, "I'm sorry that I wasn't there to help, Kath and that I didn't do better by you."

The Vicar steps forward to guide her out of the spotlight, but there is one last thing she knows she has to say while everyone's attention is on her. Taking a deep breath and trying to stop her hands from shaking,

"There's one more thing, while everyone's listening. I know that most people in this village know the story about me and Jamie, Jamie Hirst, that is...He's over there folks, on the back row," Jamie shifts in his pew as the whole congregation swivels to look at him, he waves back at them slowly, giving her a bemused smile, she shrugs at him, She can't look at Chris, Andrew or Siobhan, all of whom she knows are making frantic 'Shut up' eyes at her,

"And if you're one of the lucky few who haven't heard it, don't worry because I'm going to tell it to you now."

There is an excited murmur from the crowd. Out of the corner of her eye, she sees Chris stand up, but Josh pushes him back down. Andrew looks mortified; he's not even heard anything yet, but this is her last chance, and she's taking it.

"Most of you remember that Marie, my mum, died of cancer when I was sixteen. I handled it badly. I didn't give my dad and Kath a chance as my new family, and as you all know, I behaved badly towards my then-boyfriend, Chris, Oldswick." Chris is not happy as the whole church cranes toward him. Josh keeps his hand on his shoulder to stop him from bolting.

She remembers a bit late that it's news to Andrew that Chris is her childhood sweetheart, let alone wondering what part the annoyingly attractive Jamie Hirst, whose name keeps on coming up, is about to play in the story. The frown deepens on his already unhappy face. Josh is laughing though, he gives her a thumbs up, the Vicar looks stricken,

"I didn't give Chris a chance to help me through my grief, and he tried so, *so* hard; he was amazing, every step of the way, but as some of you will remember, I started drinking to cope. Where are you, Bill the bartender?"

She scans the crowd, he puts his hand up slowly, "Bill will tell you that I was drinking a fair bit at that time... "

Bill acquiesces with a shrug, "Now, the night of the *incident,* it was happy hour and I was making the most of it when I happened to cross paths with Jamie, who was playing pool in the backroom at The 'Horse. As we're telling the whole truth today, I'll be honest with you, I knew Jamie and I did have a bit of a crush on him, I mean, look at him, what woman in the village doesn't if they're honest ?" Everyone swivels back to Jamie, who flashes his best smile. There is a low murmur of agreement from the women in the congregation. Jamie shrugs.

"That doesn't make it right, however, what happened next? Now I know that the story *you know* has Jamie and me having sex on the actual pool table and Chris walking in and seeing us." There is a loud gasp. Could you even say sex in a church? The Vicar stands up, then sits back down again as Mel carries on, clearly not to be stopped now she is on a roll, "But although Jamie and I were admittedly…kissing…enthusiastically. (She cringes.) We kept all our clothes on. It was dead dark in there, and I think from the angle, I can imagine it looked really...bad...Anyway, in a split second Chris saw what he thought he saw, then he went back through to the bar and when Bill here saw his face and asked him what was wrong, Chris told the whole bar what he thought he saw, then he left, after which, you Bill and errr Johnny Jackson? Are you here?" Johnny half stands up,

"Right, good, stand up please..." Awkwardly, they get up,

"Now you all also know that I tried to deny what happened, but Jamie? Help me out here... "

Jamie gets up, and the whole church spins back around. "Look, I know that you all know that I've been a bit of a womaniser over the years." Several women jeer, Lindsey shouts, "Don't I bloody know it!"

"But I swear on my son's life we were not having sex, *that night*, on the pool table."

Mel could've killed him and kissed him, she carries on, "But nobody would believe me because, as well as everyone in the pub hearing Chris' announcement and spreading the rumour, there were 'witnesses' who claimed it was true... That may have made a better story, but it isn't true, is it, Bill?"

Sheepishly, he shakes his head, "Did you see us?"

Johnny says,"Jamie came into the bar, fully dressed, and it was only seconds after Chris left. I'm sorry for going along with the story all this time, we didn't think."

Mel goes in for her closing argument, "I rest my case! I just want Chris and *everyone* to know the truth once and for all before I leave. I know it's no excuse, but I was young and I was hurting. I know I still cheated on you Chris and I'm really, really sorry for that, but I never would've, with him,while we were together, but I was still a selfish, drunken idiot, and you didn't deserve it, so I hope finally hearing the truth makes it a bit better."

She trails off after looking at Chris, who looks anything but forgiving right now.

"So errr, rest in peace Kath, I hope you and dad are reunited, you know, up there." She slides away, her face burning, to hide behind the nearest pillar whilst the church erupts around her. She can't bring herself to come out for the end of the service, not quite believing she just hijacked a funeral to tell a sex story. For sure, she is going to hell for this.

She stays hidden until the scuffles and sounds of the congregation leaving have stopped, mostly feeling truly terrible but also relieved that the truth is finally out in the open. She glimpses Chris hightail it out the door without looking back. Jamie appears next to her,

"Nice eulogy, Mac!"

"Oh, it wasn't too much, you think?"Mel is spinning out,

"Not at all, you got the word sex in just enough to excite the crowd and to give the Vicar palpitations, Kath would have heartily approved." She can't stop herself from putting her head on his shoulder, "Thank you for backing me up, I know it dented your reputation as our resident sex god."

Jamie laughs," I'll let you off as it was for a good cause, not that Oldswick seems too happy, but then it has been a pretty rough week for him… It's not like we didn't have sex in plenty of other places," he ruffles her hair fondly.

Andrew coughs from behind them, completely blanking Jamie. He tells Mel coldly that it's time to leave. Jamie peels away, sensing the simmering tension.

They don't speak as they walk up to the car park. Mel doesn't know where to begin, so she chooses silence instead, which seems fine by Andrew. As they drive up the lane to the wake, Mel stares out the window. The clear day means that you can see for miles. It looks like a toy farm out there, with the dry stone walls dividing the patchwork of green fields. A kestrel swoops high on the thermals, cows and sheep dot the land. A tractor chugs its way down the lane. With a sinking heart, she knows just how much she is going to miss being here. The countryside resides like an ancient being. The wild still permitted in this ever-increasing world of buildings, technology and traffic. Even though Manchester is only over the Moors, it feels like a million miles away, and somehow, the moors viewed from the other side look ominously out of place.

Eventually, she blurts out, "I'm sorry, Andrew, I should've maybe, clearly, given you a heads up on a few things…"

"Oh, you think Melanie? How about the fact that you never once mentioned that you and Chris were childhood sweethearts, or that you cheated on him so casually, or maybe that you're still clearly in love with that guy, Jamie Hirst?" he spits out his name,

"God no, Andrew. I'm not in love with Jamie, believe me." It wasn't love; she knew that much.

"Well, you were pretty cosy back there in the church, and that was a very lingering kiss on your cheek earlier," he snorts,

"Jamie's the only person who's not mad at me or judging me

today, Andrew, that's all, and I needed his moral support, surely you can see that?"

"I don't think either of you can talk about morals, Melanie," he snipes back.

They get out of the car in awkward silence. The wake is already in full swing by the time they get to Holme End. There's a palpable hush as Mel walks in the door, but she fronts it out and goes over to the table where they laid out all the photographs. She keeps herself busy by rearranging them all, even though she's the one who put them like that in the first place. Andrew goes to get her a drink, a stiff one she directs, though currently he looks like the stiffest thing in the room.

She looks furtively around for Chris but can't see him anywhere. Bill has bought a keg from the pub, and the pints are already flowing. Mrs. Oldswick wanders about, making sure everyone has a drink. Groups gather around the paintings. Mel is pleased to see that people are claiming them. People come and look at the photos, but most of them just smile politely at her and move quickly along. Andrew hovers at her shoulder, glowering at Jamie, who is sitting with the darts team, right by the Keg, already on their merry way.

Ken Braithwaite comes over, and she admits to him that there are still some boxes that she needs to sort through. She promises she won't leave without letting him know what she finds, or doesn't. He promises to make sure everything is in ship shape for the sale. Not one person mentions her speech, to her face at least, but she knows everyone is discussing it in snatched whispers. She looks up to see someone bringing out food trays, excusing herself from sulky Andrew, and leaving him safely seated with the WI. She goes to offer her help. Crossing the cobbled yard, she slips into the farmhouse. Mrs Oldswick and Josh are in the kitchen, Mel hovers by the door, nervous for Chris's appearance.

"Nice one, Mel, that'll go down in history as the best funeral Greenleigh has ever seen!" Josh laughs, "I thought the Rev was going to have a heart attack when you said the S word...Gutted that the urban myth's busted after all these years though, very disappointing, Mel. Next, you'll be denying that the picnic blanket incident ever happened! At least Chris can finally stop squabbling with Jamie and join the darts team."

"Josh! Get on and take these through!" Mrs. Oldswick intervenes, loading him up with a large food platter.

"Can I do anything to help? "Mel asks. Sheila has competently organised all the catering and won't take any money for it, although Mel fully intends to leave payment in a thank you card after she's gone.

From behind her, Chris says brusquely, "We're good!" She steps out of his way. Brushing abruptly past, he bangs his tray down and goes to take something out of the oven, turning his back on her. Mrs. O shakes her head at Mel, mouthing good luck, hustling Josh out the door with her. Josh gives her a grimace as they shut the door behind them. Chris freezes for a minute, then turns around, his eyebrows drawn. Mel holds her breath; she's been the cause of his fury too many times, and she knows all the signs. She should sit down in a chair and brace herself, but she also dared not move from the spot.

"Just when I think you can't get any more selfish, Mel! Somehow, you always manage to raise the bar...Well done for turning Kath's funeral into a joke, it's like you can't help yourself, ruining things, you haven't changed one bit!" He pulls the hot tray out of the oven with his bare hands and doesn't even flinch.

She takes a deep breath, "That was never my intention, Chris, honestly, but do you know what else is not funny? Being blamed for something you *never* did for 20-odd years and still being judged for it by the whole village,"

"And you thought the right time to address that old stain on your character was at a funeral service?" he asks, incredulous,

"I didn't do it for me, Chris...You don't deserve to relive the humiliation again and again. I wanted you to know the truth finally. You and Mr. Nelson obviously, so he can tell anyone who might have missed it," She tries to lighten him up, an old tactic.

A brief smile crosses his face, but he shuts it down quickly, leaning back against the kitchen counter, looking at her. Are they finally having the conversation they should have had all those years ago? Back then, he froze her out, refusing all her attempts to explain and making it clear they were through, so she ran around with Jamie instead, living up to her reputation. Then, she left for Ibiza without saying goodbye to anyone, choosing not to pack her past life with her flip-flops.

Rubbing his face, he studies her, "Honestly, Mel, do you think it even really mattered whether you were having sex with him that night or not? It wasn't ever about sex, for me, I just, I loved you, and you just kept throwing it back in my face. Seeing you with Jamie, that was just the final straw."

He rearranges the platter while Mel soaks up the sentiment, searching for something to say that isn't sorry, again.

"Look, I know that perhaps I shouldn't have said all that at the church. I saw an opportunity to set things straight, and I took it. You have to believe me that my intentions were only good, Chris. Me being back and bringing it all up again, then after what Caz said. I just wanted you to be free of that stupid story for good and to hear the truth. I'm sorry for what I did, how I treated you, truly, I meant what I said, you were amazing to me when mum was sick and when she died. I wouldn't have survived without you, Chris. It wasn't that I didn't love you. I just didn't want love, then, it hurt too much, I wanted escapism."Mel's voice breaks, she stops talking, embarrassed at the outpouring, tears cloud her vision.

Chris pauses, thinking over what she said. He picks up the heavy platter, "Well, you've certainly given everyone something else to remember," he murmurs, not looking at her.

Mel picks up a plate of sausage rolls," I just want this afternoon to be perfect, you've done such a fantastic job, making it look so beautiful, the food and everything. I want to do right by Kath. I do, so can we call a truce, for today at least? I'll be out of your hair soon enough," the words catch in her throat," And then you never have to think about me again for the rest of your life."

She isn't sure, but does she hear Chris say, "I wish, " as he disappears out the door?

She'll be leaving Greenleigh in the next few days. She doesn't want to go, but she has run out of reasons to stay any longer. She's managed to rehome the remaining cats. After today, all the farm animals will be gone, and the house is empty. She can't leave Janet in the lurch much longer. Looking wistfully around her at all the familiar faces, Mel basks in how warm it is to be part of a community and to understand what home means, even if it is just for a fleeting moment.

The volume rises exponentially as the beer flows freely, the food table is bustling, and everyone is having a good time. There are shouts of laughter from the photograph table where people are spotting each other in the old photos. Despite all the hard work involved in sorting it out, Mel feels grateful that Kath kept so much of the past, allowing everyone to enjoy the memories. She hopes that this part of the day will be the bit everyone remembers, but then again, Greenleigh never forgets anything, does it?

Chris circulates, swapping stories, a charming host, Mel watches him move about the room but stays deliberately well out of his way (and Jamie's), helping where needed. She keeps Andrew safely in a corner with Kath's friends from the W.I, who are captivated by Andrew's travel tales. He is still frosty with her, but he has good manners enough to put on a convincing show. Jamie keeps catching her eye with an amused smirk, and Mel fights hard to keep her gaze from straying toward him. He's taken off his jacket, tied up his hair, and his tie hangs loosely over his broad chest, straining at his shirt. She looks hurriedly away.

Eventually, Chris gets around to their table. Mel hopes that he has mellowed out after their conversation. He shakes Andrew's hand, making polite chit chat with everyone, even including her in the conversation. It might have been just a goodwill gesture, but it was very welcome. As he moves off, she sits back relieved, bullets dodged. The W.I ladies start to tell her about some knitting challenge they've been doing, Andrew gets up to go to the buffet table,

"Marlowe couldn't make it?" Andrew asks Chris, making polite conversation as they move off across the barn together,

"We err, we broke up actually,"

"I'm sorry to hear that," Andrew commiserates,

"It's probably for the best…I guess I have to thank you, weirdly, for stopping me from making a stupid mistake."

"Oh, what do you mean?" Andrew replies, confused. Mel tries to extract herself from the table, but she isn't quick enough. Andrew shakes his head. Chris continues,

"With Marlowe? If you and Mel hadn't shown up on New Year's Eve," he sighs, "The picnic you gatecrashed?"

"Mel's picnic?" Andrew is confused,

"No... I set it up to propose to Marlowe. Mel didn't tell you?" His question hangs in the air as both men digest the situation, Mel scrambles to them, physically inserting herself between them both, not knowing who to salve first,

"I can explain," she begins, turning to them both in turn, Andrew cuts her off,

"No explanation necessary, it's pretty crystal clear, Melanie. You told me you'd organised all that to make up for missing Paris, but that was a complete lie? " he holds his hands up in disbelief.

Chris's thaw refreezes, quickly, " Mel told you what?" his voice rises,people start to stare, the W. I are agog. Mel bites her lip, there is no ideal way to spin this, "He just assumed all that when we got there and yeah, ok, I didn't deny it but I just, I felt so guilty about being AWOL all afternoon and having to cancel our trip to Paris and then with everything I had to do, I didn't get time to think about how we'd celebrate... I couldn't take him to the pub with Jamie *and* the pool table there!" Heads swivel back to Jamie, who, on hearing his name, looks over to the furious glares of both Andrew and Chris, raising his glass, bemused. Why on earth did she bring Jamie up again? Is Chris right? Can't she help herself from making everything worse?

She blusters on regardless, "You just seemed so pleased that I'd made such an effort, Andrew… I, I didn't think it would hurt. I was going to tell you," she trails off.

Andrew turns, picks up his jacket and makes for the door. The whole room is looking their way," It's time I got going, I've got work tomorrow," he says for the polite benefit of his audience,

"Don't go!" Mel puts her hand on his arm, but he side steps. Chris also backs away, "Chris, I, please, I should have told him the truth, I know. I'm sorry,"

"You're always sorry, Mel, afterwards!" he retorts furiously before stalking away. There is a sympathetic murmur of support from the crowd. Mel wishes to curl up and die, again.She trails Andrew out the door, the whole room pivots again, "Andrew, I know it looks bad, I just wanted to make you happy, I felt guilty about Paris and, "

"Let's just be honest, for once, I don't think we were ever really suited, were we? So, I think let's just call it a day, and what a day it's been. Goodbye, Melanie." He walks off into the night without looking back. Mel hesitates, should she go after him? To be honest, he's probably better off without her as well; she can't seem to stop herself from making a mess of everything.

When she goes back inside, the room falls silent. She picks up a wine glass. It isn't hers; there is nothing left for today but to get drunk.

CHAPTER TWELVE

She finds solace with the Darts team, but seats herself as far away from Jamie, as much as possible, although she knows his eye is firmly on her. He could never resist a troublemaker, and Mel has been on her A game today. They mix up shots from Kath's left over liqueurs and the lads make up names for them. Mel spits out her 'Nelson's Column', she's laughing so much. She isn't going to stop drinking until she's forgotten all the hideous events of the day. Her game plan is simply to ignore everyone else, well aware of what everyone must be thinking of her. Chris is blanking her anyway, so that makes it easier.

The wake starts to wind down, the goat man takes his leave and the goats. All of Kath's lovely paintings go off to new homes. Mrs. Oldswick pops all the old photos in the bulging condolences book. Mel keeps a few photographs of her dad and Kath, then hands them over to the W.I. It seems right that they stay in Greenleigh.

Siobhan sits with her for a while after Andrew leaves, a much-appreciated show of moral support. She tells Mel what everyone is saying about the funeral takeover. Mel is relieved to hear that most people seem to understand, and if they didn't, they were just glad of another anecdote for the village annals. Certainly, Melanie McCarthy will never be forgotten in Greenleigh. Siobhan has to pick up the girls, but hugs her for ages and makes her promise not to lose touch this time, saying that she must come back to see the kittens. Mel thinks they will be grown cats by the time she has the nerve to ever show her face around here again.

Someone suggests the pub, Sheila won't hear of her slurred

offer of help, and she knows Chris doesn't want her around anyway. He's stayed out of her way all afternoon, so she is easily cajoled by Josh, Jamie and the darts boys to come with them down to the 'Horse. Feeling like she can finally hold her head up in the pub, she agrees, though she needs to pop in and let the dogs out.

As the three of them trundle down the dark lane to the house, Josh and Jamie tell her all the funny things she's missed over the years, both begging her to reconsider leaving. Mel wonders once again if she is doing the right thing by going back to Manchester. Not that she can afford to stay in this area, which, ever since it featured in a Sunday magazine, means the locals are struggling to buy homes in the vicinity. Gentrification is haunting all her choices. But she can see now that cutting herself off from her past for all those years has led her to a pretty lonely life. She had absorbed herself in Connor, and now that he's got his own life, she doesn't know what to do with hers.

She lets the dogs out, planning to tell Chris that he could keep them today, if he still wanted. He's right, they would hate being in the city, but in all the chaos, she forgot, they might help smooth things over with him tomorrow before she leaves. God, she'll miss them and everyone.

The White Horse is the pub that time forgot. As she walks in, off the top of her head, not one thing seems to have changed since she was last here, twenty years ago. She doesn't think she's seen a horse brass or those lamp shades with the vintage hunting scenes on them anywhere since, but the fug of nostalgia and Limoncello makes them the most welcome sights she's seen. Bob cranks up the jukebox, still full of the same classics they used to play. Mel jostles with Josh to be the resident DJ. They drunkenly dance around the bar, belting out the same old songs from back in the day. Mel lets herself forget all of the drama and just enjoys being surrounded by people who feel like family, feeling more at home than she has in years.

Just as she has to leave.

She deliberately steered wide of Jamie at the wake, but as Chris firmly declined the invitation to join them at the pub, she sits down with him at the bar and they ramble drunkenly down memory lane. They talk about all the adventures they'd had, the great bands and films they'd seen or half seen. They were mainly kissing in the dark at the Odeon,

"You were always trying to get me to go watch horror films, I never got the attraction, still don't," Jamie remembers,

Josh leans over, "Chris is the same, anything gory, I don't see the appeal. You two traumatised me for life, making me watch those films when I was far too young."

Someone says 'Pool?' Jamie takes Mel's arm and says, "Shall we do the honours?" and a cheer goes up as they all troop through to the back room. A tournament hastily arranged. Mel declines to play; honestly, she hasn't been near a pool table since that night.

As it happens when you've been drinking all day, people start to disappear randomly, one by one, off into the night, like a homing beacon suddenly goes off. You could be in the middle of a game of pool or a conversation and next thing you're walking resolutely out the door off to your bed, maybe via the chippy, which you only recall when you wake up with a squashed chip stuck to your forehead. Mel and Jamie are some of the last left standing when Jamie asks her to play a game, for old times' sake. Mel hesitates,

"If you're gonna leave me again for another twenty years, Mac, at least give me something to remember you by…"

Mel gives in with a sigh. After today, the devil already has her card marked. She tries to refrain from any suggestive leaning over the table.

Bill comes through jangling his keys hopefully, "You go, Bill, we're nearly finished, I'll lock up, I've got my keys" (Perks of being darts team captain).

Bill, having had quite the day with his confession and all, is happy for Jamie to do so. He jokingly makes them promise no funny business on the pool table (the baize is new), then he leaves them to it.

Jamie chalks his cue slowly, "Are you sure you want to go back to Manchester Mac? I mean, who we 'going to talk about when you're gone?"

Mel sits down on a stool dejectedly, "I'll send video clips…The further Adventures of Melanie McCarthy, they can show them on a projector at the community centre in the interval between Mr. Nelson's travel talks,"

"I'll be on the front row," Jamie says, potting the black and sitting down next to her, "I'll miss you being around, girl, it's been good to have you home." He pulls his sad puppy face. It still works, she thinks with a sigh,

"Stop it, Jay, I'm not dying."

"You need to curb your inappropriate references at a funeral."

"I seem to live to offend people these days," She thinks about

Chris' hurt face with a pang of guilt, then Andrew's. She drains her glass,

"I saw your boyfriend make a sharp exit earlier. I take it he was one of those people?"

"In summary, he is no longer my boyfriend."

That was a fact that Mel was trying to keep to herself, not that Andrew would ever be an insurmountable barrier to Jamie, but he did serve as the first line of defence. Jamie leans back on his bar stool surveying her, his eyes flashing, "What an interesting situation we find ourselves in..."

Mel squirms out of his gaze, she'd said it many times, Jamie was like that snake in The Jungle Book, he could stare so deeply into your soul that the next thing you knew you were naked and you swore that you'd never even taken your clothes off,

"It's like some kind of wheel of destiny thing," he drawls, "Isn't it? We've ended back here, at the pool table, only we're both old enough to know *exactly* what we're doing this time, nobody's feelings are going to get hurt and nobody is going to interrupt us," he leans in, touching her cheek then cupping her chin in his hand with a slow smile, "You haven't changed a bit Mac, you're still sexy as hell."

Please, God, she prays for strength, but her insides are swimming in a very familiar, dangerously pleasant way. It's a struggle to stay focused, one touch, and all her resolve melts like the polar ice caps. He leans his face toward hers, the soft pressure of his enquiring lips inviting her with his suggestive smile. She can't stop herself from leaning toward him; old chemistry ignites. He kisses her slowly, his hand sliding round to the back of her neck, twisting in her hair, pulling her to him, and for the first few seconds, it's as intoxicating as it always was. Jamie hasn't kissed a hundred girls and not learned the tricks of the trade. He knows exactly how to make you feel like you're the only girl in the world, even when he's leaving your bed and hopping into someone else's an hour later.

Which is precisely what he did to her for weeks, until she found out directly from the other girl, Kylie from Kirkheaton, who confronted her one night in a pub in town. Kylie thought that she could stop him from cheating on her by cutting off the source, Mel. (It transpired that her mate had seen Mel and Jamie out somewhere.) Of course, it blew back in her face when she ascertained that technically, she was the one doing the cheating, having been seeing Jamie for a month or so, to Mel's year. Mel fronted it out with the girl; poor Siobhan had to hold her back at one point, but Mel was hurt and humiliated, and it made her furious. When the girl left, she went off to find Jamie, storming round the pubs until she found him holding court in a beer garden. He didn't try to deny it, claiming he was sorry, but Mel knew that he was just sorry for getting caught, so she told him Kylie from Kirkheaton was welcome to him. She cried hysterically on Siobhan's shoulder for days, weeks, even months, until she met Aaron. (Retrospectively, just trading in one distracting bad lad for another.)

It's only now that she thinks that maybe those tears weren't even for Jamie. I mean, she thought she loved him, like you do at that age, but was it more that he was just a cure for thinking about her Mum and a stopper for her crushing grief?

Everything was so intertwined, losing her Mum, moving to her Dad's, destroying her relationship with Chris, the village turning on her, missing the Oldswicks, Jamie cheating.

She left for Ibiza so quickly after her break-up with Jamie that nothing had got resolved. Chris still wasn't speaking to her, avoiding her at every turn for months afterwards. He went off to agricultural college, out of the blue, which she heard about from Mr. Nelson. "To get away from you!" Josh had said matter-of-factly when she asked him. Mel pretended she didn't care, relieved in a way that he wasn't around to witness her get her comeuppance with Jamie. But without Jamie to distract her, she was haunted by how sad she was, how stupid she'd been, and how much she missed him and the entire Oldswick family, too ashamed to go see them anymore. There was nothing to stay around for; besides, Ibiza had self-destruction written all over it. Why get off that ride now?

"Want to move to the pool table?" Jamie breaks off, his hands in her hair, running his tongue over his teeth, his eyes hungry. It would be great, probably exactly what she needs, and maybe, just maybe, Jamie's a different person. But then perhaps she is too, and maybe, for once, she isn't going to make the same mistake twice.

He walks her up to the farmhouse, "Just to the door," Mel makes it clear. She doesn't want anyone to see Jamie going inside and get the wrong idea.

"That's what they all say!" Jamie jokes, giving her his coat. They walk in companionable silence, both looking up at the clear night, the constellations more vivid than ever, just in time for her to say goodbye to them too. She sighs at the thought, her breath fogging up in the cold night, wishing on every single star that she'd done things differently back then.

Standing in the doorway, she slides off his coat and hands it back, "Thanks, Jay, for today, for everything. It's been so good to see you again." She smiles at him, quite disbelieving that she isn't going to ask him inside. He pulls her in, kissing the top of her head, hugging her tight, murmuring, "I was alright with it, you know, being a distraction for you back then, Mac, would've done it again tonight, willingly, any night, for the record, but it was always Oldswick who had your heart, and I think if you take a close look, he still does," and with that, he bows to her once again, ambling away drunkenly into the night.

She wakes up on the air bed alone with the vague taste of lemon liqueur in her mouth and thankfully no regrets. Ok, that was a lie, there were quite a few major regrets from yesterday, but at least Jamie isn't on the list.

The house is empty, save for the things she is taking back to her storage unit. Hopefully, she can squeeze it all into her car. There are a couple of last boxes to sort through, in which she threw anything that looked important. Rolling off the inflatable mattress, she cracks her shoulders, thinking how nice it will be to sleep in a proper bed tonight. She won't have to be wrapped in 5 layers, watching her breath as she shivers next to the Aga, waiting for the kettle to boil. She'll be back in Janet's immaculate, warm house where fresh coffee is just a pod popped a machine away, but then again, she won't be looking out the window to see unspoilt countryside for miles or the sun rising over the vast moors that dreamily reflect all the pretty pastel colours of the clear, cold dawn. The dip in temperature means everything is frosted. As the sun rises in the sky, the fields sparkle back in greeting. Silence, save for the birds and a few distant baa's from Mr. Oldswick's sheep.

Manchester never sleeps, never even really gets dark; all the roads are always busy, and nearly 3 million people surround you at every turn, one of whom is Andrew. Although she's broken the news to Janet, at some point, she will have to admit the whole sorry story. She hopes Janet will understand, maybe even find it funny, but it could lead to some awkward social situations if she stays at Janet's much longer.

Manchester was always Aaron's home, not hers —a good place to raise Connor with his family around to help. But now

Connor's gone, maybe it's time she did too. But where to? She enjoyed being around all the animals; perhaps she should move to New Zealand and work on a sheep station, she sighs, knowing where she'd like to be - here.

Glancing up at the fields at the cabins, she wonders if Chris will even want to say goodbye. Planning to take the dogs over later, she hopes it will go some way as a gesture of something. She isn't sure whether forgiveness is even an option.

It's too early to ring Connor, his days don't start until the afternoon and don't stop until the early hours. She remembers it well, but it makes her tired nowadays to even contemplate it. She decides on a whim to ring Aaron, Connor's answer to all of her questions is always emoji-based. Aaron will at least be able to expand on that for her,

"Everything all right, Mel?" He answers, concerned, they rarely talk these days.

"Yeah, just checking in on Connor and you guys, what are you up to? Is it a bad time?"

"No, no, just been for a run, Maya's got a check up at the hospital this morning and I'm going to the studio after that."

There was a time when Aaron never saw morning from the right end; now he's always up, doing yoga, making fresh juice, and getting to the studio by 9 am. Mel could never take credit for Aaron cleaning up his act. Anyone who wants to deal with their addiction has to make that decision themselves, but standing up to him and telling him he couldn't see Connor until he made some changes was the catalyst. She's proud of him for turning his life around, but sometimes it felt frustrating that he wasn't there for them like that, but you can't change the past; like Aaron, you have to make your amends and move on.

"Everything all right with the baby? Not long to go now?"

"A month, she's getting fed up,"

Mel sympathises, "Give her my love,"

"Connor was early, though, wasn't he?" Aaron hadn't been the most present boyfriend during her pregnancy. Connor had been early by two weeks. Aaron was out DJing, she didn't even know where. She'd got in the bath to help her backache, and when she got out, her waters broke. She completely freaked out, not knowing what to do. Thankfully, Aaron's parents came to the rescue, depositing her at the hospital with Joanne for moral support.

After several mad hours hitting Manchester's club scene, Aaron's Dad bribed a doorman to let him into the club he'd finally tracked him down to. He'd fought his way through the dancing crowds and pushed through some bouncers to get Aaron's attention. Apparently, somewhere, there's a film of Aaron announcing over the mic that he has to go and have a baby, with everyone cheering him on as he leaves through the crowd. He'd bounced into the hospital room, high as a kite. He didn't stop talking to the midwives the whole time, all of whom adored him by the time she pushed a protesting 8lb Connor into the world.

"Yep, two weeks early, I'll keep my fingers crossed for Maya." As a yoga goddess, Mel hopes she pops out the baby without too much trouble,

"I just wanted to make sure Connor isn't any trouble?"

"Not at all, he's great, Mel, honestly, he's so helpful. It's so nice to have him around."

So sons are like exes, broken in by you, trained up for the next person's benefit,

"All I ever get from him is that he's fine."

"He works hard at the bar, goes to the gym, he's learning to use the studio, and he's played a few sets now. He hangs out with Maggie; she's a nice girl. He's done a few shifts at their hotel to help out; he never stops."

"Will all that be ok when the baby comes? "

"You miss him, don't you, Mel? You know you're always welcome to come and stay with us anytime, but perhaps not with the baby? I can sort you an apartment to stay in though, anytime, no problem, just let me know. Are you still in Yorkshire?"

"Leaving today, I have to get back to work, but I don't know Aaron, Manchester… It just, it doesn't feel like home anymore, I mean if Connor's not coming back, "

"He has been looking at getting his own place," Aaron tells her guiltily, but Mel doesn't blame him; she knows she would have done the same in his shoes.

"You know we'll look after him, don't you, Mel? You don't have to worry, I won't let him make the same mistakes I did, I promise. It's your time now."

Despite his reassurances, talking to Aaron does nothing to quell her unease. To distract herself from her mood, she tips out the box of papers she's been gathering, sitting down on the floor to go through them. Unclear what exactly she's looking for, she goes through everything carefully. There are old bills, insurance letters, receipts for long-gone purchases, and some paperwork of her dad's that may look worth keeping. She puts all those things in a box for Ken. He can decide what's useful. There are also mementoes of their life together, such as tickets to art galleries and concerts, which she keeps aside to add to the memory book she's planning to make.

 She finds an old pamphlet for a David Hockney exhibition, opening it to look at the artwork, remembering that they had once visited his gallery at Saltaire with school. When a slew of letters falls out, addressed to Kath in what looks like her Dad's distinctive handwriting, she is startled, turning them over in her hands, studying the fading stamps, confused that some of the dates are from before she was even born. She hesitates to open the envelopes. Should she read them, or is it an invasion of privacy? Curiosity gets the better of her; she certainly had no idea that they'd known each other that long.

She can hear her Dad's Irish lilt as she reads,

Kathleen,

I know you must be hurting so much to have heard about the baby from someone else. For that, I'm truly sorry. I have wanted to tell you a hundred times, but I was scared because I knew it would break your heart, and all I keep doing is hurting you, the last thing I ever want to do. It's tearing me in two, but I have to stand by Marie, after she's been so sick. This baby is a miracle. I can't risk anything happening to them both because of my selfish actions. Know that you have my heart, though Kathleen and I will continue to love you, even though we can't be together. I hope you understand.

Always yours, Patrick.

Mel stares at the letter for a long time, then she reads through all the others. It is clear that her Dad loved Kath for years before he even met Marie, but then he stood by her Mum to do the right thing. Later letters reveal that her Mum knew about Kath and that she told him to leave her and be with Kath long before he ever did. She has so many questions. What did her Dad mean by her Mum was sick back then? Why was she a miracle baby? Is that why she was an only child?

She wonders if Mrs. Oldswick can shed some light on the situation. Slipping the letters in her bag, a beep in the yard signals the last of the cat's new owners coming to pick them up. After a bit of kerfuffle getting them into carrying cases, they go off to their new homes. The quiet steals over her, making her even more miserable; only the dogs still pad about the empty kitchen.

There is nothing else left to do but pack up the car, lugging her Mum's books and records and cramming the back with boxes that she plans to drop at her storage unit on her way home. She wanders around the house again, checking that nothing is left behind and that there are no more cats anywhere.

Leaning her head against the kitchen wall before she locks up, she murmurs her goodbyes to her dad and Kath with a lump in her throat, praying the house will be loved again, trying not to imagine it coming to a sticky end at the hands of some developer.

She ambles across the fields to the Oldswicks, the dogs racing away ahead of her as she carries bags with bowls and food, baskets and leads. She sees a figure working on the swimming pond, and her stomach flips over. There is so much she needs to say to Chris. Jamie's comment keeps running through her head. Is he right? And if he is right, it's now or never. She feels sick.

All she keeps doing is messing things up. How can she make amends for her latest disaster?

As she gets closer, however, she sees that it's Josh, and as far as she can see, Chris is nowhere to be seen. Josh waves, shouting to her to put the kettle on, he'll be up in a minute. She lets herself quietly into the farmhouse, not wanting to spook Chris if he's there somewhere, knowing she has to talk to him before she leaves, but unsure how it will go.

Mrs. Oldswick is pounding pastry on the kitchen top, waving her to fill up the kettle while she finishes.

"I've bought the dog's things," Mel puts them down in a corner, "Aye, Chris said you would be,"

How did Chris know? It was so infuriating, she almost wanted to change her mind and take them to Manchester just to prove him wrong, "I hope you don't mind having them?"

"Not at all, it'll keep a piece of Kath with us, I miss her, it'll be strange not to have anyone we know next door."

"Someone local might buy it? "

Mrs. Oldswick snorts," I don't think anyone local could afford it, the price of houses has gone mad in the last few years, some builder'll get his hands on it... I just hope they keep the house and don't stick a load of new ones up instead."

Of course, Mel has been looking tentatively at local property. Mrs. Oldswick isn't exaggerating, even the tiny Mill cottages she lived in with her Mum are way out of her budget. The price of rent is also astronomical. Not that there is much nearby to choose from.

"I would keep it, if I had the money to give Connor his share and do all the work, but I can barely get a mortgage on my salary to buy a bedsit, there's no way anyone's lending me the rest of the money. I'm so sorry it has to be sold."

"We understand, Mel, it's just the way it is these days. It's been a privilege to have lived by Kath and your dad all those years. It's been lovely to have you back, even for a bit. You know you'll always have a home here, don't you love?"

"Thing is," Mel blurts out, already emotional from Sheila's comments, "There's no reason for me to be in Manchester anymore, I've loved being here and to see you all and feel close to my Mum, Dad and Kath…Back then, I just wanted to get as far away from the memories as possible, you know? But now, I wish I could stay so I never forget them all." The tears leak slowly, and she blinks them away, not wanting Chris to come in and see her crying again.

Mrs. Oldswick says nothing but carries on rolling out her pastry. Mel swears there's a glisten in her eye, too. She pulls out her Dad's letters just as Josh clatters into the kitchen, sitting down at the table next to her,

"What are those? Love letters from Chris? He was always writing you soppy notes, remember, Ma? We used to tease him about it!" Chris had written her notes all the time, some silly, some sweet; he was always trying to do something to cheer her up.

"No, they're to Kath, from my dad, old letters, and I have a few questions, Sheila?"

Mel sees Mrs. Oldswick's back stiffen a little; clearly, she knew more than she ever let on, but Mel didn't blame her for keeping the past where it belonged. As these last 10 days proved, bringing the past to light is fraught with complications,

"Oooh, old Greenleigh scandal and gossip?! Pass me the teapot! "Josh picks up the letters and starts to read,

"My Dad mentions a couple of things that don't make sense to me. I thought he only met Kath when I was ten, when he left mum, but this letter is from before I was born? He talks about her being sick and me being a miracle baby?"

Sheila dusts off her hands and takes a seat at the end of the worn pine table, "I can tell you what I know, love, but I'm sure there's plenty I don't…"

"But ask Mr. Nelson, am I right?" Josh jokes, Sheila pours herself a cup of tea,

"Pat, your dad, he first came to Greenleigh when he was young, 17 maybe 18, as a farm labourer, he came over looking for work, some cousins from Ireland were working in the area on another farm. No one could understand his accent at first, but he was a handsome man. All the girls fancied Paddy McCarthy, but I was too young for him to notice me."

"Ma! You can't tell Mel you fancied her dad! Does Dad know?"

"He got a job on Kath's Uncle's farm; she was a bit older than Patrick and sort of informally engaged to one of the Shaw boys."

"Older woman, eh? There's hope for me and you after all 'Bells," Josh takes her hand and kisses it,

"Stop interrupting Josh! They fell for each other, then Kath's uncle found out and fired him, then he ended up going back to

Ireland for a few years. In the meantime, Kath married Robert Shaw and she went to live out on their farm, which was right out on' tops. Your dad came back the year after, I think, and when he found out Kath was married, he was heartbroken, but eventually he started seeing Marie. She'd not long moved here to work at Cobhams, the mill in Houghton Bridge? She'd had a tough life by all accounts, didn't have much family, but she was beautiful, your mum. A lot of men's noses got put out of joint when they got married. Your mum always knew about Kath, though, because doesn't everybody know everything in Greenleigh? The Shaw farm is so remote that no one saw much of Kath for a few years, then all of a sudden, she moved back into the village. She never talked about what happened, but there were rumours that Robert caught her with Paddy and threw her out. I think your dad would've left your mum then but your mum had been sick, she was in hospital for a long time, sepsis which caused other things, it were' touch and go for a while, it took her a long time to get better, then next thing, Marie was pregnant with you. Everyone said it was a miracle after her illness, and your dad, well, I never heard of any rumours of him and Kath for years after that. He loved your Mum, you know Melanie, but Kath just, well, she was his first love and you never really get over that, do you?"

She smiles at Mel in her knowing way, "I think they reconnected in the Art group, up at the school, that was just before he moved out. I heard it was with Marie's blessing, I mean by then it were' 20 odd years it went on for, they were childhood sweethearts of sorts and honestly, lass, that's about all I know. Kath wasn't one for gossip, and funnily enough, she's about the only one no one in the village ever gossiped about."

"Bloody hell!" Josh leans back in his chair, "Move over, Emmerdale."

Mel is quiet for a few minutes, taking it all in. She is glad she knows, but wishes that she'd known all along that her dad and Kath were star-crossed lovers. Although she felt sad for her mum, she was happy that they finally got to have a life together,

"Talking of childhood sweethearts ... Where is my brother?" Trust Josh to bring up the elephant in the room,

Sheila starts bustling around the kitchen again, "Oh...errr, I'm sorry, love, he's had to go up to Keighley to pick something up." She looks embarrassed. Mel's heart sinks. She can't believe he's avoiding saying goodbye, but then again, this is just like old times: her misbehaving, then Chris dodging her.

She stands up hastily, afraid she might start crying again. She wishes she could stay here in the warm kitchen, drinking tea, forever,

"Keighley? That could've waited. He knew Mel was leaving today. Oh..." Josh trails off, "Well, we'll miss you, Mel, it's been just like old times! Let me know when we're off to Ibiza, yeah? I've been practising my dance moves! Don't you dare leave it another 20 years before you come back again." He gives her a huge hug,

"Don't be a stranger, Melanie. Greenleigh will always be your home, you'll always be welcome, and you'll always have a place in this family love." She clasps Mel to her," You'll be alright, lass," she murmurs.

Mel makes it to the door, biting her lip, she doesn't think she'll be alright at all. Skippy tries to follow her, "Now you want me," she says, shutting the farmhouse door, gulping down a huge sob. She'll miss the animals as much as anyone.

THE TRACK BACK

She trails slowly back down the track, stupidly hoping that Chris might have changed his mind and come back to see her. She doesn't want to leave on bad terms, again. Maybe she won't see him again for another 20 years and then she'll reappear and mess up his life again, just so he keeps on hating her, and on and on until eternity.

After checking all the doors, she stands outside her car for ages, still hoping he might appear by magic, but ultimately she has to accept that whatever her feelings may or may not be, it doesn't matter. He hates her, possibly even more than he did before she got back.

She told Janet that she'd be back for dinner, and it's getting to a time where she'll be late if she doesn't get going. Shoehorning herself into the car, packed to the brim with so many memories, she sits in the yard, taking one last look at the familiar landscape. She never knew how much she needed wild places and to be amongst the kind of people that call them home.

Driving slowly down the track, she watches the house as it slowly disappears in her rear-view mirror. She doesn't stop crying until she is dazzled by the bright lights of Manchester.

CHAPTER THIRTEEN

Waking up, back in Janet's spare bedroom, it takes her a few minutes to work out where she is, as if the last 10 days have been some kind of long dream or perhaps a nightmare. Although she's warm and cosy in a nice, clean bed, she feels sad, missing the mornings when she woke up with the dogs and cats curling around her. However, she is back to work this morning, so there's no time to lie around feeling melancholy. Getting up, she tries to enjoy having a hot shower without being terrified to pull back the shower curtain. She may have been cleaner than she has been for days, but it doesn't make her as happy as she thought it might.

Down in the kitchen, Janet bustles around, offering her coffee for the commute. Mel asks for tea, two sugars, "You've changed!" Janet mocks, pushing her out to the car as Mel struggles to pick up her pace. As they inch their way to work, stuck as ever, in the glut of morning traffic, Mel stares miserably out of the window at the manufactured landscape while Janet fills her in on everything she's been missing. It feels like she's been away for a lifetime. The kids are always so fed up and restless after the Christmas term, Janet says. Mel thinks, 'same,' as it starts to sleet.

Manchester can be a bit bleak at the best of times, but never more so than in January when the Christmas lights come down and everyone feels flat and flat broke after all the twinkling promise of December. Looking out the car window at all the congestion and concrete, she finds that she can't breathe for a minute, clutching the dashboard dizzily. Janet glances at her, asking if she's ok. Mel can't articulate what's wrong; she just doesn't feel right.

She gets through the days on autopilot; it isn't boredom, it's more than that. As the weeks crawl by, she realises that she can't stand being stuck inside a classroom all day. Even standing outside on lunchtime duty (clutching her travel mug to keep warm) makes her miserable, watching the kids play on tarmac, hemmed in by roads and non-stop traffic. She becomes suddenly, overwhelmingly grateful for her wild childhood.

She spends her nights sloping off to bed like a sulky teenager, binge-watching series after series on Netflix to distract her thoughts. Janet insists that it's logical for her to stay with them until the sale of the farmhouse, when she'll have a bigger budget to play with. Mel keeps trawling Rightmove, at all budgets and still can't find anything that she wants to call home.

Connor calls her on the way home from work one afternoon, all choked up, "I've got a baby brother." Mel's throat catches, she babbles her congratulations, then makes an excuse to call him back later. Baby Gael popped out on time and easily for a first baby. (Mel adds 'yoga' to her to-do list.) Weighing a healthy 7lb something, he has his Dad's eyes, Maya's honey skin and a cute thick thatch of dark hair. Mel takes one look at the photos, thinks how much he looks like Connor, then drinks far too much gin on a school night before ugly crying on Janet. Janet hands her tissues and tells her to get dating again and "Start her own family," if that's what all this is about. When Mel doesn't even raise a smile, Janet wonders what's going on; she's not been herself at all since she came back from Yorkshire. She had presumed it was to do with Andrew, but she doesn't like to pry, much.

Seeing photos of Aaron and Connor with the baby sends her already struggling mood plummeting off the charts. Misguidedly, she goes off to the RSPCA to look at the dogs, but the thought of picking one and leaving the rest behind paralyses any decision. She leaves feeling worse than when she went in. She cries so often in her car that she keeps a box of tissues on the passenger seat. She sends baby Gael some tiny Converse all stars, whilst ignoring the goat crap that still stains her trainers.

Janet sees Andrew. She hesitates to tell Mel, but Mel assures her that Andrew is the very least of her concerns. Cindy had gone round to collect some of her things, and he decided that he'd made a terrible mistake (Mel wonders if she was the terrible mistake, but doesn't like to draw attention to the fact by asking.) Andrew had asked Cindy to marry him, and Cindy said yes. There is to be a big family party to celebrate, unsurprisingly, she doesn't get an invite but Samya sends her sneaky photos. Cindy seems to be everything Mel isn't. As such, she is sure they will be very happy together.

As the auction draws near, Mel is still toying with vague plans for her future, most of which are admittedly wildly unrealistic. She can't languish in no man's land in Janet's back bedroom forever, or can she? Making a decision is paralysing when she can't have the one thing she wants. She reminds herself daily that Aaron has moved on happily, Connor is busy making a new life in Ibiza, and even Andrew has managed to get engaged. Why is she finding it so difficult?

To get away from Janet, who has adopted a zero tolerance policy for Mel's moping, insisting that they do wholesome activities on a weekend (rather than lie in bed bingeing 'The Vampire Diaries' for the fourth time). Mel uses the excuse that she needs something at her storage unit to escape the latest stately home/ walking combo that Janet pitched for this coming Saturday. Last time, they went for a day out on Janet's insistence; she had skulked along behind her and Steve, like a reluctant teenager. Janet had refused her an ice cream until she showed some enthusiasm.

Connor wants to ship some of his things out to Ibiza, now that he's getting his own place. She decides she'll sort through his boxes and pack up some of his belongings. She also thinks that she might start a memory book of her parents and Kath to give her something to take her mind off all her current woes.

On the way back from Yorkshire, fatigued by all the tears, she'd just opened the unit door, dumped the boxes off the trolley, and left. Methodically, she starts to sort them out. The first box is full of vinyl. Mel pulls them out one by one, looking at all the artwork and recalling how her mum used to put them on when she was little. They would dance round the room together, her Mum was young too, although Mel never really thought about it at the time. She decides to buy herself a record player so that she can listen to them all again.

Each item she unearths digs deep into her long-buried memories, but they bring up happy thoughts, long overdue relief from all the sad ones. In the last box, amongst a jumble of her Mum's bits, is a bin bag they didn't bother to look through in the attic, Mel tips the contents out to get a better look and it takes a few seconds to comprehend what's in there; things of hers she threw away in a rage before she left for Ibiza, not wanting to leave any memories or incriminating evidence behind. Lying in front of her are her diaries, letters & old photographs. Her Dad or Kath must've rescued them from the dustbin.

It was an overwhelming sensation to see things you thought were lost forever. Shaking out a big envelope, a formal photo of herself and Chris from the school leavers' ball falls out. She stares at it, amazed. Chris, in his borrowed suit, his unruly hair tamed with wax, looks down on her with a smile, while she, on the other hand, looks thin and slightly sullen. Chris had tried so hard to keep her afloat that year, and yet all she had done was punish him for it.

Automatically, she reaches for her phone to share the picture with him. She and Josh are in regular contact (he tells her every week to pack up and get home), and Jamie messages her the odd cheeky comment.Siobhan sends her countless cute photos of the kittens, but there's been no word from Chris in the two months since she left, and much as she hates to admit it, it's him she wants to hear from the most. Hovering her phone over the photo, she wonders if all it might do is remind him again of how awful she is. Remorsefully, she slides it back into the envelope.

There's a bundle of cards and letters, all from Chris. She instantly recognises his neat handwriting. He would write her sweet messages to keep her going while her Mum was sick and then heartfelt ones afterwards, never afraid to wear his heart on his sleeve, despite Josh teasing him for it. As she reads through them, tears start to pour down her face, for someone so young, he had loved her so tenderly.

She flicks through her diary, long diatribes begging God for her Mum to get better, between tales of all the adventures she had with Chris on his never-ending mission to cheer her up, then months of empty pages after her Mum passed away, starting up again the night she met Jamie. After which, she started hiding her diary under a loose floorboard so she could spill all her secret longings into it. Stuck to the pages, the bus ticket from that snowy night, a ticket from the Halloween scare fest that she and Chris went to in fancy dress as Carrie and Jason, gig tickets, a dried up daisy chain, passport photos of her and Siobhan pulling crazy faces and then two of her and Chris. You'd get four in a strip, and they'd keep two each. She stares at the young couple, snuggled up together, each looking at the other with huge grins and dancing eyes. They were always so happy just being together.

She's so grateful to have all her belongings back, literally a gift from heaven, but Mel feels so sad looking at that photo. Why did she keep ruining the best thing that ever happened to her?

Recently, she has been making playlists of songs from her teenage years. She puts one on. Expecting to be plunged into further despair today by thinking about Connor living so far away from her, she finds herself instead singing (and dancing about, no one can see her) as she sorts his things into piles. It's only a 3-hour flight to Ibiza, she tells herself firmly. He's always been such a good kid, despite all the problems between her and Aaron when he was growing up. He deserves the chance to follow his dreams, and she does trust Aaron to look after him. When the farmhouse sells, she plans to go over for a weekend. Siobhan insists she's coming with her, for old times' sake.

There are, of course, photos of Jamie too, mostly in his biker jacket, staring moodily at the camera, pouting like a model. He always knew exactly how attractive he was. What if Jamie had never cheated on her and they'd somehow stayed together? There'd have been no Ibiza-no Aaron-no Connor. That was pretty unthinkable. Things happen for a reason, she thinks, wondering whatever happened to Kylie from Kirkheaton.

But what if she had never met Jamie? Would she have got over her rebellious phase and stayed with Chris, as they had always planned?

Life, or in this case, death, has given her a way back to him. She can redeem herself yet, somehow, she tells herself, tucking the photos into her purse, where they always used to be. She feels more positive than she has since returning from Greenleigh. Her future doesn't look quite so bleak because the past is in a different light. She decides to craft a message for Chris later, primarily about the dogs, just to test the waters.

On the day of the auction, she can't concentrate for toffee, kids pulling on her jumper all day to get her attention. Connor is on similar tenterhooks, having viewed a tiny studio flat near the studio that he's desperate to put an offer on. His baby brother is cute, he says, but there's not much peace anymore. Mel is helping Janet clear up the classroom after what feels like the longest day ever, when her phone rings. It's Julie, who works at the estate agents, handling the sale. She fills Mel in on the whole auction, "I mean, I thought at one point your neighbour was going to get it, then a couple of developers jumped in and the price was going up and up. I mean, good for you, I guess, but I knew he was gutted because we had a lovely chat about it before the sale started. He really wanted it, but he only had a limited budget, such a shame for him," she coos,

"Neighbour?" Mel is confused,

"*Chris Oldswick...*He said he lives on the farm next door. He looked so upset afterwards. I felt for him...Is he, errr, single, do you know?"

"Sadly not, his girlfriend is a supermodel!" Mel snaps.

She is reeling from this new information. Chris had never said that he was interested in buying the house, although to be fair, they aren't exactly best buddies. His reply to her enquiry about the dogs was 'Fine, thanks'. As she couldn't keep saying sorry, she had left it there, still unsure how she could ever make it right. Josh had never mentioned anything about the auction, though, which is not like Josh because he can't keep a secret, even if you paid him. Everyone knows that he's the natural successor to Mr.Nelson as the official village Gossip. She fires him a message about it, then rings Connor, who is over the moon with the final selling price. She is happy for him, but despite the generous addition to her budget, not so much for herself.

Insisting that they go out for dinner to celebrate the sale, Janet tries to make sense of Mel's miserable mood as she pushes her food around the plate.Somehow, having money and choices aren't nearly enough to shake the overwhelming disappointment that Chris didn't get to buy the house. She wondered why he'd never said anything. She would have much rather sold it straight to him, did he hate her so much that he didn't want her to do him any favours?

He was always very moral that way. Did he want it for another holiday let, or maybe he wanted to live in himself? He'd been living in the cabins as he finished each of them, saying it was easier so he could work all hours. He was happy to rough it, eating and washing up at the farm. Josh said living in a half-finished cabin was still a vast improvement over the bunk houses they lived in out in Australia. Josh, however, was still in his childhood bedroom, complete with a Power Rangers bedspread, now totally retro, he says.

She can picture Chris living at Kath's. He would bring it back to life beautifully. The cabins were simple but so stylishly done. He was one of those annoying types who could do anything practical, like his Dad. He'd always been building or fixing something from a young age. Mrs. Oldswick had told her proudly that to keep himself entertained in Australia, he'd worked solidly on the cabin designs and his ideas to transform the farm.

He'd come back with a full sketchbook and set to work. She's sure that's what attracted Marlowe to him. With a gift for turning his hand to anything and such natural style, he'd be catnip to anyone who appreciates aesthetics. With Chris, the added beauty was that none of it was intentional; he was just in his element, grounded in the earth that ran through his blood. He deserves to have bought it. Mel feels frustrated that, in a roundabout way, she messed up that outcome too.

Julie starts to tell her about the house going to a builder who will be trying to get planning permission, but Mel doesn't want to know any of the details; it feels too painful. She misses the house terribly. The only choice she has now is to let it go and try to move on with her life. It's all well and good daydreaming about moving home, but it's probably better to leave the past where it is. Safer, saner, for all involved. Chris doesn't want anything to do with her. Would it be too hard, eventually, to keep saying no to Jamie? And lest she forget, everyone would know all about all of it.

Now that the auction is over, Mel has no excuses to get her own life back on track. Somehow, she's been in Janet's spare room for nearly six months now. She'd hung Kath's painting of the farmhouse up in her room, but after the auction, she took it down, heartbroken that Chris didn't get to buy it. She can't stop torturing herself with the thought of it getting knocked down to make way for some ugly modern houses. Josh claims he knew nothing about the auction, she wonders perhaps if the estate agent may have made a mistake. He said he'd ask Chris, but then he doesn't get back to her. She's not heard from Chris at all; she crafts him messages about it but never sends any of them, feeling like nothing she says can ever make it right. Beyond apologising, again, she isn't sure how to get him to talk to her.

But if her 18-year-old son can crack on and buy his own home (to be fair, with some help from Aaron), then it's time she pulls her finger out too. So it's back to spending her weekends trawling estate agents and viewing properties, but even with the money from the auction to boost her budget, Manchester's nicest areas are still out of her reach. As a single person on a relatively small salary, at her age, even with a decent deposit, her mortgage offers are limited. Add to that the interest rate, which makes the monthly repayments crippling, and it's a depressing endeavour. She looks at tiny flats in nice areas and houses with gardens in undesirable postcodes, but still can't find anything that she wants to call home. Janet starts accompanying her. Mel begins to feel like a child they are trying to get out of the nest; even Steve has taken to scouring Right Move on her behalf. They trail away from another viewing, a poky new build with a view of a car park. Mel hates it before they even get inside. Janet suggests they go for a quick coffee before the next viewing, but once inside Costa, she pins Mel in a booth and starts cross-examining her,

"What's wrong, Mel?"

"The bathroom didn't even have a window, Jan, and the traffic noise would drive me mental,"

Janet wants answers, "I'm not talking about the house."

"Oh,"

"You've just been so *lost* since you came back from Yorkshire. I thought that once you'd sold Kath's house, you'd be over the moon?! Is it because Andrew and Cindy are getting married?" Mel has been pretty tight-lipped about the reason for their break-up,

"No, no, I'm happy for Andrew. Honestly, I told you, we were never really suited when it came down to it, it's not about *him*."

"If it's not him, then who is it about?"

"It's complicated." Mel sighs, stirring her tea endlessly, she can't tell Janet without admitting her awful shortcomings.

"I'm still hoping Jonathan will see sense and divorce Felicity, then you're in."

"Thanks, Jan, much as you know, I would love you for a mother-in-law, I'm not sure Jon and I are suited either."

"You're too fussy, Mel," Janet concludes,

"About men or houses?"

"Both,"

"I think when you've had the perfect one and messed it up so badly, it's hard to settle for anything less." Mel reaches for more sugars, dumping them into her tea,

"Men or houses?"

"Both." To Janet's frustration, Mel will not be drawn further on the subject.

To placate Janet, she arranges two second viewings, promising Connor that she will visit as soon as she has put an offer on a place. Janet keeps her well up to date on the baby via her WhatsApp with Aaron and has a photo of him on the fridge in the tiny United kit she sent him. Maya is holding him up; she doesn't even look tired, Mel thinks glumly every time she opens the fridge door.

The first house is in a nicer area but needs a lot of work, and as such, there is a flurry of interest, which the estate agent mentions at least three times during the first five minutes of her second viewing. It's a terrace with another row of terraces behind, so the garden is overlooked on all sides. It does have a large tree, which the estate agent suggests she should cut down to maximise the space. Mel thinks it's the property's most redeeming feature; from the back bedroom, the view of its branches gives you the vague illusion that you aren't living in a city. The agent is pressuring her to put in an offer there and then, saying, "There's another four viewings today, I'd hate for you to miss out!" but Mel remains unconvinced. She has another viewing before making any decisions.

Her phone rings just as she meets the estate agent at the next property. You do get a lot more house for your money in this part of the city, but it's so much busier. As he gives her the usual spiel about amenities and school catchments, she scrabbles through her bag for her phone, a missed call from Ken Braithwaite. He's left her a voicemail. Figuring it can't be anything urgent, Mel puts it away to concentrate on the house instead. It's a new build on a sizable estate of matching unremarkable properties. Not her cup of tea at all, but it does have a park nearby, so there are some distant views of greenery out of the upstairs windows, maybe one day she could get a dog.

As the agent shows her around again, she desperately tries to find some redeeming features, but it's all so modern and bland. No matter how realistic, she tries to keep her expectations; she knows in her heart she only wants Kath's farmhouse with those views of the moors; nothing else can compete.

"So what do you think a second time round?" the agent hovers, hoping to close the deal.

"That it's making me feel claustrophobic," Mel says, backing out the door. She sits in her car for ages, staring out at the endless rows of matchbox houses, trying to reason with herself. She can't afford a Yorkshire farmhouse with fields and an unbroken view of the hills; her job and her friends are here in Manchester, she needs to stop daydreaming and get real. The first house isn't so bad, at least there are some original features, and the commute will be direct, even though you'd be doing it at snail's pace in rush hour. Maybe she should make an offer before someone else does, if they haven't already. She fishes out her phone, remembers Ken's missed call and calls her voicemail out of curiosity,

"Hello Melanie, it's Ken Braithwaite from Braithwaite's Solicitors, I've got some, ahh, news for you, but, errr I need to see you in person because there's a few papers you need to see and err, sign, maybe... So if you can come up to the office at your earliest convenience, obviously, but the sooner the better, Monday if possible? That would be great, thank you. Look forward to seeing you soon! Ha!"

How weird, he sounds like he's laughing. She doesn't think she's even seen him smile that much. What papers would she need to see and sign? As far as she knows, all the auction paperwork's completed. Maybe there's some small print they missed, but forget all that, to be honest, what's more exciting to her is having a genuine excuse to go back to Greenleigh. I mean, *as soon as possible,* Ken said, and while she's there, it would be remiss not to go to the farm and see the Oldswicks. She is just about to message Josh to tell him, all excited at the thought, when she decides to go with the element of surprise; she doesn't want Chris to disappear on her again.

CHAPTER FOURTEEN

Mel may have exaggerated the circumstances to secure a day off work at such short notice. Janet, however, is not immune to the change in Mel's mood after her announcement, wishing that Mel could see what was evident to her, much as though she'll miss her, Mel should just go home.

Setting off for Greenleigh as soon as the rush hour traffic dies down, Mel turns up the music and drives like the wind. After a long, grey winter, it finally feels like spring. She can't wipe the smile from her face as she heads out of the city and into the countryside. Dry stone walls travel alongside her as she drives up over the moors and down into Yorkshire, a welcome committee of waving daffodils dotting the roadside.

It's only after an hour or so that she remembers she never rang the estate agent to put in an offer on that first house. Instead, she spent the rest of the weekend trying to think up things to say, or something she could do to get Chris to forgive her, or at least to entice him into having a conversation with her.

She wonders about how it might go when she gets up to the farm. Chris would be outside working on the cabins, perhaps even shirtless (despite it being early April), casually throwing timber about (obviously she was stealing her ideas from that scene in Poldark). He'll have built up a sweat, or maybe there will be some light rain. (Find me a man who doesn't look sexier with lightly tousled wet hair.) The dogs will look up, streaming toward her across the ripe corn field, strewn with beautiful wildflowers (all of which only grow in August, but hey, this is a dream sequence.) There might be some slow-motion running, maybe he might even lift her up, and they'll fall into the meadow, and he'll say that he never stopped loving her. She will say me too, then they'll live together, snugly, in a little cabin, she will learn to churn butter by hand, bottle feed orphan lambs and raise that brood of next generation Oldswick's that he always wanted.

Janet had shouted her down for dinner, breaking her from her fantasy, a tad flushed. Somehow, she had taken several large leaps, from planning how to truly apologise to Chris, to spending the rest of her life with him and "Starting a family" (she smiles to herself), the first time she had ever considered that for her future. He'd be the best Dad.

She thinks back to what Jamie said, how did he even know before she did? And what the hell is she going to do about it when Chris can't stand the sight of her?

As she drives down the hill into Greenleigh, excitement and nerves tangle up in her stomach. The countryside is waking up, spring poking out of the soil, snowdrops and daffodils litter the lanes, the sun is shining and everything has gone from grey to green. It feels so good to be back, as if she is finally home after years at sea; this is where I belong, Mel thinks resolutely. How can she make it happen? She winds down the window and takes a deep breath of country air.

To be honest, she hasn't given the visit to Ken Braithwaite much thought, more thinking about how quickly she can get away from him and get up to the farm. She left him a message to say she's coming this morning, but as she pulls in at the office, she wonders what exactly he might need her for.

She is also anxious about what she might see happening at Kath's, wondering if the builder has started doing any work yet. She hopes, whatever they are doing, it's sympathetic, thinking again about what the estate agent had said about Chris wanting the house. She'll ask him about it today, if she sees him. She'll be pretty crushed if it turns out he's out of town. She's even done her hair and worn lipstick, does it look too much? She rubs it off with a McDonald's napkin from her glove box.

As she walks into the office, Ken's secretary, Joan, goes a little giddy, telling her to take a seat in a very high-pitched voice and goes skittishly to tell Ken that Mel is here. Mel begins to fret about what she is about to find out; it would be just her luck that there's a load of debt or something that she has to pay out of her inheritance. Maybe it was a good job she didn't put an offer in on that house; she could be back looking at shabby studio flats in Salford after today. She twists her rings as she sits waiting, "Come through, Melanie!" Ken squeaks as Joan ushers her into the office, "Have a seat, have a seat, good journey? Can we get you anything? Coffee, Tea, Me?" he laughs, a tad manically, "It's from that film? Working Girl with Harrison Ford, not that I'm Harrison Ford, haha!"

This is getting super weird, "Tea would be lovely, two sugars please." Joan goes off to put the kettle on while Ken shuffles his pile of papers,

"Well, err, thank you for coming at such short notice, Melanie, I appreciate you making the journey,"

"No problem, I want to pop by and see a few people anyway, check up on the animals, see what's going on with Kath's house,"

"Well, I can tell you that the builder has been trying to get planning permission for several properties on the site but he knows he's going to be turned down flat by the planners, the whole area is opposed it, there's been all manner of protests, the Oldswick's have been rallying the village. No one wants any more executive developments in the area, it has such a knock on the local population, and the local council are in agreement. I don't know if he's done anything with the house itself. I think he originally intended to demolish it. I haven't been up there, I'm afraid."

Her heart contracts, she will be utterly devastated if it's a pile of rubble when she goes up to the farm, it doesn't bear thinking about.

"So what do you need from me, Ken?" She doesn't mean to be rude, but she is anxious to be on her way before Chris might go out for the day.

"Well, that depends! Perhaps just a couple of signatures, that's all." He giggles again,

"Sure, where do I sign?"Mel picks up a pen from the desk,

Ken shuffles the papers, "As your legal representative, I would advise you to read carefully before you sign."

Mel clicks her pen impatiently. "Can you just give me a quick summary and tell me where to scribble?"

Joan appears with the tea, hovering in the doorway, staring. Mel looks at them both, unnerved,

"Ken, what's going on? Am I in some sort of trouble? Was Kath in debt? Just tell me, please!"

Ken starts to laugh and Joan joins in, "No, No, "he chortles, "Quite the opposite!"

Mel still doesn't get it. "Meaning?"

Coughing, he sits up, adjusting his tie with a solemn look on his face,

"It took me a while to follow the paper trail, but I knew your Dad had inherited some land in Ireland when he was born. We'd discussed doing something with it years ago, but inheritance laws and other family claims complicated it. However, when he passed, it technically went to Kath. I asked her about it several times, and she told me she'd look into it, but she never got round to it or didn't want to. I could only dig around so far online. It was all pre-Internet, of course. I didn't want to raise your hopes until I had something concrete to share with you. I'm sorry it took me this long to follow the trail, but I did some research with the paperwork you unearthed, and I found out that several people have been desperate to buy that land so it has some, errr, value… "

Mel, prepared for more bad news, sits up straight. "Value?"

"If you wish to sell the land, then all you have to do is sign those papers so I can get the *value* released to you…"

"What sort of *value* are we talking about, Ken?"

Ken shuffles through his papers, "Four hundred and fifty thousand is the highest offer I've received, should you wish to sell, of course!"

Joan starts clapping ecstatically. Mel sees the desk swim beneath her. She clutches the chair,

"What?!"

"Minus a few fees, but yes, it's a good job you found that paperwork, or we may never have known the exact details,"

Mel isn't sure if she might throw up or pass out. "You're not pranking me, are you, Ken?"

"Good Lord, no Melanie! I'm over the moon for you! I take it you do want to sell? If so, I do need your signature, here and here."

Mel thinks, a plan bubbling in her mind. She doesn't want land in Ireland, does she? That money would solve a lot of her problems. She clenches her fists for a minute, trying to iron out her ideas before signing on the dancing, dotted lines. She sits back in the chair, taking some deep breaths

while Joan rubs her shoulder and passes her her tea.

"Cheers, Kath, for never throwing anything away!" She raises her mug,

"Well, I expect you'll be wanting to share the news and celebrate!" Ken shakes her hand enthusiastically. In a complete daze, she leaves the office, not knowing how to believe her luck. She climbs into her car, staring blindly out the windscreen at the valley in front of her. Four hundred and fifty thousand pounds. What the actual hell!

In a glorious rush, her fortunes frisk before her, but she knows in her heart what she's going to do. She starts driving. When she turns the corner up the track, her heart is pounding so fast that she thinks she might have a heart attack. She almost daredn't look, but apart from a van parked outside, the house looked intact or as intact as it ever had. Overjoyed, she skids round into the yard, bringing out a man from inside the barn. Legs shaking, she gets out of the car,

"Can I help you?"

"I really hope so!"

When the deal is done, they shake hands. Mel is trying not to be sick at offering such a huge sum of money, that she doesn't technically have yet, to a total stranger. At first, he thought she was another bothersome local pulling his leg. He's been completely harassed by the villagers since the day he bought it. The man in the local shop was even spreading rumours that he was building some kind of illegal gambling den.

It takes a call to Ken for him to take her offer seriously. After some back and forth, he agrees and packs up happily, leaving her to it. The whole project has been nothing but trouble, the locals contesting every plan he came up with, led by the farmers next door. It was way too much hassle compared to the easy way out Mel had just given him. She was very welcome to it and them. He hoped she had enough money left to put a new roof on it, sort out the plumbing and rewire, redo the plaster and sort out that awful bathroom that gave him the creeps. Perhaps he'll leave her his card, but on second thought, he'll be glad to see the back of Greenleigh, and yes, she can use the studio later.

After he leaves, Mel puts her hand out to touch the weathered stone, tracing a heart in the yellow lichen, "Don't worry, "she whispers. Now she just needs to execute the next part of her plan, which had come to her, wildly, in Ken's office. She looks up at the cabins. Thankfully, there is no sign of life; she needs to stay incognito until she is ready. Dragging open the barn door, she drives the Focus inside.

Josh answers, yelling cheerily, "Mels Bells!" "Shhhhh, is Chris there?"

"No, he's at the farm, I think, I'm just at the wholesalers, why? Where are you? "

"Wholesalers? Perfect…I just need a few things, but Josh, this is a SECRET, you absolutely need to keep this to yourself, ok? And can you help me sort it out later? I'll pay you whatever you want."

She spells out part of her plan to Josh, somewhat thrown by his awkward silence at the end,

"I mean it's a lovely gesture, Bells, but he's been in such an awful mood recently. We don't know what's up with him. You know what he's like… I'd hate for you to go to all that effort and for him not to stay. He's so stubborn. To be honest, I don't know what it'll take for him to cheer up."

"Trust me, I've got an idea." She isn't telling Josh *every* part of her plan.

Josh texts her when he gets Chris out of the farm on some bogus errand. In the meantime, Mel gets busy trying to replicate the look of Chris's anniversary dinner from all those years ago. Mrs. Oldswick is quick to get involved. She doesn't comment much but turns up at Kath's with food and things to decorate the space. When she leaves, she pulls Mel into a huge hug and wishes her luck. Josh ducks in, helping her string up the fairy lights. A phone call to Jamie produces a generator; he comes up in Kath's truck.

"Can't say I'm not a bit jealous, Mac," he says, looking round,

"C'mon, Jamie, as if fairy lights were ever your style."

Jamie laughs, "Not really, but I know who will appreciate it, good luck, girl. If he's not won over, then he's more of an idiot than I think…and, you know you can call me anytime." He kisses her on the forehead and guns out of the yard.

Now all she can do is wait. Once it's all sorted, Josh is going to say there's some problem down at Kath's and lure Chris out there. Josh texts her updates, her guts churning as she waits on a hay bale, rehearsing her lines over and over. She didn't bring anything nice to wear, having no clue this morning that this is how her day was going to end, but she tries to do her hair by looking in her phone, dabbing on some sticky lip gloss that's been knocking around in her handbag.

Her phone beeps, "Coming now!" Hurriedly, she switches all the power off. It's pitch black. All she can hear is her heart beating loudly in her chest. After a long few minutes, she hears Arlo barking, then the higher-pitched bark of Skippy; her heart leaps. She's missed the dogs more than anything.

She hears the murmur of voices, and for a split second, she thinks she might be sick. Arlo whines scratching at the door, she hears Josh say loudly, "You open it!" (Their prearranged cue) and as the door creaks open, Mel bangs on the switch to the generator and the room sputters out of the darkness into the warm glow of hundreds of glimmering fairy lights strung from the rafters.

Chris takes a step backwards, clearly confused by what's happening. The dogs bounded past him, throwing themselves at Mel, jumping up excitedly. Chris tries to call them to heel, but they stay stubbornly with Mel, who is overjoyed to see them. Josh coughs, "I'm leaving now."

"Hang on, you knew about this?"he waves his arm at the table, frowning,

"No, no, just thought I saw something strange going on, that's all," he backs away before Chris can tell him off,

"What is this? What are you doing here, Mel?" he says as he stands outside the door. Mel takes a deep breath. This is not going to be easy. Here goes everything,

"This is my attempt at recreating the anniversary dinner that I messed up," she says, hearing the wobble in her voice.

Chris looks around, noticing the details that Mrs. Oldswick had remembered and recreated, he steps a little further inside the room,

"Why would you do that?"

"I was hoping we could go back to that night, only this time,"

"*This time* you'd not ruin it by cheating on me with Jamie Hirst?" he snaps,

Mel takes a deep breath, "This *time*, instead of letting you down, I can make it up to you instead."

Chris doesn't say anything, but he does come inside.

"Please, Chris, can you at least hear me out?"

With reluctance, he sits down at the table opposite her. The dogs settle themselves down between them. His lack of response is killing her, the familiar frown on his face frozen,

Mel takes a deep breath, "What I did with Jamie, it, I'm not making excuses, Chris, it was wrong. Really wrong, because it hurt you. I hurt you, and you didn't deserve it, but with Jamie, somehow, I could forget all about Mum. He didn't know her or even care that I'd lost her because we never talked about it. With you, I saw my sadness reflected in your eyes every day, and I couldn't deal with it. You were in so many of my memories of her, and I just didn't want to be reminded of it anymore. It doesn't excuse what happened at all, I know that. I'm sorry I did that to you after how amazing you were to me."

She stares at him, somehow, in the two months since she's seen him, he's got more handsome or something. All she can think about right now is how he is the most welcome sight she's ever seen. He won't look at her, though, fiddling instead with a fork on the table, slowly, he responds,

"I watched your heart break into tiny pieces, Mel, while your Mum was sick. I felt powerless to help you; it didn't matter what I said or did, I couldn't change what was happening. I just wanted to make it better for you, but after she died, you stopped letting me."

Mel wishes more than anything that she could go back in time and not make such stupid decisions, but all she can do now is follow her plan through and hope that somehow it might make up for breaking his heart so badly back then.

"My dad kept all my things from back then, you know. I threw them away when I left for Ibiza because I wanted to forget everything. I didn't know until I opened a box I took from their attic last week. All your beautiful cards and notes. You saved me a thousand times by just being there, Chris. Honestly, I'm not even sure I would be standing here now if it weren't for you. I know I went off the rails, and I did some really dumb things, but it would've been so much worse if you hadn't been helping me through it. Never, ever think that I'm not grateful to you. I owe you my life, Christopher Oldswick. I messed up back then, then I came back and messed up again…I know that all I ever say to you is sorry, but I'm hoping now that my actions will speak louder than words," she peters out, looking for a response.

He looks around at all the lights, the candles, and the wildflowers on the table,

"I mean, this is very nice and all, Mel and I'm truly amazed you got Josh to keep a secret, but what are you doing in here? Does the builder know 'cos frankly he's been a 'right dickhead?"

"It's not his house anymore, I mean technically it is, until the sale goes through, but…"

"Whose house is it then? "Chris is not following,

"It's yours. If you still want to buy it, that is, I will sell it to you." She babbles nervously; this is her grand gesture, and it is all she's got.

"I'm confused. How are you going to sell it to me?"

"Well, it turns out that my Dad owned some land in Ireland, but no one knew for sure 'cos it was way back, but I found the old papers, Kath never threw anything away, did she?! Despite the hard work getting rid of it all, I'm so glad she didn't, in like a hundred ways. She kept all my Mum's stuff, my old stuff and Dad's…Anyway, it turns out that the land is, err, worth quite a bit of money now, so I made the builder an offer he couldn't refuse to buy this place, and now I'm making you one. I know that you bid for it at the auction, that you wanted to buy it. I can't change any of the things I did back then…or errr, recently…but I hope this might make up for some of it. I mean it, Chris, whatever you can afford to pay for it, you can have it."

"Well, that doesn't make any sense," he says slowly, looking right into her eyes over the flickering candlelight, his grey - blue eyes twinkling,

"I know the money thing is complicated, we can talk to Ken, he can sort it out. I don't care about losing money or anything, I just want to make things right between us finally, so honestly, it's all yours."

"... It doesn't make any sense for me to buy it from you, I mean", he says, for the first time all night, a smile hovers on his lips,

"I mean, I could rent it to you, I suppose, if you'd rather, but I thought,"

"Shhhh, Mel! Let me finish, for once! It doesn't make any sense for me to buy it *from* you because I was trying to buy it *for* you."

Now Mel is confused. He carries on, "I heard you in the churchyard, talking to your Mum...Then my Mum and Josh told me how much you wanted to keep hold of the house, to be closer to your memories, your folks, your friends. To come *home*.But I know that you couldn't afford to buy it, so I dunno. I came up with a stupid idea that maybe I'd buy it, make it a bit more habitable, and then I'd maybe offer it to you to rent or something, if you still wanted to come back. Then it went for far more than I could afford. I was going to get in touch Mel, but after it sold, I felt like I'd let you down, a developer buying it. We've been opposing his plans to knock it down and build new houses, though. The village got behind it, too, so I'm so happy it won't get destroyed. You aren't going to destroy it, are you?"

Mel shakes her head, unable to speak. Chris was willing to buy the farmhouse so that she could come home. He was still the sweet, thoughtful boy she once loved, still loved. Then it dawns on her,

"I thought I was going to be selling it back to you, but if you don't want it? You're sure you don't want it?"

" I mean, thanks for your very generous gesture, Mel. As apologies go, you hit it out of the park. I'm truly moved by your offer, but I'm sure. I mean, have you seen the state of the place?" he laughs,

"Then that makes it mine!" Mel says slowly as the realisation sinks in, "It's my house! I can come home ! " Chris pulls out a crumpled tissue just as she bursts into tears,

"Home to Holme End," Chris wipes her tears away,

"I mean, if you think about it, Chris, I've done you a favour. I'm saving you all the hassle of the DIY you'd have to do. Actually, I will need some help; that bathroom has got to go before I move in."

"I heard from the vet the other day that he's after some help in the office...I did mention that maybe you might be interested. He said only if we promise to never have another lovers' tiff in front of him." He grins at her for the first time in what feels like forever. She's quite forgotten what it's like to be on the receiving end of one of his smiles. It isn't wicked like Jamie's or over easy like Aaron's, it's warm like sunshine, and it always made her heart leap. She grins back at him,

"Lovers tiff?" Mel tries to keep her voice steady,

"His words, but you know what Greenleigh's like, everyone thinks they know the real story. You do know Josh will have gone straight to the pub tonight and told everyone about this? By tomorrow we'll be married with children? "

Is Chris Oldswick flirting with her? Mel's stomach starts doing the samba. "Well, I can provide a child," she says, "And don't you have a ring left over from?"

"Mel!"

"Do farmers do it better, though, enquiring minds wanna 'know?"

Chris laughs, blushing, then looks at her seriously, "Since you came back, Mel, I've been treating you like you're still a self-destructive seventeen-year-old, but you're a grown woman now. One who raised a son successfully, on her own. It must've taken a lot of work and sacrifice, and I'm sorry that I didn't give you a fair chance to change."

"Don't raise those expectations too high, I am still a bit of an idiot, "She pulls a face,

"Oh, I know, I saw the goat dance,"

He waves his hand around the room, "It looks lovely, it does, Mel, but I think maybe I'm done for life with fairy lights, they remind me of this terrible picnic I went on on New Year's eve."

" Chris you have to please believe me, we weren't, you know," she does a vague hand gesture, suddenly a bit shy, "Andrew was drunk and trying to get naked. Honestly I was just getting him dressed. I didn't know it was your picnic," she raises her hand to the lights, "Should've done though and should've come clean that it wasn't for him,"

"I believe you, I mean I saw his/ he was in no fit state and honestly it's a good job. You saved me from making a complete idiot of myself with Marlowe,"

"If you'd needed a photographer for the moment, you only had to ask."

"Not funny, Mel. I think, maybe, I only asked her to try and make you jealous…"

"For the record, it worked."

"Can we just pretend that night didn't happen? "

"The whole village will be talking about it for the next 20 years, so probably not."

While they are talking, he pulls out his battered wallet, thumbing through it until he finds two very crumpled and faded passport photos. "I've never been able to throw them away, is that nice or creepy, you decide?" He bites his lip. Mel could melt at his vulnerability. She puts her hand in her purse and slides out the passport photos she'd found of her and Chris, the other half of the set.

"If it's creepy, at least we're both creepy?"

They stare down at the photos lying on the table. In them, Mel is sitting on Chris's knee, his arms wrapped around her, her head tucked into his shoulder—their shape like jigsaw pieces that fit perfectly together.He bites his lip,

 "…When I saw you walking across the fields that first day, I knew then that you were probably the only girl I ever loved."

"Probably?"

"I don't want you to get big-headed. I'm so glad you've finally come home, Melanie McCarthy," he says, holding out his hand, pulling her towards him,

"Good job because I'm planning on staying," she says, sitting on his knee as he wraps his arms around her. She lays her head on his shoulder, the missing puzzle pieces fit together, and Melanie McCarthy finally feels whole again.

The End.

AFTERWORD

After finishing university, I moved to Leeds, proclaiming I was off to follow my dream of being a writer. It was so long ago that my leaving present was a giant dictionary that I've lugged around the country ever since. (Thanks, Old Orleans crew.) I wrote, in fits and starts, between life, kids, and new ideas that ambushed the last project, never quite finishing anything. I had a spell of scriptwriting, which was unexpected and a lot of fun. I can say I went to BAFTA at least. (Thanks to Andy & Russ for believing in me, it meant more than you'll know.)

Like many of us, I had time on my hands in 2020, which is when I wrote the first draft of this book. It's taken me some time to reach this point. (In my defence, I have written other books in between. Watch this space!) but finally, here we are. If you don't mind, I want to say thank you to a few people who helped me reach the finish line.

Firstly, though, thank you for reading. I hope you've enjoyed going on this journey with Mel and getting to know the people of Greenleigh. I grew up in Holmfirth, so thanks to the Holme valley, the 313 bus, and boys in biker jackets for the inspiration. I miss you Yorkshire & I hope I get home like Mel one day. Thank you to my kids (& possibly neighbours) for letting me shut myself in my room and sing with headphones on while I write. (Sorry) I hope watching me do the thing I've always wanted to do makes you determined to follow your own passions. Thanks to my Mum, Sister, and Melissa, books are in our blood. Thanks to Writing East Midlands for your feedback scheme and author Emma Pass for your encouraging comments on my early draft. Shout out to Suz for the grammar guidance (Mr. Mattingley would be proud of us both. What a long way we've come from getting told off for discussing JBJ in English, or not), & a massive thank you to all my lovely friends who've encouraged and endured my many creative endeavours over the years. Honestly, I wouldn't be doing half the things I do without the support of you lot. You're all aces, & I love you.

Find me on Instagram@wildsandfree

I'd love to hear from you X

ABOUT THE AUTHOR

Alexandra Wilds was brought up on a steady diet of Dirty Dancing, John Hughes movies & some of the best Rom Coms ever made. (Thank you, Meg Ryan). She stubbornly lives for meet-cutes, star-crossed lovers & falls in love at least once a day. She believes in the enchantment of a power ballad and the alchemy of taking off your glasses and shaking your hair. She firmly asserts that we all need some Moonstruck magic, Stand By Me friends & Princess Bride love in our lives. She will continue to happily perpetuate Rom Com tropes in all her writing, even in the YA dystopian trilogy she's working on. Love is never more needed than in the apocalypse.

Remember, "When you grow up, your heart dies." (The Breakfast Club), so maybe don't grow up. X

Printed in Dunstable, United Kingdom

64655154R00161